DEAD MAN

Rifles and pistols banged. Slugs sizzled in the night air. It did not occur to Fargo until later that while the slugs came close, the shots were either wide or high. The men shooting at them were deliberately missing.

A gully opened almost under the noses of their mounts. Fargo went down the incline in a spray of dirt and rocks. At the bottom he hauled on the reins and was out of the saddle before the Ovaro came to a stop. Shucking the Henry from the saddle scabbard, he scrambled to the top.

Cain's men were sweeping toward the gully from all sides. In their eagerness they were careless.

Fargo shoved the Colt into his holster and tucked the Henry's hardwood stock to his shoulder. He fired three times as rapidly as he could work the lever. Riders to the north, west, and east toppled. The rest were quick to scatter and seek cover.

Gravel crunched as May Ling hunkered by Fargo. Her hand found his arm and lightly squeezed. "Thank you for trying."

"We're not caught yet," Fargo said, but he was not fooling anyone, least of all himself.

A GIANT
TRAILSMAN
ADVENTURE

DESERT
DUEL

by

Jon Sharpe

A SIGNET BOOK

SIGNET
Published by New American Library, a division of
Penguin Group (USA) Inc., 375 Hudson Street,
New York, New York 10014, USA
Penguin Group (Canada), 90 Eglinton Avenue East, Suite 700, Toronto,
Ontario M4P 2Y3, Canada (a division of Pearson Penguin Canada Inc.)
Penguin Books Ltd., 80 Strand, London WC2R 0RL, England
Penguin Ireland, 25 St. Stephen's Green, Dublin 2,
Ireland (a division of Penguin Books Ltd.)
Penguin Group (Australia), 250 Camberwell Road, Camberwell, Victoria 3124,
Australia (a division of Pearson Australia Group Pty. Ltd.)
Penguin Books India Pvt. Ltd., 11 Community Centre, Panchsheel Park,
New Delhi - 110 017, India
Penguin Group (NZ), cnr Airborne and Rosedale Roads, Albany,
Auckland 1310, New Zealand (a division of Pearson New Zealand Ltd.)
Penguin Books (South Africa) (Pty.) Ltd., 24 Sturdee Avenue,
Rosebank, Johannesburg 2196, South Africa

Penguin Books Ltd., Registered Offices:
80 Strand, London WC2R 0RL, England

First published by Signet, an imprint of New American Library,
a division of Penguin Group (USA) Inc.

First Printing, February 2007
10 9 8 7 6 5 4 3 2 1

The Trailsman

Beginnings . . . they bend the tree and they mark the man. Skye Fargo was born when he was eighteen. Terror was his midwife, vengeance his first cry. Killing spawned Skye Fargo, ruthless, cold-blooded murder. Out of the acrid smoke of gunpowder still hanging in the air, he rose, cried out a promise never forgotten.

The Trailsman they began to call him all across the West: searcher, scout, hunter, the man who could see where others only looked, his skills for hire but not his soul, the man who lived each day to the fullest, yet trailed each tomorrow. Skye Fargo, the Trailsman, the seeker who could take the wildness of a land and the wanting of a woman and make them his own.

The inferno known as Death Valley, 1861—
where the air burns the lungs,
the women sizzle, and hot lead flies fast and furious.

1

The sun baked the land and the rider. It scorched the air so the rider felt as if his lungs were on fire. That was normal for the Panamint Mountains in the middle of July. The mountains bordered Death Valley. During the summer, nowhere on the continent was hotter.

Skye Fargo would rather be somewhere cooler, but this was where his quest had brought him. A big, broad-shouldered man with piercing lake blue eyes, he pushed his hat back on his head and ran a buckskin sleeve across his perspiring brow. Strapped to his waist was a Colt. Snug in his saddle scabbard nestled a Henry repeater. The Ovaro he rode snorted as he drew rein and stared down at a settlement that had not been there the last time he passed through this neck of the country.

Calling it a settlement was a stretch. Fargo counted nine buildings. The biggest was a saloon. Beside it stood a frame house in need of paint. Past the house were eight shacks barely bigger than outhouses. At first glance he thought they were sheds, but then he saw figures going in and coming out of several of them.

Fargo clucked to the Ovaro. If people wanted to live in a place with no more room than a closet, that was their business. His business was to earn the thousand dollars he had been paid by a certain well-to-do individual in San Francisco.

The Ovaro's hooves clattered on the rocky trail. It was no surprise the sound carried to the buildings below. Nor was it a surprise when four men came out of the saloon and stared up at him. Three went back in. The fourth leaned against a post and hooked his thumbs in his gun belt to make it appear as if he had nothing better to do, but Fargo wasn't fooled. Only an idiot stood outside in that heat without a damn good reason.

Fargo lowered his hand to his holster and loosened his Colt. The information he unearthed in San Francisco, the information that brought him here, had warned he was riding into trouble. He had not known what form the trouble would take, or exactly when and where it would show itself.

Not that it mattered. Fargo would do what he was being paid to do, and if anyone tried to stop him, he had no qualms about doing whatever it took to get the job done. That was part of why he had been hired.

Fargo pulled his hat brim low over his eyes to ward off the glare of the sun. The brush was a tinderbox. All it would take was a moment's carelessness to set the whole mountain range ablaze. He was reminded of that because the man leaning against the post was rolling a cigarette.

A crude sign on the saloon let the world know it was called THE WHISKEE MILL. In smaller scrawl was the tidbit THE LAST WATARING HOLE UNTIL DEAF VALLEY WET YOUR THROTE WHILE YOUR STILL BREETHING.

Fargo drew rein and leaned on his saddle horn. "That's some sign. Whoever wrote it must win a lot of spelling bees."

The man rolling the cigarette squinted up at the sign, then at Fargo. He had a mop of brown hair, a weak chin covered with stubble, and eyes that glittered

2

like a weasel's. His clothes were store-bought and had seen better days. The Remington strapped to his hip was new, though. "If you have a complaint, take it up with Pardee. He runs the place."

Six horses were at the hitch rail. Fargo kneed the Ovaro over and stiffly dismounted. Arching his back, he scanned the dusty street. "Not much to this gob of spit, is there?"

The man allowed himself a chuckle. "No, there sure ain't, friend. Which is why strangers in these parts are scarce. What might be your business?"

"I'm not your friend and my business is my own." Fargo looped the reins around the rail, shucked the Henry from the scabbard, and stepped onto the porch. Out of the corner of his eye he saw the man stiffen in resentment, then relax.

"I guess I had that coming. It doesn't do to pry into other folks' affairs." The man smiled, showing teeth nearly the same shade of yellow as the sun. "I'm Hank, by the way. What might your handle be?"

"I've plumb forgot," Fargo said.

The saloon door was propped open with a broom. Fargo strolled in and stopped just over the threshold to let his eyes adjust to the gloom. The place reeked of liquor and less savory odors. To the right was the bar, such as it was; a long plank had been placed atop stacked barrels. To the left were tables. Only one was occupied, by three men playing cards.

A sausage-shaped bartender in a dirty apron leaned on the plank, his knuckles as big as ham's knuckles. "What can I get for you, mister?"

"Coffin varnish," Fargo said. "And it better not be watered down." He set the Henry on the plank with a loud *thunk* and turned, resting his elbows on the plank. The three at the table were studying him but trying not to be obvious about it.

Hank ambled in and over to their table. Bending,

3

he whispered a few words to a beanpole with a beaked nose and a long, skinny neck. The human turkey buzzard wore a flat-brimmed black hat and a black vest.

"Hell, mister," the bartender was saying as he turned to a shelf crammed with bottles. "This isn't the big city. I don't go in for those kinds of tricks. You pay your money, you get what you pay for."

"I take it you must be Pardee?" Fargo said, accepting a bottle and a glass that could use cleaning.

The bartender smiled and nodded. "That I would. And who might you be?"

Fargo ignored the question and asked one of his own. "Why in God's name did you open a saloon in this godforsaken place? You must not want many customers."

Pardee snorted good-naturedly. "Oh, I get more than you might think. As for the why, let's just say I was made an offer that—" He suddenly stopped.

Fargo did not need to turn his head to know that the two-legged turkey buzzard had come over. Hat brims were handy for more than blocking the sun. He could peer out from under his without being noticed. The turkey buzzard was staring at him as if he were a bug that needed squashing. Without turning Fargo asked, "Do you want something, you peckerwood?"

The turkey buzzard blinked in disbelief. "What did you just call me?"

"Are you hard of hearing as well as ugly?" Fargo filled the glass.

Pardee had stepped back and was trying to shrink into the wall. "Here, now. You can't come waltzing in and insult people," he said without much conviction.

"It's the epidemic," Fargo said.

The turkey buzzard and Pardee swapped puzzled looks, and Pardee said, "What in hell are you talking about, mister?"

"The epidemic of nosiness," Fargo explained, and

4

faced the buzzard. "You were about to ask who I am and what I'm doing here. I'll tell you the same thing I told your friend Hank." He took a long sip of whiskey, using his left hand, and savored the burning sensation before saying, "It's none of your damn business."

The turkey buzzard was red in the face, and not from the heat. His left hand drifted close to a Smith and Wesson, worn butt forward for a cross draw. "I don't think I like you much."

"Who gives a damn?" Fargo snapped. "Go bother someone else before I take you over my knee."

The buzzard took a step back. "That's enough guff. Do you have any idea who I work for?"

Pardee thrust his hands out. "Hold on! There won't be any blood-spilling, Krast. It took me a whole day to clean up the last mess you made."

"I'm not the one on the prod," Krast growled. "It's this lunkhead who needs to learn some manners."

Moving so fast he was a blur, Fargo drew his Colt and slammed the barrel against Krast's temple. He had the Colt back in its holster before Krass melted like so much wax. Raising the glass, Fargo took another sip, smacked his lips in appreciation, and remarked, "You're right. This is damn good whiskey."

Pardee was gaping at the slumped form on the floor. Hank and the two cardplayers were equally dumbfounded.

"I don't suppose I can get a bite to eat?" Fargo asked.

Sputtering, Pardee found his voice. He pointed a thick finger at Krast. "Do you have any idea what you've just done?"

"Yes or no?"

With a visible effort, Pardee pulled his gaze from Krast. "Sure. I can fix you some eggs and bacon. Or a steak, if you like. Beef, not venison."

"A thick slab so rare it bleeds? With potatoes? And bread and butter?" Fargo's mouth watered at the prospect. He had not had a decent meal since leaving San Francisco. On the trail he had made do with rabbit and squirrel and the jerky and pemmican in his saddlebags.

"I'll even throw in corn and peas," Pardee offered.

"You have all that?" Fargo was surprised. Cattle were at a premium this far from ranch country, and vegetables did not grow in so arid a region.

"That, and more," Pardee said enigmatically. He started toward a door at the back but abruptly stopped.

Hank and the other two were converging on Fargo, their hands hovering near their hardware.

"Mister, you just made the biggest damned mistake of your life," Hank announced. "Our boss won't take kindly to you beating on Krast."

"Is that so?" Fargo could not tell them that he was doing what he had to in order to earn the thousand dollars he was being paid. He could not tell them he had ridden in to Whiskey Mill with a plan already worked out. "That's a scary proposition, if ever I heard one."

"Poke fun all you want," Hank glowered, "but you won't be so smug when Tobias Cain is through with you."

"Who?"

"Tobias Cain." Hank said it in the same way a minister might mention the Almighty. "He's a big man in these parts. Before long, he'll be one of the biggest hombres in all of California."

"Never heard of him," Fargo lied. Because he had, in San Francisco, a few words from a dying man, the words that led him to Whiskey Mill.

"Not yet, maybe, but you will if you live long

6

enough," Hank said. "Everyone will hear of Tobias Cain before long."

Fargo polished off the glass in a single gulp, let out a sigh, and set the glass on the plank. "If your boss wants to talk to me, you know where to find me." Snatching up the Henry, he took the glass and the bottle and shouldered past Hank and the other two and over to a corner table. They did not try to stop him. For the time being they were content to glare. Then, at a nod from Hank, the other pair looped arms under Krast and carried him out.

"Enjoy your meal," was Hank's parting shot. "It may be your last."

Fargo placed the Henry on the table. So far, everything was going as he wanted it to go. He refilled the glass and leaned back. Pardee had disappeared into the back of the saloon. About to treat himself to another swallow of red-eye, Fargo instinctively swooped his right hand to his Colt when a shadow filled the front doorway. But it wasn't Hank or one of the other hard cases.

It was a woman. An Oriental woman. Judging by her wrinkles and her gray hair, she was in her fifties, maybe her sixties. Instead of a dress she had on a long jacket or shirt and a pair of pants, with sandals. She calmly scanned the room. Then, with her small hands clasped in front of her, she came toward the corner in a sort of mincing shuffle. Bowing, she said in heavily accented English, "So sorry, please. Pardee here?" Her "sorry" came out as "solly," her "please" as "pwease."

"He's in the back," Fargo informed her. Lady Luck had smiled on him and he aimed to take advantage of it. As the woman began to turn, he said, "Don't go yet. What is your name?"

"Wen Po, honorable sir."

Again the woman went to go, but Fargo wasn't done. "Where do you come from, Wen Po?"

"I live Whiskey Mill."

"Here?" Fargo said. Then he remembered the small shacks. "Are there other Chinese hereabouts?"

"So sorry," Wen Po said. "What be hereabouts?"

"In the settlement. In Whiskey Mill."

"Some, yes. Others—" Wen Po did not finish.

Pardee was stalking toward them with a scowl on his face and his fists clenched. "Damn your yellow hide. What are you doing? I've told you before not to come in here without my say-so."

Wen Po bowed halfway to the floor. "Sorry, honorable sir. Need help. Lu Wei, she be ill."

Taking hold of the old woman, Pardee roughly propelled her toward the front door. "I'll check on her when I'm done with my customer. Don't you ever set foot in here again without permission, Wen Po. You hear me? Not if you know what's good for you."

Fargo spoke up. "My meal can wait if someone is sick."

"It's only one of the Chinese," Pardee said. "And a shirker, at that. This makes the third time this week the contrary bitch has claimed she's not feeling well." He shoved Wen Po so hard, she stumbled. "Now off with you."

Fargo controlled his temper. A lot of whites treated the Chinese exactly as Pardee was treating the old woman. He must be careful and not show any sympathy. "I never expected to find Chinese way out here in the middle of nowhere."

Pardee came over to the table. "Mister, you would think you were in China. Why, we've got a passel right here." Leaning down, he grinned lecherously. "Eight are young fillies you can bed for as long or as short as the mood moves you. Provided you pay first."

"Chinese whores?" In all of Fargo's wide-flung wan-

8

dering, in all his countless visits to saloons and his dealings with fallen doves, he hardly ever met ladies of Chinese extraction who sold their flesh for money.

Pardee gleefully nodded. "They'll do anything you want. If they don't, I'll kick their teeth in."

"You don't say."

"There's more to Whiskey Mill than you might reckon," Pardee said by way of bragging. "It's worth your while to stick around a day or two. But that might not be wise. When Krast comes to, he's liable to have a hankering to buck you out in gore."

Just then spurs jangled, and into the saloon stormed the gentleman in question. The turkey buzzard was mad as hell and out for blood.

2

Krast was not alone. Hank and three others cut from the same coarse cloth were with him. Krast stalked halfway to the corner and made a show of planting himself, his hand poised to draw. "On your feet, you son of a bitch!"

Fargo sipped some whiskey. "What for?"

"You damn near caved my skull in!" Krast snarled, and jabbed his thumb at the side of his head where a scarlet rivulet ran from a gash in his temple to his chin. "I aim to repay the favor."

"Your head must be harder than most," Fargo commented. "Usually they stay out longer."

Almost beside himself with fury, Krast hissed like a riled rattler. "I won't tell you twice! You can die sitting or you can die standing. It's your choice."

Fargo had no desire to kill him. He had knocked Krast down to draw attention to himself, not to complicate things by being forced to gun him down. "What about your boss, Tobias Cain?"

"What about him?"

"He might not take it kindly," Fargo said. "But if you don't care what he thinks, I'm more than happy to oblige you."

Krast's weasel eyes narrowed. "How is it you know Mr. Cain? Who the hell are you, anyhow?"

"I'm nobody."

Hank opened his mouth to say something, then closed it again. He studied Fargo intently, then shook his head as if he could not quite make up his mind what to think.

As for Krast, he curled and uncurled the fingers he was about to use to draw, then rasped, "I don't quite know what to make of you, mister. But I damn sure don't want to make Mr. Cain mad. So I'll go have a talk with him, and if he doesn't know you from Adam, I'll be back to put windows in your skull."

"I can hardly wait."

Wheeling, Krast jangled out, the others in tow.

Hank halted in the doorway to look back and smirk. "You're either the cleverest cuss I've ever come across, or an idiot. I can't make up my mind which."

Fargo swirled the whiskey in his glass and said, "Give my regards to your employer."

"The man you told me a few minutes ago you never heard of?" Hank chortled. "Don't worry. I will. I'm anxious to see whether he lets you go on breathing or feeds you to the worms." He strolled out.

Pardee let out a long breath. "Whoooeee. I thought for certain Krast would fill you with lead. I've never seen him sheathe his horns."

"There's a first time for everything," Fargo said. "Now what about that food you mentioned?"

"Oh. I almost forgot. Do you want a slice of pie, too? It's fresh baked."

"Did you bake it yourself?"

Pardee laughed. "My woman did. Tilly. She's not good for much except cooking and under the sheets at night, which is all any woman really has to be good at."

"I'll take that slice," Fargo said. He was listening to hooves drum off down the street.

"There goes Krast," Pardee mentioned. "It will take him a couple of hours to reach the Oasis. Figure two

11

more to return. That gives you four hours to eat and light a shuck if you know what is good for you."

"I might stick around," Fargo said.

"Suit yourself. But I wouldn't want to be in your boots if Mr. Cain gives Krast permission to curl your toes." Pardee swiveled on a heel. "Give me fifteen minutes and your supper will be ready."

"What was that about an oasis?" Fargo wanted to know.

"Not *an* oasis. *The* Oasis. It's the name of Tobias Cain's farm."

"A farm in these mountains?" Fargo scoffed. "As dry as they are?"

"Not in the mountains," Pardee said. "In Death Valley."

Fargo absorbed that. "Are you joshing? I've been across Death Valley. Nothing can grow there except mesquite, creosote, and desert holly."

"That used to be the case, yes," Pardee said, "but Tobias Cain doesn't let an inconvenience like a desert stop him. He's licked it, mister. Licked Death Valley. He makes it do what he wants it to do."

"How does he manage that miracle?"

All Pardee did was chuckle.

"A farm in Death Valley?" Fargo fished for more information. "When there is plenty of fertile land west of here to be had dirt cheap?"

"I know. It sounds loco. But trust me. Tobias Cain isn't the least bit crazy. Fact is, he's smarter than most ten men, and meaner than most twenty. You might keep that in mind the next time you toss his name around to wriggle out of a scrape."

The instant the door at the back closed, Fargo was on his feet and hurried out. Only one other horse beside the Ovaro was at the hitch rail. Wen Po was nowhere to be seen. He left the shade of the overhang in a beeline for the shacks. He had to pass the frame

12

house. The windows were open to admit the snail of a breeze, and from one drifted a husky voice.

"Howdy there, handsome. What's your rush?" The speaker had flaxen curls down to her slender shoulders, eyes the same hue as emeralds, full lips like ripe cherries, and was sheathed in a red dress tight enough to qualify as skin. She was in a chair, her arm draped along the windowsill, her cheek in her hand, looking as bored as a person could look and still be alive.

Fargo stopped and leaned on the Henry. "Howdy yourself." He grinned. "What is a vision like you doing in a dump like this?"

The blonde brightened and regarded him with keen interest. "That was an awful nice thing to say. I bet you have a knack for wooing the ladies." She giggled. "I'm Tilly, by the way. Tilly Foster."

"Pardee's woman?"

"So he would like to believe," Tilly said flatly. "But between you and me, if I ever get the chance, I'm heading for Denver."

"What's stopping you?" Fargo asked. He imagined it was money.

"I'm not too fond of being dragged back by my heels," Tilly informed him. "Or of being tied to a post and whipped."

"Pardee would do that?"

"Oh no. He can be rough but he's a kitten compared to Tobias Cain. Now, there's a man you don't want mad at you."

"I don't understand," Fargo admitted. "You're with Pardee. How does Cain figure in?"

"I'm with Pardee because Tobias Cain wants me to be," Tilly revealed. "You could say I come with the territory." She poked her head out, glanced at the saloon, and said quietly, "Pardee was working as a bar-dog in Sacramento when Mr. Cain offered him this job. Pardee declined at first, like a lot of others. There's not much to do here except watch the grass grow." A sound from the saloon caused her to glance over sharply. When no one appeared, she went on. "But Mr. Cain never takes no for an answer. It's not in his nature. He threw in a house and a woman to sweeten the deal. The house being this one and the woman being me."

"What did Cain offer you?"

"Offer?" Tilly said, and cackled. "Mister, he had some of his men jump me and gag me and throw me over a horse, and here I am."

"You were brought here against your will?" The more Fargo learned of Tobias Cain, the more worried he became for the person he had been hired to find.

"What Tobias Cain wants, Tobias Cain gets. Any way he can," Tilly said bitterly. "He is not someone you can cross and live to tell about it."

Fargo had been told the exact same thing in San Francisco, where a lot of Chinese had gone missing. Many were women. Young women. The father of one of them, a jade merchant, had heard of Fargo's reputation as a tracker. The father sought him out and offered a thousand dollars for Fargo to find the daughter. Fargo was honest with the father. He told the man he might not be able to do it, that it was not the same as tracking, but he would do his best.

That was good enough for Shen Ling. "She is all the family I have left," he said sadly in his clipped English. "My wife died of smallpox two years ago. My son was found stabbed in an alley. I want her back. I want her safe. Do whatever it takes to find May Ling."

Fargo had asked for a description of the girl. "Is there anything else you can tell me that might help? Anything at all?"

That was when Shen exploded a cannonball. "The

first man I hired sent word to me before he disappeared—"

"Wait a minute," Fargo had interrupted. "You hired someone else before you sent for me?"

"A local man. Harry Maplewhite. He was highly recommended. He searched for over a month. Right before he disappeared I met with him. He told me that he believed a man named Cain was responsible. Maplewhite was to leave for a place called Whiskey Mill to find out more." Shen had frowned. "That was the last time I saw Harry Maplewhite."

"I've never heard of any Whiskey Mill," Fargo had said.

"Be utmostly careful," Shen cautioned. "Maplewhite said that Cain is very dangerous."

"Don't worry. I can handle myself."

Shen's thin lips had curled in a wry smile. "Maplewhite made the same claim. But I fear he is dead, and I would rather the same does not happen to you."

A comment by Tilly brought Fargo back to the here and now.

"I'm not the only one Cain has shanghaied. But I've said too much. Prying ears are everywhere."

Fargo glanced up and down the deserted street. "There was a Chinese woman in the saloon a few minutes ago. Wen Po. Did you see where she went?"

"Sorry, I didn't pay much attention," Tilly said. "Most likely she's with one of her girls."

"She has kids?" Fargo said. The woman had seemed too old for that.

Merry laughter tinkled from Tilly Foster. "Mercy me, no. She helps oversee the girls for Tobias Cain. From what I hear, she ran an herb and tea shop in San Francisco before she wound up here. Can you imagine?"

"What girls are you talking about, then?" Fargo feigned ignorance.

Tilly leaned out the window and gestured at the shacks. "Pick one. Any one. Knock on any door. You'll get your answer." She rose. "I must go."

The curtains closed, and Fargo turned. From behind the curtains came a final comment. "It doesn't do to ask too many questions in Whiskey Mill, mister. The last gent who did regretted it."

"Do you know that gent's name?" Fargo asked, thinking of Maplewhite, but he received no answer. Shrugging, he walked to the first shack and lightly rapped. Almost immediately the door opened.

"How do you do?" The young Chinese woman who addressed him wore a plain calico dress and brown shoes. Her hair had been clipped short and was in curls, like Tilly's. Powder and other cosmetics had made a travesty of her face in an attempt to have her appear more Western. Her smile lacked genuine warmth. "Five dollars for first hour."

"How's that again?"

"Five dollars first hour. One dollar each hour after." The young woman held out her hand. "Five dollars, please. Then you touch."

Fargo estimated the shack was seven feet long by five feet wide. A small bed was against one wall, a chair close to the door. Above the bed, hanging from a short peg, was an unlit lantern. A shaft of sunlight betrayed a crack in the roof. "This isn't where you live, is it?"

"Five dollars first hour," the young woman repeated, wagging her palm.

"Thank you, but no."

Her dark eyes mirrored relief. "You not like me? Try other girls. Maybe so find one you think pretty." She quickly closed the door.

Fargo had every intention of doing just that, but a hail from the saloon nipped the notion in the bud.

"There you are!" Pardee hollered. "I thought you left without telling me. Do you want that meal or not?"

Reluctantly, Fargo ambled back. He would investigate the rest of the shacks later, and hope he didn't find May Ling. From what her father had related, she was as sweet and innocent as a new-grown daisy and had never been with a man in her life.

The tantalizing aroma of the food reminded Fargo of how hungry he was. A steaming pot of coffee had been placed in the center of table to wash everything down. He buttered a thick slice of bread, sprinkled salt on the sizzling steak, and dug in. Whatever else Pardee might be, the man could cook. Fargo ate with relish, savoring the delicious taste of a juicy piece of fat, the creamy tang of the butter, and coffee thick enough to float a horseshoe.

Fargo was so famished, and so intent on his meal, that he did not realize someone had entered the saloon until he looked up and saw Wen Po. She was not alone. A much younger Chinese woman was with her, dressed much like the one in the first shack except that her raven hair fell loose past her shoulders and she did not use as many cosmetics.

Pardee had gone behind the bar and was arranging bottles. He looked up when Wen Po coughed to get his attention. "Damn it." Wiping his hands on his apron, he came around the end of the bar. "Didn't I just tell you never to come in here again without asking first?"

"So sorry, so sorry," Wen Po said politely. "But Lu Wei much sick. She want rest."

"Does she, now?" Pardee gritted, and rounded on Lu Wei. "You've been sick a lot of late, missy. If you ask me, you're trying to get out of earning your keep."

"Oh no, sir," the younger woman said, bowing. "I am really sick."

"Convince me," Pardee snapped. "What is supposed to be wrong with you?"

Lu Wei smiled. "I am with child."

For some reason, both Pardee and Wen Po reacted as if they had been punched in the gut. Pardee even took a step back, then blurted, "You stupid cow. You've just made yourself maggot bait."

"Sorry?" Lu Wei said.

It was Wen Po who enlightened her by sliding a finger across her neck as if slicing her throat.

3

Skye Fargo went on eating as if nothing out of the ordinary were occurring. As if a young woman had not just been told she would be murdered for being pregnant. Over the rim of his coffee cup he watched as Lu Wei burst into tears and pleaded with Wen Po in Chinese. Her appeal had no effect. The older woman might as well have been carved from stone for all the emotion she showed.

Pardee tapped his foot, impatiently listening, and when he had taken all he could, he snapped, "Enough of that gibberish. You're supposed to speak English, remember?"

Lu Wei bowed, tears dampening her cheeks. "Please forgive me, venerable Pardee. I did not want to be with child. It just happened."

"How can that be?" Pardee glared at Wen Po. "Haven't you been giving the girls those herbs and whatnot? The stuff that fixes it so they can't be like she is?"

"I give potions each morning," Wen Po said, sounding offended that he would think otherwise.

"You damn well better be," Pardee growled. "That's why Mr. Cain brought you here. Whores aren't any good to him if they're having a kid. They're sick all the time, like she is. They bloat up like cows, and no one wants to bed them." He jabbed a finger at the two women. "Mr. Cain told you how it is. He warned you what would happen if you broke any of his rules."

"Sometimes potions not work," Wen Po said. "Not my fault. Not fault of potion. Not fault of girl."

Pardee laughed scornfully. "That's not how Mr. Cain will see it. He doesn't accept excuses."

"Surely he will not kill me?" Lu Wei said plaintively. "Not when I did not mean for this to happen?"

"You stupid cluck." Pardee snorted. "Do you honestly think Mr. Cain gives a hoot whether you did or didn't? The important thing is that you *are*, and that makes you of no use to him, and whatever is of no use to him, he gets rid of." He shook his head in disgust. His eyes alighted on the corner table and he stiffened as if he had forgotten Fargo was there. "Both of you skedaddle," he gruffly demanded. "I'll get word to Mr. Cain and he'll deal with this as he sees fit." Taking a step, Pardee poked Lu Wei in the bosom. "But don't you think of running off, girl. You wouldn't get far in these mountains. Mr. Cain's trackers would hunt you down and bring you back."

The women left. Pardee hesitated, then walked to the table. "How is everything?" he asked.

"Right fine," Fargo complimented him.

"Listen, about that business with those China-women," Pardee said, with a vague wave. "I hope you won't take it into your head that it's anything you need fret about. They are Mr. Cain's property, and he does as he pleases."

Fargo shrugged. "Like you say, they're his girls."

Pardee smiled. "Good to hear you say that. Some men wouldn't be so sensible."

"How many painted cats does Cain have working for him?" Fargo was wondering if May Ling might be among them.

"One in each shack," Pardee said. "You're welcome

to take your pick. Any give you sass, you come to me and I'll beat them within an inch of their lives."

"You don't sound like you care much for them," Fargo observed.

"They're Chinese," Pardee replied, as if that were explanation enough. "But there's more to it than that. When I hired on, Mr. Cain didn't tell me I'd have to ride herd on a bunch of whores. I thought all I'd have to do is run this saloon and serve drinks."

"You could have refused the job."

Pardee nervously lowered his voice. "Mister, you don't seem to savvy yet. No one tells Tobias Cain no. Not ever. What Tobias Cain wants, Tobias Cain gets. Any way he has to."

"You sound scared of him," Fargo said matter-of-factly so Pardee would not take offense.

"I am, and I don't mind admitting it. You would be, too, if you knew what I know or had seen some of the things I've seen." Pardee shuddered. "I agreed to run this place for five years. As soon as the time is up, I'm heading east. As far away from Cain as I can get. Some place like New York or Philadelphia."

"I'd like to meet him," Fargo remarked.

"Believe you me, you wouldn't if you had any sense," Pardee said. "And don't forget about Krast. In three hours or so he's liable to show up looking to separate you from your hide." He walked off into the back.

Fargo considered what he had learned so far. He was more certain than ever that he had come to the right place. May Ling was there somewhere, either in Whiskey Mill or at the Oasis. Finding her should not prove too difficult. Then it was a simple matter of returning her to San Francisco, and her father, and being paid the thousand dollars Shen Ling had promised.

As he leisurely ate the pie, Fargo's thoughts strayed

to Lu Wei. She could not be more than twenty, if that. From the sound of things, she was in for a hard time when Tobias Cain found out about her condition. She might be open to a suggestion he would make.

When he finished, Fargo pushed his chair back and patted his washboard stomach. There was nothing quite like some whiskey and a hot meal to wipe away fatigue. He hollered for Pardee, and paid. Taking the half-empty bottle, he announced, "I think I'll take a gander at these girls of yours."

"Two and a half hours," Pardee reminded him.

Whiskey Mill blistered under the afternoon sun. Fargo hoped to catch sight of Tilly, but the frame house was quiet and still. He knocked on the door of the first shack.

The young Chinese woman with the curly hair was sweltering. "You back?" She did not sound happy about it. Holding out her hand, she said, "Five dollars, please."

"Lu Wei?" Fargo asked.

The woman frowned, stepped out, and pointed at the last shack in the line. "Lu Wie there. But she not do you. Lu Wei no feel good." Forcing a smile, she tugged at his sleeve. "You kiss me, hug me. Same, same."

"Maybe another time."

Clinging to his arm, she said, "I make very happy." Her "very" was more like "velly." "I Tu Shuzhen. Try me."

Shaking his head, Fargo said, "I need to see Lu Wei."

"You like me," Tu Shuzhen insisted, her painted nails digging into his arm. "You see."

Fargo was mystified. Earlier she had shown no interest. Now she was trying to pull him into her shack. "No, thanks," he said, and sought to pry her fingers off.

Tu Shuzhen clung on. "Lu Wei not well. Take me. Please. I be good."

It hit Fargo, then, why she was behaving as she was. Removing her hand, he gently held it in both of his. "She's your friend, isn't she?"

"Yes. Good friend. Like sister."

"Don't worry. I only want to talk to her," Fargo whispered. "I know about the trouble she is in and I might be able to help." He thought that would suffice, but he was mistaken.

Wariness gripped Tu Shuzhen. "Why help Chinese girl you not know? This first time you here, yes?"

Fargo enlightened her. "I don't work for Tobias Cain, if that's what you're thinking."

"You white. Lu Wei Chinese. Many whites not like Chinese. Many whites kill Chinese."

"I don't care what color a person's skin is."

Tu Shuzhen went to say something. She glanced past him, gasped, and shut the door so fast she nearly snagged her dress.

Thinking that Krast had come back sooner than he expected, Fargo spun, his hand dropping to his Colt. But it was only the inscrutable Wen Po, standing and staring with her small hands clasped at her waist. "You shouldn't sneak up on folks like that," Fargo said gruffly.

"What you do, mister?"

Slightly annoyed by her tone, Fargo answered, "I'm looking for a girl."

Wen Po nodded at the shack. "Tu Shuzhen nice girl. Why not do her?"

"I want to take my pick." Fargo strode off but the old woman promptly fell into step beside him, taking three short steps for every long stride of his. "I don't need a nursemaid."

"I help," Wen Po offered. "I show you girls."

"I can do it myself," Fargo made plain. He figured

23

she would take that as a hint, but she stayed glued to his elbow.

"Me hear you mention Lu Wei," Wen Po said. "Why you want see her? You in saloon. You know she with child."

Suddenly stopping, Fargo faced the old woman. For all her mild bearing, she was like a wolf with its jaws locked on a haunch of meat. "Mind explaining why it matters to you?"

Wen Po encompassed the shacks with a sweep of an arm. "All girls mine. Mr. Cain say I watch."

"I've heard that's Pardee's job," Fargo said.

"Pardee run Whiskey Mill. I run girls. Mr. Cain run all. You understand what I say?"

"I didn't come squalling into this world yesterday."

"That mean yes?" Wen Po studied him. Apparently she did not like what she saw, because she frowned. "You not make trouble, mister. You go. Leave Whiskey Mill before you hurt."

Her threat rankled. "I'll leave when I'm damned good and ready," Fargo said. "Now go pester someone else."

Wen Po stepped in front of him. "You listen, please. Girl do bad, Mr. Cain punish girl, Mr. Cain punish me. Same, same."

Fargo understood. Whenever the girls acted up, Wen Po was held to account. No wonder she was worried.

"Last time, Mr. Cain have Wen Po whipped. Wen Po not like whip. Not like pain, not like blood. You, how you say, savvy now?"

"I savvy," Fargo assured her. But it did not change anything. He felt sorry for her, but he would still do what he had to. "I only want to talk to Lu Wei." The lies were piling up.

A hint of regret touched Wen Po's wrinkled countenance. "You talk, then," she said quietly. "Remember

I try." With that, she wheeled and short-stepped into the narrow gap between the second and third shacks.

Fargo continued on. The doors to all the shacks were closed. Inside, the shacks had to be ovens. He came to the eighth and raised his fist to knock. Soft sobbing fell on his ears, giving him pause until he remembered May Ling, and the thousand dollars. He knocked loudly.

The sobbing ceased. There was sniffling, and the rustle of movement, and the door opened a crack. A single brown eye widened. "Oh." Lu Wei opened the door the rest of the way. "I thought you were someone else."

"Like Pardee or Wen Po?" Fargo said, and doffed his hat. "I'd like to come in, if you don't mind."

Lu Wei misconstrued. "Five dollars first hour," she recited, holding out a hand. "One dollar each hour after that."

Fargo had had no intention of paying for her services. Then he saw Wen Po watching from near the saloon. Fishing in his pocket, he gave Lu Wei the money.

"After you, sir." Lu Wei stepped aside and bowed. "Please forgive these humble surroundings."

"You speak English better than Wen Po or Tu Shuzhen," Fargo said by way of praise. He sat on the edge of the small bed, his hat in his lap.

"I was born in America. They were not." Lu Wei closed the door and without preliminaries commenced working at her dress.

"You're getting ahead of yourself," Fargo said. "I only want to talk."

Lu Wei cocked her head, her smooth brow furrowing. "I am afraid I do not understand. You gave me five dollars."

"And you can keep it," Fargo said. "It's money well spent if we can help one another."

"Again I do not understand." Lu Wei turned the chair so the back was to him, and straddled it.

"I was in the saloon a while ago."

"I saw you."

"It's not right they punish you. They're to blame. Not you. They dragged you and the other girls here against your will."

Fear twisted Lu Wei's features and she put a finger to her lips. "It is not permitted to discuss such things. Those who do are severely beaten."

"No one will ever know," Fargo promised. "This is between the two of us. I would like to help you and your baby."

"How?" Lu Wei asked suspiciously.

"By helping you escape. In return, you help me find the woman I'm hunting for. Her name is May Ling. She's a sweet young thing. She was kidnapped in San Francisco about two months ago. Her father hired me to fetch her back. Have you seen her?"

"Everyone has seen her."

"Good. Then what do you say? Do we have a deal?" Fargo held out his hand for her to shake.

Lu Wei stared at it but did not move. "Does May Ling know you have come to take her home?"

"Not yet. Not that it matters. She'll be glad to be shed of this hellhole," Fargo predicted.

"Perhaps not," Lu Wei said. "Perhaps she will refuse to leave, and if you try to take her, she will fight you."

"Why in God's name would she do something like that?" Fargo rated the notion ridiculous.

"Because the sweet young thing, as you call her, that you have come so far to save, is Tobias Cain's woman."

4

To say Fargo was stunned was an understatement. Nothing Shen Ling, the father, had told him, and nothing he had unearthed, hinted at anything like this. "Are you sure?"

"Quite sure." Lu Wei smiled thinly. "May Ling lives in Tobias Cain's fine house. She sits at his supper table and eats from his fine china. She sleeps in his fine bed. She is very much his woman."

"But she has only been here a couple of months."

Lu Wei's smile widened slightly. "Your sweet young thing worked fast to get where she is."

Fargo felt like a water skin that had just been punctured. Spiriting May Ling back to San Francisco was not going to be as easy a chore as he reckoned.

"As for helping you in return for you helping me," Lu Wei said, "I must respectfully decline. I do not want to leave yet."

"But you are in danger," Fargo reminded her. "I heard what Pardee and Wen Po said. If you are pregnant, you are of no use to Cain."

"Then it is good I am not with child."

"What?" Fargo had just taken three verbal kicks to the gut, and this latest had him completely confused. "But you told Wen Po—"

"Today is the day the workers from the Oasis come

27

to Whiskey Mill," Lu Wei revealed. "Many men would want to bed me. I would rather not do that."

"So you made up a story about being pregnant?"

"Tobias will be mad that I tried to avoid my duty, but not as mad as if I were of no use. The worst he will do is have me whipped."

"You say that as if it you don't mind."

"It will not be the first time," Lu Wei said, and shifting her shoulders, she grimaced. "I have endured much here. I will endure more until I have done what I have set my mind to do."

"What would that be?" Fargo asked.

"You should go now," Lu Wei said, and held out the five dollars. "Here. It is not right I take your money and not pleasure you."

Fargo pocketed the money. "My offer still holds, though. If you want to get out of here, I will take you with me when I go."

"You have not been to the Oasis, have you?"

"No. Why?"

Lu Wei leaned toward him and placed her hands on his knees. "You should leave while you still can. Your purpose is noble but you have no idea of what you are up against. You are one and they are many. Even if May Ling wants to leave, which I very much doubt, the two of you would not get far. Tobias Cain would see to that."

"He's not the Almighty," Fargo said.

"Cain is as close as mortal man comes. You will understand why when you see him. And he has many killers working for him. Forty-one in all, I believe."

A soft whistle escaped Fargo. He had not expected to go up against a small army.

"There is another reason escaping with May Ling is impossible," Lu Wei said. "Tobias Cain has two men working for him, brothers from somewhere in the South. They are trackers. The best alive, Cain likes to boast. They can catch anyone, anywhere, anytime. It is no idle boast, either. They catch everyone they go after."

Fargo was not without skill as a tracker, himself. "These brothers have a name?" he asked.

"Shote and Vale Viktor, with a 'k.' "

Another unwelcome revelation. Fargo had never met the Viktor brothers but he had heard of them. They were indeed two of the best. They also had no scruples about working on the shady side of the law. Saloon gossip had it that for sport they liked to hunt down Apaches.

Fargo sat up and donned his hat. Lu Wei had given him a lot to think about. "Thanks for the information."

"There is one other you should know about. A Modoc they call Captain Jim. He is vicious, that one. He never speaks, except to Cain. He is like a ghost, that one. When he walks, you do not hear him. Among all those who work for Tobias Cain, Captain Jim is most feared."

"If you have any more bad news," Fargo said, "I don't want to hear it."

Lu Wei grinned. "I am sorry. You have been kind to me and I would not have you come to harm. Leave before it is too late. Leave before you are one of the many Cain has had killed."

"I can't," Fargo said.

"Why not? Is it the money her father is paying you?"

"No, it's not that. I don't get a cent until I hand her over to him." Fargo stood and arched his back to relieve a cramp.

"Then why?"

"I gave her father my word."

Lu Wei was silent awhile. Then she did a remarkable thing. She kissed him on the cheek.

Her lips were exquisitely soft, and her scent reminded Fargo of high country flowers in the bloom of spring. "What was that for?"

Before Lu Wei could answer, a low rumble filled the air and rapidly grew louder, swelling until it became pounding thunder. Riders trotted past her shack. A lot of riders.

Fargo sprang to the door and peered out. Dust enveloped him, and he coughed. The new arrivals came to a stop in front of the saloon but did not dismount. All eyes were on the man in the lead, who wore an expensive brown suit and a wide-brimmed brown hat.

"Tobias Cain," Lu Wei whispered in Fargo's ear.

The lord of Death Valley was a giant. When he swung down and unfurled, he stood close to seven feet tall. His shoulders were twice as broad as those of any of the men with him. His barrel chest bulged with muscle. Tree trunks for legs lent him the stature of a human redwood. He had a square face, a chin like an anvil, and fingers as thick as spikes. Gesturing with those fingers, he boomed in a voice as deep as a well, "That pinto must be his. Spread out and find him."

Among those dismounting was a familiar face. "Pardee told me it would take Krast four hours to get to the Oasis and back," Fargo mentioned.

"Krast probably met Cain on the way here," Lu Wei said quietly. "The wagons will not be far behind."

"Wagons?"

"I told you, remember? This is the day the Chinese workers are treated to a night in Whiskey Mill. Cain often comes with them and brings at least half his killers. The rest stay at the Oasis."

The riders were fanning out in twos and threes; Krast, Hank, and more of their flinty-eyed ilk, bristling with weapons.

Tobias Cain stood under the saloon overhang, his enormous arms folded across his huge chest. Flanking him were several men who did not take part in the search. Two were scruffy scarecrows in loose-fitting homespun, enough alike to be brothers. Shote and Vale Viktor, Fargo guessed. The third was short, stocky, and swarthy, and wore a faded army jacket, a breechclout, and moccasins. It had to be Captain Jim.

"You cannot escape them," Lu Wei whispered fearfully.

"I don't aim to try." Fargo pecked her on the forehead. "If anyone asks, I was great in bed."

Her surprise at the kiss was matched by the surprise of the searchers at what Fargo did next. He walked boldly out and strolled toward the saloon, the Henry at his side. As he was the only stranger in Whiskey Mill, it was obvious he was the man they were looking for. Within moments he had acquired a dozen shadows, some with rifles, some fingering their pistols. No one tried to stop him. He rounded the hitch rail, patted the Ovaro, and turned to the giant. "What's all the fuss?"

Tobias Cain was unusual in another respect besides his size. His eyes were deep, penetrating pools of silvery gray, a quicksilver hue not possessed by one person in a million. When those eyes bored into someone, as they now bored into Fargo, they gave the impression they could see right through him. "So you're the one who tangled with my men." It was a statement, not a question.

From among the pack of curly wolves stepped Krast and Hank. "That's him!" barked the turkey buzzard. "He's the one who damn near busted my noggin."

Tobias Cain looked Fargo up and down, his silvery eyes twin daggers. "Do you know who I am?"

"You're not Abe Lincoln." Fargo should know. He had met Lincoln not long ago and been impressed by Honest Abe's quiet dignity.

Cain chuckled, then leaned toward the swarthy

Modoc in the army jacket and said, "Do you hear, Captain Jim? He's not scared of me. I can tell. That is quite rare. This promises to be interesting."

The Modoc did not answer. Up close, he had a cruel cast to his countenance. Here was a natural-born killer if ever Fargo met one.

Tobias Cain stepped from under the overhang. Few men ever towered over Fargo, but Cain did. He was taller and broader and more heavily muscled. "Suppose you explain why you did what you did?"

"Krast has a big nose," Fargo said levelly.

"Hank and him are under orders to question strangers," Cain rumbled. "*My* orders. So when you bucked them, you were bucking me. And I don't like to be bucked. I don't like it at all."

Krast moved to Fargo's right and tapped the pearl grips to his Smith and Wesson. "Let me have him, Mr. Cain. I owe him. And I don't want you thinking I can't do my job."

Whiskey Mill was astir. Pardee had appeared in the saloon doorway. Tilly emerged from the house. Most of the Chinese women, including Lu Wei and Tu Shuzhen, were interested spectators.

Tobias Cain raised a hand twice the size of Fargo's. "All I have to do is this"—he snapped his fingers—"and my men will turn you into a sieve."

A glance showed Fargo that Cain's men had trained their rifles and revolvers on him. His life hung by a leaden thread. Unless he thought of something, and fast, he could count the minutes he had left to live on two hands. "Is this how you treat everyone who wants to work for you?"

Cain placed his huge hands on his hips. "Perhaps you better explain."

"The law is after me. I had to leave San Francisco in a hurry." Fargo made it up as he went along. "I'd heard about this place. Heard you have a lot of men working for you. Heard you hire on with no questions asked."

"That won't wash," Cain said. "I've gone to considerable lengths to keep what I am up to a secret."

"Did you really think you could go around kidnapping people and no one would notice?" Fargo countered. "The missing women are the talk of Chinatown. How many Chinese have you kidnapped, anyhow?"

"Three hundred and twenty-seven."

Fargo was dumfounded. That was far more than he expected, far more than Shen Ling had said were missing.

"That's where you heard about me? San Francisco?"

"Whispers," Fargo said. "A mention of Whiskey Mill. Of someone in need of hired guns."

"He's lying, boss," Krast flatly declared.

"Maybe not," Cain said. "There's bound to be talk. It could be he did hear something."

"I don't trust him," Krast persisted.

Tobias Cain turned and asked in a deceptively mild tone, "Are you questioning my judgment?"

Krast blanched and shook his head so vigorously, it was a wonder he didn't shake it clean off. "No, sir. Not ever. Whatever you say or want is always fine by me."

"I would hope that's the case," Cain said. "I would hope I have made it clear to you and everyone else that my word is to be obeyed without question or quibble."

"You have," Krast said, and was echoed by Hank and others.

Cain shifted toward Fargo. "As for you. I already have enough men in my employ. What skills do you possess that would persuade me to add you?"

"I'm more than a fair hand with a shooting iron," Fargo said.

"So is Krast and half a dozen others," Cain rejoined. "I need an extra gun like I need an extra nose."

"I can track."

The giant nodded at the Viktor brothers. "So can they. Better than most anyone alive, as a matter of fact." He sighed. "If those are all the skills you have, then you have come a long way for nothing."

"I can think," Fargo said.

Tobias Cain snickered in amusement. "Can you, now? Well, that is a rare talent. Most of my men are as dumb as stumps."

Krast and Hank and some of the others looked uncomfortable, but not one objected to the insult. It showed the sway Cain had over them. They were hardened killers, but they were afraid of him.

"Am I hired?"

"Not yet." Cain began removing his jacket. "Every man I take on has to pass a test first."

Sadistic smiles sprinkled those watching. Krast licked his thin lips and smirked in anticipation.

"What kind of test?" Fargo asked, suspecting the answer and hoping he was wrong.

"A measure of his mettle." Tobias Cain folded his jacket neatly and gave it to Hank to hold. "The only measure I rate as worth a damn."

"That doesn't tell me much."

Cain flexed his thick fingers, then balled them into fists the size of hams. He tucked slightly at the knees. "If you want the job bad enough, you have to fight me."

"Does anyone ever refuse?"

"A few have. Usually I break a few bones, the price they must pay for wasting my time. I trust I won't need to break any of yours."

5

Excitement rippled among the toughs and cutthroats as they formed a circle around Fargo and Tobias Cain. Wagers were made. Fargo noticed few were willing to bet on him. A space was cleared for Lu Wei and the other Chinese women as they made their way to the front.

All the while, Tobias Cain limbered up by boxing an imaginary adversary. For a man his size, he was lightning with his fists. He had been at it a couple of minutes when he pivoted in Fargo's direction and stood stock-still. "Why are you just standing there? I thought you wanted to work for me."

"Working for you is one thing," Fargo said. "Being worked over by you is another." He had no hankering to fight. Cain outweighed him by at least a hundred pounds and had fists twice as large as his own.

"Can you think of a better way for me to tell if someone is yellow?" the giant asked.

"I might hurt you," Fargo said.

Tobias Cain burst into hearty mirth. Some of his men added their brays. "*You* hurt *me*? How wonderful. I admire a sense of humor. But to be honest, if you land even one punch, I will be impressed." He paused. "That reminds me. You have not told me your name."

Fargo had been debating whether to use his own or

another. Since his was fairly well known throughout the frontier, he elected to err on the side of caution. "The handle is Kit Bridger."

"Off with the Colt," Tobias Cain commanded. "I am unarmed. You will be the same."

"I wish you would reconsider," Fargo said sincerely as he pried at his belt buckle.

"That will not happen, so you might as well resign yourself to the inevitable. Your reluctance puzzles me. You do not impress me as a coward. It could be you have more common sense than most, but I am afraid you are overlooking a pertinent fact." The giant flexed his huge arms. "I enjoy these bouts. They are the best exercise I know of."

Left with no choice, Fargo carried his gun belt and the Henry past Cain and held them out to Lu Wei. "Would you hold these for me?"

Taken aback, the young woman stared at them as if they might bite her. "Why me?"

"You're prettier than Krast," Fargo responded, and some of the hired guns chortled.

Krast put his hand on his Smith and Wesson but did not draw it.

"I don't have all day, Bridger," Tobias Cain said. "Let's get this over with. I promise not to harm you any more than is necessary."

Trying not to sound too sarcastic, Fargo replied, "I'm obliged." He raised his fists and slowly circled. "I'll do the same."

The giant laughed some more. "You amuse me. You truly do."

Fargo thought he was ready. He was wrong.

One instant Tobias Cain was motionless and smiling. The next he was a human tornado. His arms driving like steam engine pistons, he closed in. Fargo was forced to retreat to keep from having his face caved in. Cain's blows were incredibly powerful. They jarred him down to his toes. In fact, Fargo soon came to the conclusion that Tobias Cain was the strongest man he had ever fought.

Fargo blocked, ducked, weaved. Cain pressed him fiercely, giving him no chance to throw a punch of his own. Then an opportunity came. Cain's guard opened, if only a few inches. Instantly, Fargo swung a fist at Cain's middle. But Cain had deliberately lured him in, and was ready.

A ten-ton boulder smashed into Fargo's jaw. He was vaguely aware of tumbling, of the sky and the ground switching places. The next he knew, he was on his back and mocking cackles pealed on all sides. His head ringing, he rose on his elbows.

Cain was not laughing. He was waiting. "If that is the best you can do, I am afraid I have no use for you."

Fargo rubbed his throbbing jaw and forced his mouth to work. "I'm just getting warmed up."

"Prove it."

The taunt seared Fargo like a red-hot poker. No one had ever manhandled him like the giant was doing, and it rankled. He put his hands flat on the ground and pushed up as if he were about to stand. Instead, he whipped his legs out and around and had the satisfaction of connecting with the back of Tobias Cain's legs and sweeping them out from under him. The pain was excruciating, but it was worth it.

Tobias Cain landed hard on his back.

A collective gasp came from the onlookers. Apparently they had just witnessed a miracle.

In a twinkling, Fargo was up and waded in. A kick narrowly missed his kneecap. Another flicked at his groin. He was forced back, unable to land a blow. The next second, Tobias Cain was on his feet with those great fists cocked.

"That was clever of you, Bridger. My compliments. No one has ever knocked me down before."

The man thought highly of himself, Fargo reflected. He responded with, "There's a first time for everything."

"Now that we have each taken the other's measure, what do you say we find out which one of us has the most grit?"

Like two bulls charging headlong, Fargo and Cain hurtled forward. They planted themselves, and would not be moved. Punches rained furious and fast. They countered, they blocked, they slipped jabs and deflected uppercuts.

Cain fought with the methodical precision of a machine, never once making a mistake, never once letting a solid blow land. Fargo was not so fortunate. He caught a straight-arm to the ribs that came within a whisker of cracking them. A right cross to his hip almost buckled his legs. A left to his shoulder rendered his arm numb. He was doing his best, but it was not enough.

Fargo had been in a lot of fights, a lot of brawls. Usually he was the one in control. Usually he kept the other man on the defensive instead of the other way around. But in Tobias Cain he had met his match, and then some.

Soon Fargo was sweating and battered and bruised, yet Cain showed no more strain than if he were out for a Sunday stroll.

Cain's men whooped and hollered in vicious delight, Krast the loudest of them all. "Bust his head open, boss! Spill his brains!"

With his next punch, Cain nearly did.

Fargo saw it coming and ducked, but he was a shade too slow. It was a wonder his head stayed on his neck. The world exploded in pinwheeling bright lights and for a few harrowing moments he could not see. Backpedaling, he shook his head to clear it, which made the pain worse. A wave of dizziness washed over him, and he stopped to catch his breath. Just when he thought he would collapse, his vision cleared and his legs steadied.

Tobias Cain was advancing.

Fargo dipped his chin to his chest and swayed. He wanted Cain to think he was about to drop. It worked. Cain grinned, swept his arm back, and unleashed what he no doubt counted on being the last punch. Ducking, Fargo felt Cain's fist knock his hat off. Above him, unprotected, was Cain's face, Cain's chin. His own fist was close to the ground. In a flashing arc Fargo brought it up, throwing all of his weight and every ounce of strength in every sinew in his body into as perfect an uppercut as any man ever threw. He nearly broke his hand.

The *crack* of knuckles on jawbone was like the snap of a tree limb. Tobias Cain staggered. His huge fists drooped. Blinking and shuffling, he appeared to be on the brink of consciousness.

Seizing the moment, Fargo sprang. His fist was a flesh-hued streak. But it did not land. Cain's hand darted out and caught hold of his wrist. Undaunted, Fargo swung his other arm, only to have that wrist seized, as well.

"No more."

Fargo wrenched and pulled and almost succeeded in breaking loose.

"Didn't you hear me? It's over, Bridger. You have proven yourself." Tobias Cain let go and stepped back. Gingerly rubbing his anvil jaw, he said without malice, "That was some punch. I have never been hit that hard by anyone. Were we in earnest, the outcome might be in doubt."

The praise surprised Fargo. There were aspects to the giant he did not expect.

Cain's gaze sought Krast. "You exaggerated, Asa. You claimed Bridger tried to bash in your brains, to use your own words. But I daresay if he had tried, your brains would be on the saloon floor."

Krast was a boiling pot ready to overflow. "Are you taking his side, boss? After all I've done for you?"

"I do not deny you have rendered valuable service from time to time," Cain said. "But do not presume to trade on my good graces to get me to do something I shouldn't. I am always fair in my dealings with those under me, am I not?"

Krast did not answer.

"I didn't hear you, Asa."

"Yes, sir," Krast spat.

"Then I suggest you drop your grudge," Cain advised. "As of this moment, Bridger, here, works for me, the same as you. He is entitled to the same consideration you would be." Cain held out a huge hand to Fargo. "That is, if you are still willing."

The more Fargo learned, the more puzzled he became. He had not tried to win the giant's confidence, but now that he had, he saw how it could work to his benefit. "Count me in," he said, and shook.

"The job pays a hundred dollars a month to start. Plus a place to hang your hat at night, and free meals."

Fargo remembered Lu Wei telling him that Cain had over forty men riding for him. If Cain paid all of them the same, that came to over four thousand dollars a month. Where did all the money come from? he wondered. Surely not from the doves or the farm.

Tobias Cain was shrugging into his jacket. "I intend to head back to the Oasis at six this evening. Until then, your time is your own." He strode toward the saloon, the onlookers moving quickly aside.

Hank came up to Fargo. "No hard feelings? Now that we're working together, we might as well get along."

Krast, Fargo noticed, was not willing to bury the

tomahawk. The scrawny buzzard glared, then tramped off toward the shacks.

"I'm afraid Asa won't ever forgive and forget," Hank said. "It's not in his nature."

"Why does Cain keep him on if he's so hot-headed?" Fargo asked.

"Oh, Krast has his uses," Hank answered with a sly smile. "But don't ever turn your back on him. Accidents have been known to happen to people he doesn't much care for."

Since Hank was being so friendly, Fargo sought to confirm his hunch. "Do all of us make the same amount?"

"Exactly the same. Except for the Viktor brothers and Captain Jim. Mr. Cain never shows favorites except for those three."

"Cain makes that much money from selling vegetables?"

Hank chortled. "The Oasis is only part of it. He has his fingers in several pies at once. He'll tell you about them himself when the time is right."

"You like working for him, I take it?"

"I've never had it better," Hank admitted. "The grub is good, the work ain't too god-awful hard, and the Chinawomen are there when we feel the need."

"Are all the workers at the Oasis Chinese?" Fargo continued to probe.

Hank nodded. "Coolies, every single one. Even the cook and the butler Mr. Cain has."

"A butler?" Fargo said in amazement.

"You'll find that Mr. Cain likes to live high on the hog. He has the best of everything. Wait until you see his mansion. You'll think you were in Georgia."

"I can't wait," Fargo said.

"You're in for a heap of surprises," Hank predicted. "Why don't I introduce you to some of the boys? The first drink is on me."

The saloon was jammed except near the corner table Fargo had occupied earlier. Tobais Cain sat there now. Everyone gave it a respectful berth.

Conspicuous in their dresses, the Chinese girls mingled with the hard cases. Tu Shuzhen was talking to Krast.

Lu Wei saw Fargo staring at her, and smiled demurely.

Hank made a circuit of the room. Soon Fargo had met the likes of Stoney Loftis, a Texan from the Staked Plain country. He met bushy-bearded Merle Twern, who had lost the use of a knee to an Apache arrow and had a pronounced limp. There was beefy Benjamin Cavendish, who wore two bowies, and who, according to Hank, could split a melon at ten paces. There was Kid Fontaine, whose pockmarked face was enough to give a child nightmares. And others, all cast from the same hard mold, and all held on a tight rein by the one person in the world they feared: Tobias Cain.

Eventually, the weasely Hank drifted to a table to take part in a poker game and Fargo found himself alone at the end of the bar. He was not alone long. Perfume wreathed him. He had caught a whiff of the same scent when he took his stroll. "So you don't stay in that house all the time."

Tilly leaned on the counter. "If I don't put in an appearance, Mr. Cain will take it unkindly. And I'm hoping he'll ask Pardee and me out to his mansion for supper. I always go along. The woman Mr. Cain has taken up with loves to entertain."

"A friend of yours, is she?" Fargo played dumb once more.

"I hardly know her. Her name is May Ling. She came in with the last batch from San Francisco. Tobias took one look and claimed her for himself. Don't ask me why."

"You sound jealous."

"Hell yes, I'm jealous," Tilly declared. "I'd rather live in luxury than in that hovel. All those nice clothes. A four-poster bed. Waited on hand and foot. I could get used to that real quick."

"So this May Ling has it easy," Fargo remarked.

"She better enjoy it while it lasts," Tilly said, fluffing her hair. "None of the girls Cain picks ever last long. He always tires of them."

"Then what?" Fargo asked. "They're sent to work in the shacks?"

Tilly made sure no one was eavesdropping. "No. It's the strangest thing. They always disappear."

6

Fargo had added incentive to find May Ling quickly.

Over at the corner table, Pardee was saying something in Tobias Cain's ear. Whatever it was, Cain did not look happy when he replied. Pardee, grinning, stepped forward and raised his arms.

"Quiet down! Mr. Cain wants your attention!"

A hush instantly fell. All eyes focused on the giant. Tobias Cain had been treating himself to scotch. Now he slid the bottle to one side, folded his huge hands, and said in his rumbling manner, "It has been brought to my attention that one of you is not happy working for me."

Some of those eyes shifted to Lu Wei. Those nearest her suddenly wanted to be somewhere else.

Cain beckoned imperiously and Lu Wei came meekly to the table, her head bowed. "What is this I hear from Pardee? You're going to have a baby?"

Murmuring erupted. Wen Po looked like a cat that had just been jabbed with a fork.

Lu Wei met Cain's gaze. "No, great one, I am not."

There was a lot more murmuring, silenced only when Tobias Cain raised an enormous hand. Cain leaned back and drummed his thick fingers on the table. "What are you playing at, girl? Why did you tell Wen Po and Pardee you were with child?"

Lu Wei did not answer.

"Let me guess," Cain said. "You knew the wagons were due today and you wanted to get out of earning your keep."

"A strange choice of words, great one," Lu Wei responded. "Is it earning one's keep when one is forced to do something against one's will?"

Shock spread like wildfire. Even more space was cleared around her. Tu Shuzhen looked stricken. Others plainly expected a dire outcome.

But Tobias Cain did not rear up in anger or indulge in petty threats. He sat and studied her, then remarked, "I don't quite know what to make of you, Lu Wei. You are aware of the punishment for disobeying. You have only been with us a short while, yet you have been whipped twice. Why invite a third blistering with the lash?" When she did not reply, he went on. "It's not that you are stupid. On the contrary. You are more intelligent than most of the girls."

"The great one is mistaken," Lu Wei brazenly said. "I am as ordinary as rainwater."

Cain stopped drumming his fingers. "When you were brought here I assigned you to the shacks because of your looks. You are uncommonly pretty, and the shacks are for the pretty ones. A lot of girls would be happy doing that rather than working the fields all day."

"I do not mind hard work."

Cain gave no sign that he heard her. "The first time you were whipped was because you refused to spread your legs. We cured you of that. But then you refused to sleep with Mr. Twern, whose habit of never bathing has made him a bit rank. Now this." Cain rose, came around the table, and cupped her chin. "Explain yourself. And make it good."

"It is simple, great one. I am not a whore."

Cain's arm flashed. The *smack* of his palm on her cheek was like the crack of a derringer. Lu Wei rocked

45

on her heels and stumbled against a table. Before she could recover, Cain had her chin in his hand again.

"Use that tone with me again and I will snap your neck. The one thing I will not abide, ever, is disrespect." Cain leaned down until his nose practically touched hers. "What are you up to?"

Lu Wei would not meet his gaze.

"You do this on purpose," Cain said slowly. "You want me to assign you to field work. But not because you hate working a shack more than most. There's something else. Something you are not telling me."

"I would not—" Lu Wei began.

Cain's huge fingers clamped hard, gouging her flesh. "Don't insult my intelligence, girl. I am wise to you now. And I have a surprise for you." He stepped back. "Pardee?"

"Sir?" Pardee came briskly up to them.

"As of this minute Lu Wei is no longer under your charge."

"Sir?"

"I am granting her wish. She goes back to the Oasis with me. From here on, she works the fields."

"You're letting her get away with lying to you?" Pardee was astounded.

"You know me better than that," Cain said harshly. "Little miss is in for a surprise." The two of them were talking as if Lu Wei were not right there in front of them. "Lock her in her shack until I'm ready to leave. I'll send a new girl to replace her."

"Yes, sir." Pardee took hold of Lu Wei's arm and marched her out, none too gently.

Tobias Cain reclaimed his seat. Gradually, conversations resumed. Bottles and glasses tinkled.

"That was darned peculiar," Tilly said, half to herself.

"In what way?" Fargo asked.

"Cain never lets anyone manipulate him. Unless I am very much mistaken, he has something special planned for that poor girl. Something nasty." Tilly stopped and twisted her head. "Hear that? Here come the workers."

Loud rattling and creaking accompanied the thud of hooves.

Fargo went to the window. Half a dozen wagons were rolling into Whiskey Mill. All the drivers and four heavily armed riders ahead and behind were white, but the wagon beds were crammed with Chinese. The lead wagon came to a stop in front of the saloon and the Chinese spilled out.

"The workers who behave themselves are allowed to come here once a month, fifty or sixty at a time," Tilly explained at Fargo's side. "They almost seem happy, don't they? You would never guess to look at them that they are being held against their will."

Krast and Hank and the rest of the hard cases who had ridden in with Tobias Cain were gathering up rifles. Some filed out. Others took up positions around the saloon.

"Now and then a drunk worker will take it into his head to try and escape," Tilly said. "The guards see to it they don't get far." Tilly placed her warm hand on his and spoke softly. "Listen. Pardee will be busy as hell for the rest of the day. What say you pay me a visit in half an hour or so? Come to the back of the house." She paused. "Make sure no one sees you."

"What do you have in mind?"

Tilly smiled seductively, and winked. "To get better acquainted. As if you didn't know." She lightly ran a fingernail across his wrist. "I'll make it worth your while, handsome. I promise."

"Half an hour, then," Fargo said. He waited a couple of minutes after she sashayed off. By then the saloon had filled with Chinese. Some clamored for drinks. Others flocked to the tables to gamble. Fargo strolled outside.

Merle Twern and Kid Fontaine were by the hitch rail. Twern was a grimy ghoul who reeked worse than a pigsty. Kid Fontaine wore a derby and a pair of black-handled Remingtons.

Merle Twern was saying, "—two hours or so. We're to ride up to the ridge and escort him down. Mr. Cain's orders."

"You would think, after coming all the way from Los Angeles, he could manage the last mile on his own," Kid Fontaine complained. He had buckteeth and big ears that stuck out from under the derby.

"Don't let Mr. Cain hear you grouse," Twern warned. "He treats the fat man special for a reason."

"I'll be ready," the Kid said.

Fargo began unwrapping the Ovaro's reins from the hitch rail. The street bustled with activity. Lines of Chinese had formed in front of every shack except the eighth, the one Lu Wei was in. They were waiting their turns. Fargo went to lead the Ovaro to a water trough in the shade on the north side of the saloon, but his way was blocked by Kid Fontaine. The Kid's small hands were on the butts of the Remingtons.

"I want you to know something, mister."

"What would that be?"

"Krast is my pard. Him and me go back a ways, and I don't much like what you did to him."

"Keep standing there and I'll do it to you," Fargo said.

Kid Fontaine took a quick step back. "I'd like to see you try. I surely would. I've put windows in the skulls of more gents than you can count."

In his travels Fargo had run into more young upstarts like the Kid than *he* could count. "Brag a lot, do you?"

The Kid glowered and nipped at his lower lip with his buckteeth. "For two bits I'd prove it. But you're off-limits so long as you're of use to Mr. Cain."

"Don't let that stop you," Fargo said.

Merle Twern intervened, saying, "Enough, Kid. Don't let him goad you. The boss will have you skinned alive if you make maggot bait of this jasper without his say-so."

"I'm not dumb," Kid Fontaine snapped. Reluctantly, he stepped out of Fargo's way. "But this ain't over between you and me, mister. I'll be keeping an eye on you. Step out of line like you did with Krast, and I'll go to Mr. Cain and ask his permission to bed you down permanent."

"Whenever you feel lucky." Fargo did not take his eyes off the Kid until he was around the corner. For all his bluster, Fontaine struck him as the kind who was as likely to shoot him in the back as the front.

Other horses lined the trough. Fargo made room for the Ovaro and waited while it drank. He was alone. It would be simple to mount up and ride off and forget the whole thing. Simple, and smart. The odds against him were too high. But he had given Shen Ling his word. Come what may, he would see it through.

After a while Fargo pulled the pinto from the trough and toward the rear of the saloon. A rusty nail sticking from the wall was handy for wrapping the reins around. Backing to the corner, he slipped from sight.

No one was behind the buildings. The saloon windows were all at the front so Fargo need not worry about being seen as he walked to the frame house and knocked on the back door. After a minute he rapped again. Still no Tilly. He was turning to leave when a bolt rasped and the hinges creaked.

"Took you long enough."

"I was washing up." Tilly took his hand, glanced

both ways, and ushered him inside. "No one saw you?"

"Just Cain and Pardee."

Tilly took a step back, then frowned. "That's not the least bit funny. Do you have any idea what Cain would do to us if we're caught together? I'm supposed to be Pardee's and Pardee's alone."

"Cain hasn't ever shown an interest? As good-looking as you are?"

Tilly patted her blond hair and playfully wriggled her hips. "Thank you, kind sir. I've received my share of compliments. But you wouldn't know it by Tobias Cain. My hair isn't dark enough and my eyes don't slant enough to suit him." She closed and bolted the door. "It's the strangest thing. But from what I've learned, Cain only beds Chinese girls, and only the prettiest, at that."

Fargo had known white men, bigots mostly, who would only bed white girls, and a few Mexicans who would only bed Mexican girls, and a gambler of French descent in New Orleans who swore black women were the best lovers in all creation. But he had never heard of a white man who liked only Chinese girls. He wasn't all that fussy, himself. Females were females. So long as a filly had lips and breasts and the rest, he was happy to oblige whatever amorous notions she had.

"It's the same with the workers," Tilly was explaining. "Why Cain prefers the Chinese over all others is beyond me. It's not all that far to the border, and Mexican workers come dirt cheap."

"You've never asked?"

Tilly had moved to a cupboard. From a middle shelf she took a half-empty bottle of whiskey and two glasses. "I like breathing too much to pry into Cain's antics. He does speak Chinese, though. Maybe that has something to do with it."

Fargo sat on the edge of the kitchen table. "Where did he learn their lingo?"

"How should I know?" Tilly rejoined. "According to Wen Po, he speaks it real well. Yet he always makes the Chinese speak English. Does that make any sense to you?"

"No," Fargo admitted.

Tilly placed the glasses on the table and filled them to the brim. Raising hers with care, she treated herself and smacked her lips. "Here's to Tobias Cain. May he wind up in an early grave."

"You hate him that much?"

"I was happy in San Francisco. The place I worked was called the Nugget. The money was good. Real good. The customers were high class. No drunken sailors or other riffraff." Tilly gulped half her glass, her features softening with sorrow. "I was happy there. Happier than I've ever been my whole life long. I'd have stayed at the Nugget until I was a shriveled old prune. But no. Cain tore me away from the best job I ever had."

"If it bothers you so much, don't talk about it."

"I want you to know. I was walking home late one night when his men jumped me. I had no idea why. I was scared to death. I tried to scream but they stuffed a gag in my mouth, rolled me up in a rug, and carted me off." Tilly uttered a cold, hard bark of a laugh. "Do you want to hear why they picked me out of all the women in San Francisco? Because Pardee told Cain he likes blondes."

"That's the only reason?"

Tilly finished off her drink and wiped her mouth with a swipe of her sleeve. "That's why. Cain wanted to hire Pardee, and Pardee wanted a blonde, and I was the first blonde Cain's boys came across. Pitiful, isn't it? If I had come along that alley ten minutes sooner or ten minutes later, they'd have missed seeing me." Tilly slapped the glass onto the table. "But enough about me and my bad luck. I didn't invite you here to bend your ears. I want you to help me forget for a while." She sidled over and pressed herself against him, bosom to chest, hip to hip. "What do you say? Are you in the mood?"

Fargo answered her honestly. "Haven't you heard? Men are always in the mood."

7

Tilly Foster had the most luscious lips. Full and ripe like plump cherries, they curled in invitation as she rose onto her toes and molded her mouth to Fargo's. Her breasts swelled like melons about to burst. Grinding her hips, she cooed deep in her throat.

Fargo had not feasted on feminine charms since San Francisco. A familiar hunger coursed through his veins, a familiar stirring occurred below his belt. His tongue met her tongue. She tasted of whiskey, with an underlying savor of chocolate. He sucked on her tongue and she sucked on his. Her fingers kneaded his shoulders and arms like they were clay.

When Fargo cupped her pert bottom, Tilly moaned and dug her fingernails into his biceps. He kissed her neck, her ear, her earlobe. She shivered as if cold but actually grew hot to the touch.

"Mmm. I knew you would be good. You've had a lot of practice, haven't you?" Tilly grinned.

"No more than most men."

"I wish Pardee had more. His idea of lovemaking consists of a couple of kisses and a minute of grunting. It's over before I can blink." Tilly sighed. "He gets his jollies but I never get mine. Is that fair, I ask you?"

Fargo had no interest in hearing about her bouts with other men. He kissed and licked her throat to take her mind off her bedroom woes. It didn't work.

"Some men are like that. They think only of themselves. When Pardee is done, he rolls off me, and that is that. I don't dare suggest he try to please me like I please him. I tried once and he shook me by the hair until my teeth rattled, saying as how only a slut would talk like that."

Fargo ran his hands from her shoulders to the base of her spine.

"I'm not no saint but I'm not no slut, either. So what if I like to be with men? I should think Pardee would be grateful to have me."

"You talk too much," Fargo said, and once more covered her mouth with his. He let the kiss linger until she was squirming with impatience. Then he brought his hand up and cupped her right breast.

At the contact, Tilly's eyes grew hooded with lust. "Like that, yes," she husked. "Don't be timid. I like it rough. The rougher, the better."

"In that case," Fargo said, and squeezed hard enough that she cried out. Her nipple tried to poke through her dress.

"Yesssssssss." Removing his hat, Tilly set it on the table and entwined her long fingers in his hair. "You stoke my fire and I'll stoke yours."

Fargo gave her other breast the same treatment. Tilly arched her back, sank her teeth into his shoulder. When next her lips found his, they were molten coals. Her hand did things, low down, and his manhood became an iron bar. A constriction formed in his throat and he coughed to clear it.

Tilly deluged him with fiery, passionate kisses. She was starved for caresses, for the intimacy Pardee denied her. Swept up in an inferno of desire, she stroked him with raw abandon.

It was all Fargo could do not to explode. He began undoing her buttons and stays. She took that as her cue to pry at his buckle and loosen his belt so his pants fell down around his ankles.

"Oh my," Tilly breathed. "You must be part stallion."

Fargo lathered her neck, her ear. Her dress parted, admitting his hand. He covered a wonderfully soft breast with his callused palm, then pinched her erect nipple between his thumb and forefinger.

Tilly's rosy lips were a delectable oval. "I want you inside me." She clutched at his pole. "I want you inside me *now*."

Gripping her shoulders, Fargo spun her around so her back was to him.

"What are you doing?"

Fargo did not answer. Instead, he bent her over the kitchen table. Looping his right arm around her waist, he slowly slid it higher. At the same time, he hiked at her dress with his other hand.

Tilly giggled and swished her bum from side to side. "You're just as naughty as naughty can be."

Her dress was up over her waist. Bunching the folds so they would not slip back down, Fargo positioned himself. Under her dress she had on the usual female impediments, and it required a minute for him to gain access and run a fingertip along her nether lips. She was wet for him, so very wet, and when his finger lightly brushed her swollen knob, she threw back her head as if to scream.

"Don't hold off any longer. Please. I need it."

Sliding his rigid member between her silken thighs, Fargo rubbed the tip where his finger had just been. The sensation was heavenly. Bit by gradual bit he inserted his manhood until he was all the way in.

"Oh! Oh! There!" Tilly husked. "Take me hard. Take me fast. But for God's sake, take me."

Placing his hands on her hips, Fargo commenced a

stroking rhythm as instinctive as breathing. He went slowly at first, sliding almost out and then sliding back in, using her hips for leverage. She had her hands flat on the table. Bit by bit they moved faster, increasing the friction, and their mutual pleasure, by rising degrees.

Suddenly Tilly cried out. She thrust against him in a frenzy of release. Her inner walls rippled and squeezed, and a different sort of deluge took place. She lost herself in ecstasy. Her head tossed back and forth, her legs quivered. Tiny mews kept cadence with their strokes.

Fargo stopped stroking as Tilly crested the pinnacle. At length she coasted down to some semblance of her normal state.

"Thank you," she breathed. "You were everything I hoped you would be. You put Pardee to shame."

"We're not done yet."

Only then did Tilly realize he was still rock-hard. "Oh my. Where have you been all my life?"

Fargo grinned and resumed stroking. She-cat that she was, she thrust against him with renewed vigor. The table creaked under their combined weight, its wooden legs grating on the floor.

Tilly looked over her shoulder, her eyes widening. "I'm almost there again! Oh! Oh! What you do to me!"

Fargo could say the same about her. His body was on the cusp of release. Every nerve, every pore tingled. A whirlwind formed inside his head. Then he was there, plunging over the rim into inner space and falling, falling, falling. The world blurred. His thoughts became a jumble.

The table made a racket but it couldn't be helped. Tilly's hands were wrapped around the edge, her head bowed. She mewed and cooed nonstop, adrift on currents of carnal rapture.

Eventually, mutually spent, they lay half across the table, Fargo cushioned on Tilly, Tilly blissfully smiling.

"Thank you, kind sir."

"Anytime." Fargo was close to dozing off. He might have, too, if not for a slight sound. Opening his eyes, he glanced toward the next room.

Framed in the doorway was Wen Po.

"What the hell!" Fargo exclaimed. Unfurling, he hitched at his pants, but he was much too slow.

Wen Po bolted. For someone her age, she exhibited the speed and agility of an antelope. Within heartbeats she was at the front door and whipped out into the bright light of day.

"What did you see?" Tilly asked, sluggishly rising and clasping her dress about her.

Fargo moved to a front window. All the curtains were drawn so there was no danger of anyone seeing inside. "The old Chinese woman."

"Wen Po? That witch!" Tilly exploded. "I should have known. She's always spying on me. She walks into my house any time she feels like it. I've complained to Pardee, but he says I'm making too much of it."

"Will she tell him?"

"I don't know. She's a strange duck. She always treats me nice even though I've yelled at her for snooping around like she does."

Fargo had his belt buckled and his Colt where he liked it to ride on his hip.

He parted the curtains and peeked out. Nothing had changed, except that Merle Twern and Kid Fontaine were about to mount up. Of Wen Po, there was no sign. "She's gone."

"That's another maddening habit she has," Tilly complained. "Pops up out of nowhere, then disappears like a damn rabbit down a hole."

"Does she do her spying for Pardee or Cain?"

"I can't rightly say. Either. Both. Hell, maybe she spies for her own self. Like I told you, she's a strange duck." Tilly was arranging her underthings as they should be. One breast hung out, full and round and inviting.

Fargo closed the curtain. "I have something to do. Join me in the saloon later and I'll treat you to a drink."

"We have time for more fun if you want," Tilly suggested. "Pardee will be busy as a bee until the wagons head back to the Oasis."

"As much as I want to, I can't," Fargo said. He kissed her and hurried to the back door.

"Bridger? Did you mean it? What you said about taking me away from here?" Hope lit Tilly's face.

"When I go, you're welcome to come with me. I'll take you anywhere you want. No strings attached."

"Thank you." Tilly's eyes were misting.

Fargo got out of there. No one saw him and soon he was on the Ovaro and heading north away from Whiskey Mill. Once under cover he looped to the west. Twern and Fontaine had said the man they were to meet was coming from Los Angeles, so that was the logical direction.

Tobias Cain was out in front of the saloon, talking to them. Twern kept nodding. Then the pair applied their spurs, and as Fargo had figured, they headed due west.

Hunching over his saddle, Fargo stayed hidden until they were out of sight. Cain went back inside. Lines of eager coolies still waited their turn at the girls. Fargo spotted Wen Po, just coming out of Lu Wei's shack. That puzzled him but he had no time to ponder what it meant.

For the next couple of hours Fargo trailed the two hired guns up into the mountains. A well-worn trail made the going easy. It soon became apparent they were making for a ridge. They were not in any great hurry. It enabled Fargo to circle wide at a trot and get ahead of them. He paralleled the trail to the top of the ridge, hid the Ovaro, and crept to a cluster of boulders within spitting distance of where the trail started down the other side. He had guessed right. Not five minutes later Twern and Fontaine arrived, and drew rein.

"No sign of the fat bastard yet," the Kid said. "He better not keep us waiting. I have more drinking to do."

"He's usually here when he says he will be," Merle Twern commented.

Saddle leather creaked. They were dismounting. On his side with his back to a boulder, Fargo was glad he was in the shade.

"Where do you suppose they met?" Kid Fontaine asked. "Cain and Miles Endor?"

"No one has ever mentioned," Twern said. "It's not too healthy to poke into their past."

"I'm just amazed, is all, at how slick Cain runs things. At the rate he's going, in another five years they'll have their own little empire. This whole corner of the state will be theirs."

"Mr. Cain thinks big—that's for sure," Twern agreed. "How he came up with the idea is beyond me. I would never have thought of it."

"That's because he has more brains than the both of us," Kid Fontaine said, "and I'm not too proud to admit it."

"All that matters to me is that he pays well," Twern said. "The work is easy enough, all things considered."

"We can thank the Chinese for that," the Kid said, and tittered. "They're yellow in more ways than one."

"What can they do? We have guns and they don't."

"There are forty of us and over three hundred of them," the Kid said. "They don't need a lot of guns, but they're too dumb to realize that."

"It's not in their nature. Over in China they always have to do as they're told. They're used to being bossed around." Twern paused. "That, and Mr. Cain fills their heads with promises he won't ever keep."

"Who ever thought you could get rich kidnapping a bunch of miserable Chinese?" Kid Fontaine said. He tittered again. Evidently it was a habit of his.

"It wouldn't work if they were whites or Mexicans," Twern said. "No one cares about Chinamen, though. Hell, there are anti-Chinese leagues all over the place. I reckon—" He stopped. "Did you hear that?"

Hooves clattered on stone. Riders were approaching. Fargo slid his hand to his Colt, just in case.

"There they are," Twern said. "Let me do the talking, remember? Mr. Cain told me what to say. He's fussy that way."

"He's fussy in a lot of ways," Kid Fontaine said. "That rule of his about no drinking at the Oasis is one I can live without."

"You and me and the rest of the boys," Twern said. "But it won't kill us. And Mr. Cain has his reasons."

"I still say we should sneak a bottle back."

"The last hombre who did that was sent packing," Merle Twern mentioned. "But only after Mr. Cain busted the bottle over his head and broke all his fingers on the hand he had been holding the bottle with."

The riders were near enough that Fargo heard a horse snort. Suddenly he froze. They weren't the only things approaching. Gliding sinuously toward his hiding place was a small rattler.

8

Rattlesnakes did most of their hunting at night. During the day they were fond of lying in the sun to warm their cold-blooded bodies. The small rattler had apparently been doing just that and was now seeking shade. As the whims of fate would have it, the snake was crawling toward the boulder Fargo was behind, and the very patch of shade Fargo was lying in.

Not everyone was aware that juvenile rattlers were as venomous as adults. Fargo was. He knew a bite from the small rattler could prove deadly.

Head low to the ground, the snake darted its forked tongue in and out. It was entirely possible the young rattler did not realize Fargo was there.

Ordinarily, Fargo would shout or stomp to scare the snake off. But he dared not utter a peep with the two cutthroats so close, and the riders from Los Angeles about to reach the top of the rise at any moment. All he could do was lie there, helpless.

The rattler slithered within spitting distance and abruptly stopped. Its head rose a few inches and its tongue darted faster. It had sensed Fargo's presence but was unsure what to make of him.

Fargo prayed to God the snake would not use its rattles. The Kid and Twern were bound to hear and might venture around the boulder.

The clomp of hooves grew louder. A horse whinnied.

"Howdy, Mr. Endor. It's good to see you again."

The hooves thudded to a stop. Puffs of dust swirled past the boulder. Someone made a sniffing sound.

"Twern, isn't it? I take it Tobias has extended the courtesy of sending you to meet me?"

"Yes, sir, Mr. Endor," Merle Twern responded. "He thinks highly of you, Mr. Cain does."

"Tobias thinks highly of money," Endor said. "I happen to be in a position to enrich his coffers."

"His what, sir?"

"I help him put money in his pockets," Endor clarified. "You could say much of the success of his entire operation hinges on me."

Kid Fontaine spoke up. "You and that other gent from San Francisco. The two of you bring in the most Chinese."

For perhaps a minute nothing else was said. The rattler did not move or hiss or strike. Then Endor, sounding distinctly displeased, remarked, "Am I to understand Tobias has other sources besides me?"

"Don't pay any attention to the Kid, here, Mr. Endor," Twern answered. "He doesn't know what he's talking about."

"Spare me your feeble attempt to cover for his mistake," Endor said resentfully. "I am not a simpleton." He sniffed again. "I am riding back to rejoin my wagons. You will return to Whiskey Mill and inform Tobias I expect to arrive by nightfall. Inform him I am most displeased."

"Yes, sir, Mr. Endor, sir," Twern said.

The riders from Los Angeles departed. Hardly were they over the crest when Merle Twern swore a mean streak, ending with, "Now you've done it!"

"What's put a burr in your britches?" Kid Fontaine demanded. "All I did was mention that other gent from San Francisco, and the fat man looked like he had swallowed a porcupine."

"You lunkhead!" Twern was furious. "Mr. Cain has been keeping it a secret. He doesn't want Endor and Proust to know about one another."

"Why in hell not?" the Kid snapped. "And why in hell didn't someone tell me?"

"Cain will rip our innards out," Twern said. "You, for having a leaky mouth, and me, for not stopping your mouth from leaking."

"It can't be as bad as all that."

Twern roared like a stricken bear. "It's worse, damn your hide! I told you to let me do the talking, but you didn't listen."

"Don't talk to me like that," Kid Fontaine bristled.

"It's nothing compared to what Mr. Cain will do," Twern predicted. "Jesus, Kid. You've stepped into it. I fear for you. I truly do."

"Stop it. You're starting to scare me."

"Let's head back. Mr. Cain will want to hear this as soon as possible." Twern's spurs jangled.

The Kid sought his advice. "What should I do? If I'm in as much hot water as you say, I should light a shuck."

"How far do you think you would get with Captain Jim and the Viktor brothers after you?"

"Then what?"

"Ride back with me and take your medicine. I'll explain that it wasn't entirely your fault. Maybe Mr. Cain will go easy on you."

"You'd do that for me, Merle?"

"We've been friends awhile now, haven't we?"

Once again drumming hooves receded with distance. Fargo was alone on the ridge. Or almost so.

The hoofbeats had agitated the rattler. It hissed, but did not bare its fangs, while crawling slowly toward him. Toward his face. Fargo scarcely breathed. The snake was within striking range, and when rattlers struck, they were quicksilver fast. There would be no dodging it, no evading its lethal fangs.

All Fargo could do was lie there and hope it crawled off.

But the snake kept coming. The vertical slits of its eyes fixed on his with mesmerizing intensity. It did not stop until its tongue almost brushed him, and then it suddenly coiled and raised its head higher in the typical striking posture. The buzz of its rattles confirmed the worst.

Fargo broke out in goose bumps. He was nose to snout with one of the most dreaded serpents alive. He could draw the Colt, but the snake's fangs would sink into his face before he cleared leather.

The rattler moved its blunt head to the right, then to the left. It opened it mouth, revealing its curved fangs. Drops of venom dripped from the tips. All it would take was the tiniest amount of that venom to stop a human heart from beating.

Fargo fought an urge to scramble to his feet. He would not make it. The snake swung to the left, toward his throat.

The rattler closed its mouth, but its tongue continued to probe.

Fargo could not say what made him do what he did next. Maybe it was the likelihood that the next time the snake bared its fangs, it would strike. Maybe it was the feeling that he had to do *something* or he was a goner. Or maybe it was simply frayed nerves. But whatever it was, he suddenly lunged, his own mouth wide open, and bit down behind the snake's head. Scales crunched and crackled under his teeth. So did the rattler's backbone. His mouth filled with blood and who-knew-what-else, and some of it trickled down his throat. He nearly gagged.

The rattlesnake went into a paroxysm of thrashing

and lashing. Its tail whipped wildly, the bony rattles striking Fargo's cheek, his brow, his neck. He saw the rattler try to bend its head to bite him and he clamped his jaws tighter. His teeth sheared deeper. More of whatever juices were inside the snake seeped down his throat. In a gag reflex, he nearly opened his mouth to throw up. Force of will smothered the impulse.

Ever so gradually the rattler's thrashings grew weaker and slower and finally stopped entirely.

Slowly, carefully, Fargo reached up and gripped the snake, next to his teeth. Only when he had a firm grip did he pry his teeth apart. Scales and pieces of flesh and blood dribbled over his lower lip into his beard. "Damn!" The head had been nearly severed and flopped against his wrist. He gave a start when one of the fangs brushed his skin.

Taking the rattler by the tail, Fargo threw it as far as he could. He examined his skin but did not find puncture marks. Removing his hat, he ran his fingers through his hair, then jammed his hat back on. After what he had just been through, he could use a whiskey. Better yet, an entire bottle, if only to wash the lingering aftertaste of the snake from his mouth. Thinking of it, he spat on the ground a few times, then hurried to where he had left the Ovaro.

The pinto's head was down, its tail limp.

"This heat is a son of a bitch, isn't it?" Fargo stepped into the stirrups and gigged the pinto to the west. He had not gone far when he spied six riders winding down the ridge. In the distance, so far away they were little more than specks, were a line of wagons and more men on horseback. The rest of Endor's party, no doubt. Fargo would have dearly liked to find out what was in those wagons, but he had already been gone long. He reined east and clucked to the Ovaro.

Fargo figured Merle Twern and Kid Fontaine would

take their time. He could easily beat them to Whiskey Mill. But spirals of dust showed they were riding hell for leather. Fargo went faster, as fast as the terrain allowed. But the two men had too large a lead. He had no hope of overtaking them before they got there.

Fargo tried his utmost anyway. When the squalid buildings reared like so many dust-caked tombstones, he swung to the north and came out of the woods near the water trough.

Quite a ruckus was taking place. A crowd had gathered in front of the saloon and more were streaming from the shacks. Coolies and girls and hired guns did not want to miss the spectacle.

Dismounting, Fargo left the Ovaro by the trough, hooked his thumbs in his gun belt, and sauntered to the front.

Kid Fontaine lay on his back in the dirt. His derby lay nearby. His nose was bleeding, scarlet flecked his mouth, and his ear had been smashed to a pulp. "Please, Mr. Cain!" he squawked. "I didn't mean anything by it!"

Tobias Cain was livid. His huge fists clenched, he glowered at the Kid. "Your stupidity is inexcusable."

"How was I to know?" Kid Fontaine wailed.

When he wanted, Tobias Cain could move incredibly fast. He did so now. Bending, he grabbed the Kid by the front of the shirt. One-handed, he lifted Fontaine into the air and held him at shoulder height. "I am afraid I must make an example of you."

"No one told me it was a secret!" the Kid bleated.

"Now you know," Tobias Cain said, and hit him. Not with a fist but with an open palm. It was a wonder Fontaine's head did not go tumbling in the dust.

"Please!" the Kid blubbered. His lips were pulped and the tip of one of his buckteeth was missing. "No more!"

"I am just getting started." Cain slapped the kid again, as casually as if he were swatting a fly.

Many winced at the fleshy *splat*.

More blood and part of another tooth oozed down the Kid's chin. Barely conscious, he feebly moved his hands as if to ward off the next blow. He muttered something, but no one could hear.

Tobias Cain effortlessly lifted Kid Fontaine higher and cocked his huge fist. If the blow landed, there was but one outcome. Then Cain saw Fargo, and Fargo's expression. Cain's arm lowered a trifle. "You don't approve?"

"Do you pull wings off flies, too?" Fargo rejoined.

"He did something he shouldn't have," Cain said.

Fargo cared little whether Fontaine lived or die. The Kid lived by the gun; he was no choirboy. But Fargo was curious as to how the giant would react when someone stood up to him. "I take it you have never made a mistake."

"I try not to if I can help it," Cain rumbled. "Mistakes get you killed."

"We're none of us perfect," Fargo said. "If you expect me to be, you might as well let me ride off right now."

Whispering spread, and quickly died when Cain raked the ring of faces with a piercing glare.

Merle Twern made bold to say, "The boy didn't mean no harm, sir."

Cain drew himself up to his full impressive height. He thoughtfully regarded the slumped figure of Kid Fontaine, then glanced at Fargo and let the stripling fall in a heap at his feet. "Happy now?"

"You're the boss," Fargo said.

"And you are one devious son of a bitch," Tobias Cain declared. Cain did the last thing Fargo expected; he smiled. "But you have a point. Killing someone who doesn't know any better doesn't teach him or anyone else much of anything." Cain slapped the Kid's cheeks a few times, so lightly the slaps were almost gentle.

Fontaine stirred and groaned.

"Can you hear me, boy?" Tobias Cain asked. "This is your lucky day. Bridger, here, has persuaded me to permit you to live. But don't think I've gone soft. Make another mistake like this one, ever, and I promise it will be your last." Straightening, Cain barked a dozen names, including those of Krast, Captain Jim, and the Viktor brothers. "I want all of you in the saloon. The rest of you stay alert. When Endor gets here, there promises to be trouble."

Fargo wondered why he had not been included among those called inside. He noticed Tilly talking to Tu Shuzhen. Acting casual, he threaded through the dispersing Chinese and hard cases.

Tu Shuzhen walked off before he got there.

"Where have you been?" Tilly asked. "I've been looking all over for you."

"I went for a ride." Fargo did not elaborate. "What can you tell me about this Endor?"

Before Tilly could answer, a hand fell on Fargo's shoulder.

"I wanted to thank you," Kid Fontaine said. He was bleeding and bruised and could barely stand.

"No need."

"Yes, there is. I didn't hear much of what you said to Mr. Cain, but Merle tells me you saved my bacon." The Kid managed a twisted smile, the best he could do with his mouth smashed and his gums and teeth rimmed with scarlet. "I don't know why, and I don't care. I won't forget it. If I can ever repay the favor, you let me know."

"I'll keep it in mind," Fargo said. He was amused. Not all that long ago, the Kid had threatened to kill him. Not that he imagined he would ever be so bad off he would need the Kid's help.

Little did he know.

9

The wagon train arrived in Whiskey Mill an hour before sunset. In the vanguard were six riders, rifles in
hand. Then came five covered wagons. On either side
of each wagon rode more men with rifles. Behind the
wagons came another dozen. The wagons were similar
to Conestogas except that the beds were longer and
the canvas tops were not as high.

Before the wagons got there, Whiskey Mill under-
went a change.

Tobias Cain had all the coolies rounded up and
herded into the junipers. He ordered the Chinese girls
to stay in their shacks. Tilly was sent to the frame
house and told not to show her face until she was sent
for. Next Cain had most of his men spread out the
length of the dusty street.

"Keep your rifles handy but don't make it look like
we're ready for a war even if we are."

Fargo was among a handful instructed to stay close
to Cain at all times. Krast and Hank were included,
along with the Viktor twins and Captain Jim. The
Texan, Stoney Loftis, and Cavendish, the man who
was partial to bowies, stood at the north corner of
the saloon.

The wagon train from Los Angeles rattled to a halt.
The man in the lead weighed close to four hundred
pounds. He had a face the size of a pumpkin and three

rolls of fat where his chin should be. For all his bulk, he was dressed in a finely tailored riding outfit. A pair of revolvers in a custom-crafted gun belt were around his tremendous middle. He was on one of the biggest horses Fargo ever saw, a roan that could bear the man's great weight with the same ease the Ovaro bore Fargo.

Flanked by the six riflemen at the front of the train, the mountain of lard drew rein a few yards from Tobias Cain. His pumpkin head swiveled on his thick neck, and his dark, glittering eyes took everything in. "Tobias."

"It's good to see you again, Miles," Cain said. "Any difficulties along the way?"

"No." Miles Endor leaned on his saddle horn. "You have brought a lot of men with you, I see."

"Don't I usually?"

"You also usually bring some of your Chinese, but I don't seem to see any," Endor observed.

"Oh, they're around somewhere," Cain said vaguely.

Endor's gaze alighted on Kid Fontaine. "Isn't that the boy you sent out to meet me? His face was in much better shape when I saw him last."

"He tripped," Tobias Cain said.

"I thought perhaps a building had fallen on him." Endor's pudgy hands shifted to his holsters. "Shall we quit bandying words, Tobias? We have been business associates for too long to indulge in petty games. I thought I was your only supplier and now I find out I am not."

"I won't deny it," Cain said.

"Why, in God's name?"

"You can't supply enough to meet my needs. It's nothing to become upset about, I assure you."

Endor's triple chins quivered with anger. "Damn it, Tobias. Don't patronize me. How many other cities are involved?"

"San Francisco, mainly. The Chinese community there is quite large. Larger even than in Los Angeles."

"Mainly?" Endor said. "How greedy are you? And why wasn't I told? You have put me at great risk."

"I don't see how."

"We can be hanged for what we are doing. The more of these wretches you kidnap, the greater the chance someone will go to the law."

"You worry too much, Miles."

"And you do not worry enough."

"Why don't we talk about it over a drink?" Cain suggested. "Once I explain, you will simmer down."

"Don't you want to see the latest merchandise first?" Endor raised an arm, and two of his riders went from wagon to wagon, pulling on ropes that dangled from each canvas. The canvas tops came off and slid to the ground, revealing iron bars. They were prison wagons. Huddled in four of the wagons were Chinese men. In the fifth were Chinese women. Most were slumped in misery and despair.

"You've brought more girls," Tobias Cain happily noted.

One of the men in the first wagon pressed against the bars. Of short stature, he wore clothes of fine quality. "Are you in charge here? What is the meaning of this outrage?"

Cain looked at Endor. "Who would this firebrand be?"

"I can speak for myself," the young man said. "I am Li Dazhong. My father is Ke Dazhong, one of the foremost merchants in Los Angeles. I demand that you free me this instant."

"Do you, now?" Tobias Cain said, smirking. "Tell me. Does your father care whether you live or die?"

"What a ridiculous question," Li Dazhong said. "Of course he does. I am his only son."

"Good. Then he'll be willing to pay through the

nose to keep you alive. And you will stay alive so long as you do as you are told."

"That is what this is about? Money?"

"What else?" Cain retorted. "We don't just take anyone. Mr. Endor, here, picks those with families with deep pockets. The men, anyway. With the girls it doesn't matter as much. They have a different use."

"I am being held for ransom?" Li Dazhong was indignant.

"You're not paying attention, boy. No one said anything about returning you to your father. We keep you here, and we keep you alive, so long as he keeps paying us to do so."

An awful insight had struck Fargo. He was wrong in thinking the abducted Chinese were coolies used as slave labor. There was more to it, much more. Yes, they were put to work at the Oasis, but they were held captive for one reason and one reason only: to make a rich man of Tobias Cain.

It was diabolical.

It was dastardly.

It was the brainstorm of a sick and twisted mind.

The Chinese were known for their close-knit families. They were also known for handling their problems themselves. They rarely went to the law. Factors Cain was exploiting.

But perhaps the most important factor was the one mentioned by Merle Twern up on the ridge. No one else would care. Most whites wanted nothing to do with the Chinese, and treated them as outcasts. Small wonder the Chinese kept to themselves.

Fargo had to admit that Cain had picked the perfect victims for his scheme. Even if, as Endor feared, someone did go to the law, missing Chinamen would not light a fire under most lawmen. The tin stars might nose around a little, ask a few questions, but that would be it.

Li Dazhong closed his eyes and pressed his forehead to the bars. "This can not be happening to me. I was born in this country. I am an American citizen."

"To me you are nothing but worm bait," Tobias Cain said. "Keep that in mind and we'll get along just fine."

Cain and Endor went into the saloon. The six riflemen went with Endor. Krast's bunch trailed after them, Krast snapping over a shoulder at Fargo, "What are you waiting for? A special invite?"

Fargo entered and drifted over near the front window. Now that he knew what was going on, he had a crucial question to answer: What was he going to do? He did not have a personal stake in any of this. He was there to do what he had been hired to do. Find May Ling and return her to her father. To do anything else, to try and bring Cain's web of greed and bloodshed crashing down, was certain suicide. He was outnumbered. So much so, it was ridiculous. One man could not hope to prevail against forty guns.

Then there were the Chinese. There were too many of them. Far too many to slip away in the middle of the night, with him to lead them to safety. They wouldn't get ten miles before the Viktor brothers and Captain Jim tracked them down. Even if they did somehow elude the trackers, it was doubtful many of the Chinese could live off the land. They would starve or die of thirst long before they reached a town or settlement.

It didn't help that Whiskey Mill was so far from civilization. In effect they were cut off from the outside world. They could rely on no one but themselves.

The more Fargo thought about it, the more obvious his choice became; he would spirit May Ling to San Francisco, collect the thousand dollars, and let the law know about Tobias Cain. Then it would be out of his hands.

There was one hitch. Or actually two. Fargo had promised to take Tilly and Lu Wei with him when he went. Pulling it off would take some doing, but if he helped himself to a few horses, it could be done.

His mind made up, Fargo paid attention to what was going on around him.

Tobias Cain and Miles Endor were at a table in the middle of the saloon. Ranged behind Endor were the six riflemen. Behind Cain were Krast and Hank and a few others. A bottle had been opened. Cain was pouring.

"Now then, let's hash this out. You're worried that I'm getting too big for my britches, that if I'm not more careful, you can end up behind bars. Is that the gist of it?"

Endor bobbed his triple chins.

"You should have more faith, Miles. Look at the precautions I have insisted you take." Cain slid the glass to him. "You make two trips out here a year. Everyone thinks you are in the trade goods business, so they don't think twice if they see you leaving Los Angeles with five or six wagons. You snatch only Chinese. Only certain Chinese, at that. Then you get word to their families. But the Chinese never know you are involved. They never know I am involved. They hand the money to your man, he hands it to you, and you take your cut and bring the rest to me."

Endor held up a hand. "I admit you have it well thought out. But the wrong word in the wrong ear and it will all collapse like a house of cards."

"I repeat. You should have more faith. My operation in San Francisco is as well thought out as the one you run in Los Angeles. And I started it long before I made you a partner."

"You keep too many secrets."

"You should be grateful I know how to keep my mouth shut," Cain countered.

"You can't keep this up indefinitely, Tobias," Endor said. "You realize that, don't you?"

"I don't intend to try," Cain assured him. "Once I have enough money, I plan to leave the country. Maybe live in Europe or on one of those tropical islands where the native girls wear grass skirts."

"How much is enough, if you do not mind my asking?"

"A million dollars."

Fargo was as stunned as everyone else. It was beyond belief, and yet, so far, Cain was pulling it off.

Miles Endor picked up his glass and set it back down. He flicked dust from his jacket. He looked about the room as if to assure himself it was there. Then he said mildly, "One of us is insane, Tobias, and I fear it isn't me."

Cain laughed. "You've seen how much some of the families are willing to pay to keep their loved ones alive."

"Yes, but—"

"What would you say if I told you I am a quarter of the way to my goal?" Cain nodded. "That's right. I already have a quarter of a million dollars. In four years, maybe five, I will have my million."

"I had no idea," Endor said.

"So are we cross? Or will you stick with me? You won't have a million, but your end will come to one hundred fifty thousand, at least. Isn't that worth a few risks?"

Endor drained his glass in two gulps and motioned for more. "You might well prove the death of me, but yes, damn you, I will stick with you."

"I figured you would. Now why don't you and your men enjoy yourselves? In the morning we'll head for the Oasis."

Now that the crisis was past, everyone visibly relaxed. Since no one had said he couldn't, Fargo went outside.

The sun was perched on the ridge and would soon relinquish its reign to the stars and a quarter moon. Haunted eyes gazed at Fargo from the prison wagons.

Li Dazhong, still pressed against the bars, stared down at him. "Help us, whoever you are. My father is rich. He will reward you handsomely. I give you my solemn promise."

Fargo was about to reply but a guard with a rifle came around the end of the wagon.

"Hush up, if you know what's good for you."

Fargo kept walking. The last wagon contained the women, eight in all, all young, all of them pretty, all of them bent in sorrow or quietly weeping. The wagon was parked near the last shack. Fargo leaned against the front wall, near the door. "Lu Wei?" he whispered.

"Who is that? Are you the big man with the blue eyes?"

"I want you to know I'll keep my promise to get you out of this. Whatever they do with you at the Oasis, I will find you."

"Do not trouble yourself," Lu Wei said.

"Would you rather break your back working in the fields?"

"Yes," Lu Wei answered. "I do not want or need your help. If you try to take me away, I will do all I can to stop you."

Footsteps warned Fargo that two of Cain's men were approaching. Nodding at them, he headed for the saloon. He glanced back, trying to make sense of Lu Wei's threat, just as a figure stepped out of the shadows on the other side of Lu Wei's shack.

It was Wen Po.

She had heard every word.

10

The rest of the night was uneventful.

Fargo stayed in the saloon until midnight, drinking and waiting for the other shoe to drop. Nothing happened. Cain did not call him over to demand he explain himself. Krast wasn't ordered to buck him out in gore. Either Wen Po told no one what she heard, or Fargo was mistaken and she had not heard anything.

Fargo didn't know what to make of it, just as he did not know what to make of Lu Wei's refusal to be rescued. But if that was what she wanted, fine. He would find May Ling, collect Tilly, and fan the wind.

Deep in thought, Fargo did not hear someone come up behind him. He almost gave a start when a hand fell on his shoulder. Spinning, he started to drop his hand to his Colt.

"Whoa, there!" Kid Fontaine exclaimed. "It's just me."

"What do you want?" Fargo felt half foolish, and was glad Tobias Cain had not glimpsed his display of nerves. Cain might wonder why he was so jumpy.

"To buy you a drink, is all," the Kid said amiably. He had cleaned off the blood, but he did not look much better. His lips would never be the same shape and his ear would bear a jagged scar from top to bottom. "What's your poison?"

Fargo was about ready for a refill anyway. "Whiskey."

Kid Fontaine leaned his forearms on the bar. He was much more subdued than before, much more withdrawn. He did not speak until Pardee poured their drinks. Then he raised his and said, "How about if we drink to stupidity?"

"If you can't think of anything better."

"I'm serious," the Kid said. "I learned a lesson today. Never trust a soul until he proves he can be counted on."

"Do you have anyone particular in mind?"

Kid Fontaine glanced at the center table. "Three guesses. I would have done anything for that man. I thought he was the greatest thing since this red-eye we're drinking. And look at what he did to me."

Fargo offered no comment.

"I would kill for him. Hell, I *have* killed for him. I'd have run naked through brambles, given my life for his, yet because I made an innocent slip, he pounded me near to mush."

"I heard a saying once," Fargo mentioned. "We're known by the company we keep." He was a fine one to talk. Most of his time was spent in saloons drinking, gambling, and making the acquaintance of fallen doves.

"He would have killed me and not batted an eye after," Kid Fontaine said. "I'm nothing to him. No more than the manure he steps in." The Kid flushed. He was working himself up, and that could prove dangerous for both of them.

"Where do you come from?" Fargo asked to take the Kid's mind off Cain.

"What's that got to do with anything?" Fontaine demanded. But he went on with, "From Virginia. I came west with my folks when I was knee-high to a

78

calf. My ma was put under by fever. My pa took to drink and broke his fool neck falling from a buck-board. I was eleven. I've been on my own ever since."

"When did you take up with Cain?"

"About a year ago. I had drifted west to San Francisco. I was in a saloon when a drunk bumped into me, then began pushing me around like it was my fault. I reckon he figured I'd be easy pickings, me being so puny and all."

"Were you?"

"I should say not. I slugged him so hard he fell on his bottom. That made him mad, so the fool went for his hardware." The Kid shook his head. "He was a turtle. I could have been asleep and beat him to the draw. And before you ask, no, I didn't kill him. I shot him in the shoulder and the leg and he flopped around like a fish, screaming and blubbering."

"Where does Cain come in?"

"I'm getting to that. Cain happened to be in the saloon. He's always looking for new men worth a damn, and he figured that was me." The Kid gazed glumly into his glass. "A hundred dollars a month sounded like all the riches in the world. I thought he walked on water . . . until this." Fontaine touched his face.

"You shouldn't let anyone hear you talk like that," Fargo warned.

"I ain't scared of Tobias Cain nor anyone else," the Kid boasted, although in a small voice. "Still, I reckon you have a point." He finished his drink. "Don't forget what I said about if you ever need help. I never meant anything more."

Fargo watched the bucktoothed stripling walk off, thinking that the world was a peculiar place at times. Circumstance had turned an enemy into an ally.

A commotion outside stilled every tongue. Loud

voices, and the sound of blows, preceded the door flying open. In spilled a young Chinese man in black: Li Dazhong. He pitched to his hands and knees.

After him came four of Endor's men with rifles, along with Merle Twern, Stoney Loftis, and the brutish Cavendish.

"We brought the Chinese like you wanted, Mr. Cain," Twern said. "But he didn't come easy. He's a hellion with his hands and feet."

Tobias Cain rose and pushed out an empty chair. "There's no need for any of that. Have a seat, Li. I can call you Li, can't I?"

Li Dazhong slowly rose. He had a bruise on his cheek, but the ones who had brought him had more. "Are you ready to release me?"

"Be serious," Cain said. "You're here to write a letter." He indicated the chair. "Would you care for something to drink or eat?"

"We have not been fed in two days," Li said. "We are given water but once a day. What do you think?"

"I'll take that as a yes." Cain snapped his fingers and Pardee hurried over with a tray bearing a pitcher of water, a glass, and a loaf of bread. Pardee placed the tray down and scurried away.

By then Li was in the chair. He glared at Endor, then fingered the bread with distaste. "Have you any rice?"

"You'll get plenty of rice at the Oasis." Cain sat back down. Almost immediately, Krast and Hank and Merle Twern ringed the table.

Li filled his glass. He smiled contentedly between swallows, and when the glass was empty, gently placed it down. "You mentioned a letter."

"To your father," Cain said. "Miles tells me he's made his money in the opium trade. Has more than a few opium dens, I understand."

"I am not involved with them. I disapprove."

"A man with morals. I can respect that," Cain said. "Me, I have none. Never have, never will. I killed my first animal when I was six, my first man when I was twelve." He snapped his fingers a second time and Pardee appeared carrying another tray; only on this one were paper, a bottle of ink, and a pen. "I mention that to impress on you the consequences of refusing."

"What would you have me say?"

"Tell your father you are alive and well. Tell him you will remain that way only so long as he pays a thousand dollars a month for as long as I see fit to hold you here." Cain smiled. "And no tricks."

Li placed a hand on the pen but did not pick it up. "You can not honestly expect me to comply?"

"You won't like what I do if you don't."

"Beat me if you wish. Torture me as you will. I will not write your letter," Li declared.

"Oh, I wasn't thinking of harming you," Cain said. "You're too valuable. But those women in the last wagon. Would it upset you much if I had one staked out and whittled on until you couldn't tell what she had been?"

"You are hideous," Li Dazhong said.

Tobias Cain laughed and smacked the table in delight. "I've been called a lot of things, and a lot of them none too flattering, but that is the first time anyone has ever called me that."

"You would harm the women to force me to write your letter?"

"I just said I would, didn't I?" Cain reached across and tapped the bottle of ink. "Get started."

"What if my father will not pay?"

"You're stalling," Cain said. "He'll fork the money over to keep you alive. They always do."

"He might demand proof that you hold me," Li mentioned.

"You were frisked after Endor's men knocked you

81

out in Los Angeles. Or maybe you haven't noticed your rings and that medallion you wore around your neck are missing."

"I wondered what happened to them."

"We'll send the medallion as the proof," Cain said, and grinned. "Problem solved."

Li picked up the pen and placed a sheet of paper in front of him. "What would you have me write?"

"I've already told you," Cain growled.

"Very well." Li removed the stopper from the bottle of ink and set it next to the bottle. He held the pen over the bottle, looked Cain in the face, and said quietly, "I would rather die than be humiliated by captivity." And with that he came out of the chair in a blur. He whirled so fast that none of Cain's or Endor's men had time to react. The pen was still in his hand but held like a knife instead of a writing implement. With a lightning thrust, he stabbed the pen deep into Stoney Loftis's right eye. The Texan howled and stumbled back, his revolver rising, but he did not complete the draw before his legs buckled.

Without slowing, almost in the same motion, Li Dazhong kicked Cavendish in the knee. Cavendish howled and unlimbered his bowies, but Li was out of reach, streaking past the riflemen toward the door.

"Stop him!" Cain roared.

One of Endor's men snapped a rifle to his shoulder.

Cain surged upright, bawling, "Don't shoot, you idiot! Take him alive!"

Other hired guns were between Li Dazhong and the door. They moved to stop him. Li became a whirlwind, using his hands and feet in ways Fargo had never seen a man use them, kicks and punches that were as incredibly effective as they were incredibly swift.

Fargo had to stifle an urge to run to his aid.

More men rushed in from outside. So many, they

jammed the doorway, making it impossible for anyone to get through.

Li realized that. In the middle of a swirling melee, he spun toward the window. He drove his right hand, his fingers held rigid, into the throat of one foe, leaped high into the air, and lashed his foot into the face of another. A path cleared, and he would have made it, except that Hank darted out of the bedlam and brought the barrel of his revolver crashing down on the back of Li's head.

Li Dazhong folded without a sound.

"That will teach you, you damned jackrabbit," Hank gloated.

Tobias Cain came around the table and over to Loftis. The Texan had thrown his last lead. Blood welled from the ravaged eye. The other eye was wide in shock, and death. Furious, Cain walked over to the unconscious Li and viciously kicked him in the ribs. Cain drew back his boot to kick Li again but lowered his foot without doing so.

One of Endor's men was also dead, his throat crushed by a hand blow. Endor flicked a finger at the body and said, "Someone kindly remove that, will you? And close the door on your way out. We don't want to tempt our reluctant guest more than we have to."

Li was hauled to the table and roughly shoved into the chair he had occupied. Cain growled at Krast and Krast dashed a glass of water in Li Dazhong's face. Li blinked and sputtered and slowly sat up.

Tobias Cain leaned toward him. "Try that again and I will have one of the women brought in. Then I will personally cut her throat in front of your eyes."

Li's mouth became a slit.

Cain uncoiled. Brutally, coldly, he struck Li as he had struck Kid Fontaine earlier, an open-handed blow that nearly took Li's head off and almost caused the chair to topple over. "That's for killing my men."

Li touched a finger to blood trickling from a corner of his mouth. "Such courage," he said thickly.

"What?" Cain responded in surprise.

"You hit a man who dares not fight back," Li said in undisguised contempt. "At least the men I killed had a chance to defend themselves."

Cain became a tower of rage. Stepping back from the table, he snarled orders, "Clear a space! Everyone stand back. This is between Dazhong and me." He removed his jacket and his hat and handed them to Krast.

Miles Endor heaved his enormous bulk erect. "Why bother, Tobias? You have nothing to prove."

"Except to him."

Li spread his legs and crouched in a peculiar stance. He held his hands in front of him, his fingers curled into claws.

"Whenever you are ready, little man," Cain said. His huge hands hung at his sides.

Li never hesitated. In a dazzling display of speed, he took two steps and vaulted high with his leg rigid. By rights he should have rocked Cain on his heels. But a hand as big as Li's head flashed out and seized Li's ankle. Li kicked with his other foot, and twisted. The kick had no effect, the twist failed to wrench his ankle free, and the next moment Li's lithe form arced toward the rafters.

As easily as Fargo might swing a feather duster, Tobias Cain swung Li Dazhong, slamming him onto the floorboards with an impact that seemed to shake the saloon. Not once, not twice, but three times the giant smashed the much smaller man to the floor, and after the third time Li lay limp and barely conscious with blood streaming from his nose and an ear.

Straddling him, Tobias Cain jabbed a thick finger into Li's chest. "I swat my own flies."

11

The Oasis, they called it.

A farm where the Chinese were forced to labor for as long as Tobias Cain saw fit, while their families paid for the privilege of Cain keeping them alive.

Fargo had imagined a plot of five or ten acres with ramshackle buildings to house the Chinese and not much more. He had underestimated by a considerable degree.

The Oasis encompassed over a hundred acres. Since this was Death Valley, one of the hottest, driest, dustiest, and brownest spots on the planet, the lush greenery was all the more startling. Crops were being tilled and tended by hundreds of Chinese in drab work garb. Every crop conceivable, from corn to turnips to beets to oats. Even rice, in a five-acre plot that, amazingly, was more marsh than desert.

Fargo, riding near the head of the column of men and wagons, blurted the first thing that came into his head. "How in God's name?"

Tobias Cain heard, and slowed his mount so Fargo could come up alongside him. "An impressive sight, is it not?"

"An impossible sight," Fargo said. "Death Valley only gets a few inches of rain a year."

"Two inches, to be exact," Cain said. "Some years less."

"Then how—" Fargo marveled, and gestured at the verdant expanse of green. In the middle reared buildings, a full dozen, including a mansion and a stable with a corral, and four long buildings with barred windows and one without. Near the stable were pens for a couple of dozen cows. All the buildings, the corral, the pens, had been painted white. The effect, in the bright sunlight, was so dazzling as to hurt the eyes.

"I have a prospector to thank," Tobias Cain said. "He was one of the forty-niners. Came to California from Indiana or Illinois in the hope of striking it rich. But like most of those lunkheads, he never did." He chuckled as if that amused him.

Fargo waited for the tale to continue.

"One night I was at a saloon in Barstow and I met the old buzzard. He had prospected for gold here in Death Valley, but instead of gold he stumbled on something just as valuable."

"A spring," Fargo guessed.

Cain smiled and nodded. "Not a piddling little spring, either. A spring with no bottom. A spring that puts out water by the gallon. It was hidden by a rock slab as big as a house." Cain raised an enormous arm and pointed.

Where the Panamint Mountains and the floor of Death Valley met were low black hills sprinkled with boulders and rock formations worn by the elements. At the base of one of the hills a gigantic slab jutted skyward at an angle. A shack had been constructed under it.

The tilled fields began within a stone's throw of the slab and extended across the valley floor to the east.

"The old prospector found it when he wandered under the slab to get out of the sun," Cain related. "The moment he told me, I knew I had the perfect place for a scheme I had in mind. Hardly anyone ever comes here. Those that do don't stay very long. I pretty much have the valley to myself."

Beyond the tilled fields, stretching for as far as the eye could see, was Death Valley's baked, parched landscape. Shimmering waves of heat served as a warning that anyone who attempted to cross the valley would be roasted alive.

"You see, I had the idea of extorting money from the Chinese years ago. But I couldn't figure out how to work it so that I didn't attract attention. I needed some place out of the way."

"You can't get more out of the way than this."

Again Cain nodded. "I hired men, kidnapped my first bunch, and was in business. Since then the Oasis has grown until we have all the food we need, and extra besides." He swept a huge arm at the tilled fields. "Hell, I could get by living off the farm alone. But that wouldn't be enough. I have plans. Big plans."

"The million dollars," Fargo said.

"Exactly. Spending the rest of my days in luxury appeals to me. Never having to work. Only the best clothes. Waited on hand and foot by servants. If that isn't the best life a man can live, I don't know what is."

"And when you have your million?"

"Eh? Oh, you mean the Chinese? And the Oasis?" Cain sobered. "I won't have any use for either. I already have a site picked for the grave for the Chinese. The rest can rot, for all I'll care."

Fargo kept his tone level to disguise his disgust. "You have it all worked out."

"Did you think I wouldn't? I never leave anything to chance. Not a blessed thing. It's why in a few years I'll be as rich as Midas. Me. Tobias Cain."

Since Cain was being so obliging with information, Fargo ventured, "You said you had the idea for years. What made you think of it in the first place?"

"I've never exactly lived on the right side of the law," Cain related. "Except the first ten years of my life, before my mother killed herself and my father shot himself because he couldn't live without her." He lowered his rumbling voice so only Fargo would hear. "I'm about to tell you something no one else knows." He paused. "My mother was Chinese."

A puff of wind could have blown Fargo from his saddle. "What?"

"You heard me. My father worked on the docks. He'd take his clothes to a Chinese laundry to be washed every now and then, and that's how he met my mother. You wouldn't know I have any Chinese blood to look at me. I take after his side of the family. He was a big man, too, although not as big as me."

"But if your mother was Chinese—" Fargo began.

"Why am I kidnapping her people for money?" Cain scowled darkly. "My mother's side of the family wasn't too happy about her marrying my father. This might surprise you, but there are Chinese who hate whites for being white, just as there are whites who hate Chinese for not being white."

Hatred, Fargo reflected, came in all guises.

"My mother's parents and brothers and sisters treated me like I was scum," Cain went on. "I never understood why until after she died. She took a knife to her belly. I was the one who found her lying in the kitchen with her guts on the floor. She left a note saying she was taking her life because her father and mother did not want anything more to do with her. They had put up with my father and me—their own words—as long as they could stand it."

Fargo could think of nothing suitable to say.

"My father didn't want to go on living so he put a pistol to his temple and blew his brains out." Cain shifted in the saddle and stared back at the wagons with the iron bars. "And you ask me why I'm doing this to the Chinese?" He shook himself, then glanced quizzically at Fargo. "What I don't understand is why in hell I'm telling you all this. Maybe it's because I respect you."

"You do?"

"You're one tough son of a bitch, and I admire toughness," Cain said. "You're the only man who has ever lasted more than a minute against me."

First Kid Fontaine, now Tobias Cain. Next thing Fargo knew, Krast would want to become blood brothers.

The Chinese workers in the fields, Fargo observed, did not stop working to stare at the new arrivals. Overseers with bullwhips had something to do with it. The overseers prowled ceaselessly, ready to use those whips on workers who slacked.

"You keep the women and men separate," Fargo noted.

"Less trouble if we have them work apart," Cain said. "There's nothing like a woman being whipped to cause men to rush to help her."

A lot of the Chinese, Fargo now saw, were working on an extensive irrigation system that accounted for the garden of green in the sea of brown.

The mansion was magnificent. It was made of stone and mortar, the door and the window casements and the shutters of pine.

Cain stared in the direction Fargo was gazing and commented, "I had fifty men working on it for over a year. Wait until you see inside. Which reminds me. I always have a special supper when Endor visits. You're invited to the one tonight."

Fargo had been debating how best to go about talking to May Ling, and here a perfect opportunity had been dropped in his lap.

"Dress as you are. We don't hold on ceremony."

"We?"

"A Chinese girl who lives with me. Her name is May Ling. She has the mistaken notion I'm in love with her, but all she is to me is a bed warmer." Cain laughed, then used his reins. "See you at seven o'clock."

Fargo slowed to mull over all he had learned, and the first of the wagons came abreast of the Ovaro. It was the wagon with the women. Among them was Lu Wei. Unlike the rest, who were portraits of melancholy, Lu Wei had her face pressed to the bars and was eagerly taking everything in. He gigged the Ovaro in close to the wagon and said out of the corner of his mouth, "If you change your mind, let me know."

"Go away," Lu Wei said angrily.

"I only want to help."

"Did I ask you to?" Lu Wei responded. "If you are not careful, you will spoil everything."

About to ask her to explain, Fargo fell silent when hooves drummed and someone came up beside him.

"What are you two whispering about?" Krast snapped.

"Nothing that concerns you," Fargo said.

Krast's buzzard face was alive with spite. "That's where you're wrong, Mr. High and Mighty. I pretty much run the Oasis for Mr. Cain. When I tell you to do something, it's the same as him telling you to do it. When I ask you something, it's the same as him asking you."

"I didn't know that," Fargo said. "I'll have to ask him why he didn't tell me when I go to his place for supper later."

Krast had the look of a man who had just been slugged in the gut. "Mr. Cain invited you to his mansion?"

"At seven."

"He's never invited me," Krast said resentfully. He quickly recovered. "Not that it matters. Just do as I say and we'll get along." He trotted ahead.

Lu Wei nodded at Krast. "Do you see why you must stay away from me? You attract too much attention."

"If you change your mind, I'll be around a few days." Fargo figured it would not take much longer than that for a chance to slip away with May Ling to present itself. He pricked the Ovaro with his spurs and passed the wagons.

About twenty Chinese men were filing along the edge of the dirt track, all with shovels or rakes or hoes over their shoulders. The last two in line were shackled about the ankles, but the rest were not.

Fargo slowed next to a hard case with a bullwhip at the head of the line. "I've just been hired on."

"Good for you."

"How many hours a day do you work in the fields?"

"The Chinese work from sunup until sunset," the man said. "We work eight hours out of every twenty-four, with one day off every two weeks to visit Whiskey Mill. That's the best part. You wouldn't reckon those Chinese girls would be any good under the sheets, but they have to be, or else."

Fargo rode on. He was taken aback to discover that a handful of the Chinese were older men and women, like Wen Po. That they survived in the heat was a testament to their endurance. Theirs, and everyone else's. For although the Oasis had the appearance of a Garden of Eden, it was an inferno. The temperature was above one hundred, the air as still as death. Sweat caked Fargo, and he had to pull his hat brim low against the harsh, blinding glare of the sun.

Trees had been planted in the vicinity of the buildings, but they had not grown high enough yet to amount to much. Various flowers in a bed along the side of the mansion struggled to bloom.

Fargo kept an eye on the mansion in the hope of spotting May Ling. Her father had described her in detail, and Fargo would know her on sight. But she did not come out to greet the wagon train or appear at any of the windows.

The long building that housed Cain's small army was furnished about the same as a ranch bunkhouse. Fargo chose a bunk near the back door. He left his saddlebags and bedroll on the bed and went out the rear. A washbasin, lye soap, and a half-empty bucket of water piqued his interest. Removing his hat, he stripped to the waist, filled the basin, and gave his face, chest, and back a good scrubbing. No towels were provided, so after soaking and wringing out his red bandana, he stood and surveyed the Oasis while the air dried his tingling skin.

Tobias Cain had accomplished a miracle. He had transformed an admittedly small part of Death Valley into fertile farmland. The rest of Death Valley was as inhospitable to life of all kinds as it had always been, but here life thrived. The fact that Cain's miracle was wrought with wicked ends in mind did not diminish the achievement.

It was not the first time human hands had wrested the impossible from a hostile desert. The Mormons had done the same in the region of the Great Salt Lake, and settlers in Arizona were taming more of the dry landscape there each year.

Fargo did not have a watch. He never felt the need. He had lived in the wild for so long that he could tell with a fair degree of accuracy what hour of the day it was just by squinting at the sun. His next squint goaded him into putting on his shirt and hat and strapping on his Colt. He tied the red bandana around his neck, adjusted it as he liked it, and ambled toward the mansion.

A middle-aged Chinese dressed as a butler admitted him and led him along a hallway to the dining room.

Others were already there: Tobias Cain, Miles Endor, Shote and Vale Viktor, and Captain Jim.

Fargo was surprised to see the two trackers and the Modoc. But his surprise was short-lived. A few seconds later it gave way to bewildering shock as the woman he had come so far to save, the woman whose father had described her as a "sweet, young innocent," came through a door at the other end of the dining room, walked up to Tobias Cain, embraced him warmly, and gave him a passionate kiss.

Fargo had found May Ling.

12

Skye Fargo had been with his share of ladies. More than his share. Tall ones, short ones, skinny ones, round ones, blondes, redheads, brunettes, and every other shade. American women, Canadian women, women from France, women from England, senoritas from south of the border. Many were pretty, many were more than pretty, some were stunningly beautiful.

May Ling fell into the last and extremely small group. Everything about her was exceptionally exquisite, from her luxurious hip-length black hair to her delicate lips to the flawless symmetry of her face. She was tall for a Chinese girl, almost six feet, her body a shapely hourglass, her legs, as hinted by how her satin dress clung to them, the kind of legs men dreamed about.

May Ling greeted Miles Endor but did not so much as acknowledge that the Viktor brothers or Captain Jim existed. Tobias Cane pulled out a chair for her and she gracefully sat.

Fargo cleared his throat.

"Bridger!" Cain said with what seemed like real warmth. "I was hoping you would come." He introduced Fargo to May Ling.

"How do you do, Mr. Bridger? Anyone my husband thinks highly of, I think highly of, too."

For the second time that day, Fargo could have been knocked over with a feather. "You two are married?"

Tobias Cain laughed. "She wishes we were. So she goes around calling me her husband. Isn't that cute?"

Fargo's word for it began with an *s* and ended with a *p*. "Well, I hope it works out for you one day," he said to May Ling.

"It will. I know what I want, and when I want something, I get it. That is one of the traits Tobias likes most about me."

"If you say so, my dear," Cain said, and claimed the chair at the head of the table. "Everyone. Sit. All of you must be hungry after the long day we spent in the saddle."

Endor sat on Cain's right, next to May Ling. The Viktor brothers and Captain Jim sat on the left.

Fargo sat across from the Modoc, whose dark eyes regarded him as coldly as the rattlesnake's. "Do you always invite the hired help to your table?"

"Hardly ever, except for the three you see right there," Cain answered. "Captain Jim has been with me from the start, and Shote and Vale amuse me."

"It's our accent," Vale Viktor said.

"Our Southern drawl," Shote echoed. "We're from Virginia."

"And perfect gentlemen," Cain said, "although you would never guess it to look at them, or how they dress."

"Not everyone likes runnin' around in penguin suits, suh," Vale remarked.

"That's a strange thing to call them," Miles Endor said.

"Have you seen the way you waddle?" Shote Viktor responded.

Cain laughed and said to Fargo, "See what I mean? They are constantly saying things like that."

"We can't help it, suh," Vale said.

Shote nodded. "We've tried saying it out our ears and it doesn't work."

Again Cain roared. Then he put his huge hand on May Ling's and asked, "Did you miss me?"

"Of course." May Ling's smile was as ravishing as the rest of her. "I tossed and turned and could hardly sleep."

"Isn't she sweet?" Cain asked Fargo.

So I had heard, Fargo almost answered. "You're a lucky man."

Cain sat back. "Luck has nothing to do with it. My men in San Francisco and Los Angeles know they are to send me the best-looking girls they can find. They outdid themselves with her."

"Your flattery, husband, makes my heart sing," May Ling cooed.

Fargo wondered if her fawning over Cain had a secret purpose. Some men were more susceptible to praise than others. Maybe she hoped that by treating Cain as if he were everything she ever wanted in a man, she would stay in his good graces longer.

The door opened, and in came Merle Twern and Kid Fontaine. But they were not there to eat. They had brought someone else.

"Ah. My other guest. Come join us," Cain said, with a grand gesture. "Take a seat, won't you?"

May Ling looked fit to choke.

The new arrival was none other than Lu Wei. She timidly approached the table, then hesitated.

"Don't be shy," Cain coaxed. "No one will bite you. Sit next to Bridger, there. I'm sure he won't mind your company."

Fargo did not comment. His instincts warned him that this was no coincidence, that Wen Po had told Cain about the conversation she overheard. Yet Cain did not show the least little hostility.

"I do not understand why I am here," Lu Wei declared.

May Ling was as stiff as a plank. "Nor do I, husband. Am I not good enough company that you must invite this woman as well?"

"Sheathe your claws," Cain told her. "I invited Lu Wei because there is more to her than you might think."

"How so?" May Ling asked.

"We'll get to that later," Cain said. "First, the food."

It was fitting, Fargo supposed, that the man who had set himself up as the kingly lord of Death Valley should eat like royalty.

The food just kept coming. The meal started with two types of soup, chicken and rice. Fresh-baked bread and butter were laid out, and then the main course was brought. Beef steaks, roast suckling pig, potatoes in cheese sauce, onions in cream, a thick gravy, squash, celery, radishes, and corn, mince pie, and brown Betty. To wash it down, either piping hot coffee or steaming tea.

Fargo ate until his gut was fit to burst. Endor outdid him, eating twice as much as anyone else. Cain and the Viktor brothers all had healthy appetites, but Captain Jim, strangely enough, was content with a single slice of bread without butter and a small portion of suckling pig.

The Modoc was not the only one who did not eat much.

Lu Wei ate a small bowl of rice soup and picked at the onions in cream, but that was all. She was apprehensive, and Fargo couldn't blame her. She was the fly invited into the spider's parlor, or to his supper table, to be more exact.

Throughout the meal, May Ling cast frosty glances at Lu Wei. Evidently she regarded Lu Wei as potential competition for the affections of her lord and master. Her jealousy suggested to Fargo that she did, indeed, want to become Mrs. Tobias Cain.

As for their host, Cain said very little during the meal. Like many big men, he liked to eat. He liked it so much that he did not let anything interfere with his enjoyment. Only after he had finished his second helping of mince pie and pushed his plate back did he turn his attention to his guests. Specifically, to Lu Wei. "You are not eating. I should think you would have quite an appetite."

"Why am I here?" Lu Wei bluntly asked.

Ignoring the question, Cain turned to May Ling. "Do you want to know what made me curious about her? She's pretty enough that I had her working the shacks in Whiskey Mill. But she would rather work in the fields."

"Some are like that," May Ling said. "They refuse to sell their bodies." She made it sound silly.

"True," Cain said. "But our guest had a different reason." Leaning on his elbows, he smirked at Lu Wei. "Didn't you?"

"I have no idea what you are talking about."

"There is something you should know," Cain said. "Better yet, how about if I show you?" He glanced at the man in the butler uniform and for the first time since Fargo had met him, barked words in Chinese. The butler hastened off.

Merle Twern and Kid Fontaine were still there, on either side of Lu Wei's chair. The Kid caught Fargo's eye and his pulped lips curled in a friendly smile.

Cain reached over to pat May Ling's hand. "You see, my dear, Lu Wei is a recent arrival from San Francisco. When I picked her to work in Whiskey Mill, she raised a fuss, but no more so than most girls do and far less than some. But she wasn't at Whiskey Mill a week when she caused trouble. She claimed she was sick. Then she claimed she was pregnant. Anything to get out of spreading her legs. Some women do that even though I warn them what will happen. So I thought no more of it until I confronted her in Whiskey Mill."

"And?" May Ling said when Cain stopped.

"That was when she told me she wanted to work in the fields."

"But you just said others have done that."

"It was the way she acted," Cain said. "Even those who don't want to work the shacks aren't happy about working all day under the hot sun at the Oasis. Lu Wei, here, was much too eager."

"That is silly," Lu Wei said.

Just then the butler returned with a leather-bound volume of the kind used to keep journals or diaries or business accounts. He placed it on the table in front of Tobias Cain. Cain tapped it and grinned.

"Do you know what this is?"

"How would I?" Lu Wei asked defensively. "I have never seen it before."

"Few have," Cain said, and opened it.

From where Fargo sat, he could see a long list that covered an entire page. Some of the writing was in Chinese. There were a lot of numbers.

"This is a record of everyone I've ever had brought here," Cain disclosed. "Their names, where they're from, the names of relatives, addresses, all the information I need." He flipped pages, doing them one at a time, drawing out the suspense. "Ah. Here's the one I'm looking for." He ran his finger along an entry. "Lu Wei. San Francisco. Father's name, Zhu Wei. Mother's name, Xu Wei." Cain made a show of bending over the page. "Why, what's this? You have a younger sister, too, by the name of Luo Wei."

Lu Wei squirmed uncomfortably in her chair.

"Oh my." Cain slapped a hand to his forehead as

if in great surprise. "Will you look at this? How could I have missed it when you were brought in?" He was acting. He had already uncovered what he was about to reveal.

"Missed what, husband?" May Ling asked.

Cain tapped the page. "The sister, Luo Wei, was brought here six months ago."

At last Fargo understood why Lu Wei had refused his help.

"This is troubling," Tobias Cain said. "Very, very troubling."

"How so, husband?" From May Ling.

"Don't you see? Lu Wei is here to rescue her sister. She deliberately had herself brought here. That's never been done before."

"How could she manage that, boss?" Merle Twern piped up.

"That is exactly what I would like to find out," Cain said. "The identities of the men who do the snatching are supposed to be a secret. Yet somehow our dainty friend here got them to snatch her."

Lu Wei had stopped squirming. Now that her secret had been revealed, her features reflected only bitterness and loathing. "You are not as smart as you think you are. I tricked your men easily."

"Mind sharing how?" Cain requested.

Lu Wei did not respond.

"Then I guess you don't want to see your sister?" Cain said. "Here I thought she was the reason you came."

"Wait," Lu Wei said. "If I tell you how I did it, I can see her?"

"I give you my word you will be taken straight to her," Cain promised. "Captain Jim will tend to it personally." He looked at the Modoc and touched his sleeve. Captain Jim nodded.

Fargo had a nose for danger, and his inner sense

warned him that Lu Wei was in great peril. But when Captain Jim just sat there, and Tobias Cain smiled at Lu Wei and motioned for her to begin, it dulled his concern.

"All right. I will tell you," Lu Wei said. "You are right. I am here to save my sister. My parents did not want me to try. They pleaded with me. But Luo and I have always been close. I had to do something."

"How touching," the giant remarked.

"Mock me all you want. But you would understand if you ever loved anyone. If you ever had a family."

A slight flush spread from Cain's collar to his brow.

"We knew my sister had been taken by four men. Four white men. They were seen tying and gagging her and forcing her into a carriage," Lu Wei related. "One of the men wore white pantaloons and a stovepipe hat. It was not much but I asked everyone I met if they had ever seen such a man. It took many weeks but at last I talked to a baker who had a customer who often wore a stovepipe and white pants. The customer was fond of sweet pastries. He came in once a week to buy some. The next time he came, I was hiding in the back. I followed him. I learned where he lived. Once I knew that, it was easy to watch him day and night."

"Rufus Stine wears a stovepipe," Cain said.

"Was that his name? He spent a great deal of time in Chinatown, watching the daughter of a money lender. I knew that she would be taken so I went to her and told her about my sister. She wanted to go to the authorities, but I begged her not to. She let me take her place on her evening walks in a nearby park. I changed my hair to match hers and she let me wear her clothes."

"But how did you know when she would be snatched?" Cain asked.

"It was the only time she was ever alone. It seemed

logical that was when your Rufus Stine would abduct her."

"And Stine abducted you instead." Tobias Cane sat back. "I'm impressed, girl. I truly am. That was damned clever."

"May I be with my sister now?" Lu Wei requested.

"I always keep my word," Cain said, and nodded at Captain Jim.

There was nothing Fargo could have done. It happened almost too swiftly for the eye to follow. The Modoc's arm flashed, and a silver streak flew from his hand into Lu Wei's bosom.

13

Lu Wei gaped at the hilt of the knife and the blood oozing around it, and then at Tobias Cain.

"I promised you would be with your sister. She was disposed of two months ago. Or didn't you know your father refused to pay any more money?"

Sagging in her chair, Lu Wei tried to speak. All that came out of her mouth were crimson ribbons. Her last act was to look at Fargo in mute sorrow. Then the light of life faded from her eyes and her forehead thunked onto the table.

"Good riddance," May Ling said.

Regret and disgust filled Fargo. Regret he had not done something to prevent Lu Wei's death. Disgust with Tobias Cain and his total disregard for human life. And disgust for the woman he was there to save.

Captain Jim calmly rose and walked around the table. He raised the body, slowly drew the knife out, and cleaned the blade on Lu Wei's sleeve. He did not smirk or smile or otherwise show emotion. He had slain Lu Wei as dispassionately as someone might swat a fly.

It took all of Fargo's self-control not to draw his Colt and shoot the Modoc dead.

He avoided looking at anyone else as Captain Jim came back around and sat down. He was afraid his expression would give him away.

"Have someone take the little fool away, will you?" May Ling requested.

"Right away," Cain said, and snapped his fingers.

Merle Twern and Kid Fontaine slipped their arms under Lu Wei's shoulders and dragged her out.

Fargo held his coffee cup in both hands, wishing it was Tobias Cain's neck. But Cain was not his foremost problem now. It was the woman he had been hired to bring back. May Ling was nothing like her father claimed. She was not sweet, and she certainly was not innocent. He debated leaving her there. He could slip away from the Oasis in the middle of the night, ride to Whiskey Mill for Tilly, and report Cain to the law. There was only one hitch. The thing he kept coming back to: He had given his word to May Ling's father.

"Are you all right, Bridger?" Tobias Cain unexpectedly asked.

"Never better," Fargo said gruffly, raising the coffee cup to his mouth. "What makes you ask?"

"You look peaked," Cain said. "I hope my little indulgence didn't spoil your digestion."

"I've seen a lot of people die," Fargo said. Too damn many, if the truth be known.

"Such is the nature of things. As you know, I learned at an early age that life is all too short. We're born, we blink, we die."

Miles Endor, who had been unusually quiet this whole time, snorted. "You are too much of a pessimist, Tobias. It's not dying that counts. It's what we do before we die."

"I couldn't agree more," Cain said. "Which is why we must wrest what we want from life before death comes calling."

At a command from Cain, the Chinese butler brought drinks. Endor liked brandy. The Viktor brothers were given ale. Captain Jim refused any liquor with a curt shake of his head. Fargo settled for whiskey. So did one other.

"My father always said this was bad for me," May Ling commented, swirling the amber liquid in her glass. "But he was as wrong about alcohol as he was about so many things." For the first time that evening, she looked at Fargo. "Have you told the new man the rules yet, husband?"

Cain was sipping scotch. "Not yet. But now that you bring it up, I suppose I should." He wagged a finger. "The mansion is off-limits unless you are invited. Anyone who steps foot inside without my permission dies. No exceptions."

"Understood," Fargo said. Given the violent natures of the men Cain had working for him, the precaution was called for.

"The spring is off-limits, too. Not that anyone can get anywhere near it with the guards I keep posted. But don't stray too close or they'll part your hair with a slug."

"Why the spring?" Fargo was curious.

"One of the Chinese in the first bunch I kidnapped came up with the brainstorm of filling the spring with dirt and rocks," Cain explained. "He figured if the water stopped flowing, the Oasis would dry up, and I would have to let everyone go. I caught him in time and had him whipped to death. Ever since, the spring is guarded twenty-four hours a day."

Fargo decided he should act as if he were interested in the work he was to do. "Who do I answer to around here?"

Cain's eyebrows met over his nose. "Three guesses. If none of them is me, you're dumber than I took you for."

"Krast told me I answer to him." The way Fargo figured it, as the old saying went, one good turn deserved another.

"Oh, did he, now?" Tobias Cain said. "Was that when I saw him talking to you on the way in?"

Fargo nodded. The giant never missed a thing. Yet more cause to be as careful as he could be.

"Pay Krast no mind. He likes to think he's more important than he is. Everyone answers to me. No exceptions. I might pass on orders through Krast now and again, but I won't do that with you. All your orders will come directly from me. Report to me every morning at seven and I'll give you your work for the day."

May Ling shot Cain a puzzled look. "That is most unusual, husband. You must think highly of Mr. Bridger."

"He is in a class by himself, my dear," Cain replied.

Fargo was flattered, but he was also mystified. He had done nothing to merit Cain's praise other than not be knocked out during their fisticuffs. "Don't make more of me than I am. I'm as ordinary as spit."

"I admire your humility, sir," Miles Endor said.

"I don't," Cain spat. "Humility is for Bible-thumpers. The only thing the meek will ever inherit from me is the backside of my hand."

Endor made a clucking sound in reproach. "I don't share your arrogance, Tobias. I never grasp for more than I can hold."

"Don't put on airs with me, Miles. You have lived on the wrong side of the law for as long as I have."

A petty argument ensued, with Endor trying to prove he wasn't a hypocrite, and Cain taking him to task.

Fargo paid little attention. He was studying May Ling without appearing to do so. She sat and sipped her drink with an air of utter contentment. If she was shamming, she was doing an outstanding job. If she wasn't, returning her to her father would take considerable doing.

Suddenly May Ling looked right at him. She had caught him studying her and was returning the favor.

Fargo met her gaze. If he had to wager, he was willing to bet Tobias Cain was not the only one without a shred of meekness. He began to wonder if her father had lied to him, and if so, how he was to go about earning the thousand dollars.

Suddenly shouts rent the gathering twilight outside. A pistol cracked. The heavier boom of rifles answered. A woman's terror-struck scream rose to an earsplitting shriek.

"What the hell?" Tobias Cain shoved up out of his chair and started across the room, but he was only halfway to the far door when in burst Merle Twern, out of breath. "What's going on out there?" Cain demanded.

"One of the Chinese knocked out one of our men, took his revolver, and is hightailing it for the mountains."

"What was that scream?"

"A woman got in the way and was shot by mistake."

"Call out the men. Half will stay here, the rest will come with me." Cain smacked his right fist into his left palm. "I will personally break every bone in the body of the bastard who is trying to escape."

"You might not want to," Twern said.

"Why the hell not?"

"He's worth an awful lot of money to you," Twern said. "It's Li Dazhong."

Whatever else might be said about Tobias Cain and those who worked for him, they were efficient. Within twenty minutes a search party was ready. Cain, himself, was at the head of the riders. The Viktor brothers were going, naturally. So was Captain Jim, Krast and Hank, Merle Twern and Kid Fontaine, and Cavendish. So was Fargo. Cain had bellowed at him to saddle the Ovaro as Cain rushed from the dining room.

Full canteens were given to every man. Rifles and revolvers were checked and loaded if necessary. A packhorse was brought from the stable and the lead rope handed to the last rider in line. The packhorse was laden with water skins and packs of food.

The hunt began near one of the long buildings with barred windows and doors. A knot of overseers and a few Chinese were gathered around a Chinese woman who was on her back on the ground. They moved aside as Cain rode up. A man Fargo had not seen before was on one knee, a black bag at his side, bandaging the woman's shoulder.

"How is she, Doc?" Tobias Cain asked.

"She'll live." The doctor was getting on in years. His features bore the ravages of dissipation. In the open medical bag, along with a stethoscope and other items, lay a large silver flask. "But she'll be laid up for a week to ten days."

Cain addressed the overseers. "Which one of you lost your six-shooter?"

The question need hardly be asked. The man stood out like a mouse in a room full of cats. His lean face was twitching and he was nervously wringing his hands. "It was me, Mr. Cain, sir," he squeaked.

"Tell me what happened, Wilson."

"I was taking this Chinese, Li Dazhong, to show him where his bunk would be," Wilson said, "when he did something with his feet. I ended up in the dirt and he ended up with my revolver. He didn't take my whip although he could have."

"Weren't you warned to be careful around him?" Cain asked.

"Yes, sir. I was told he had given you trouble, and that he could fight like a drunken sailor. Honest to God, I didn't take my eyes off him. He's fast, sir. So very fast."

Cain looked at the wounded woman. She was young and quite attractive even though worn down from her toil in the fields. "How did she get shot?"

"It was the Chinese. He began shooting wildly after he knocked me down, then lit out of here like a scared rabbit."

"I hate liars," Tobias Cain said.

Wilson gulped air. "Sir?"

"You did take your eyes off Li Dazhong. To look at her. Dazhong saw his chance and tried to kick your head off and it's a damn shame he didn't do it. That's the lump you have on your temple. You drew your revolver and fired wildly and he hit you again and took your revolver from you. That's why your cheek is swelling up. It was you who shot the girl, not Li Dazhong."

"That's not true!" Wilson belated.

"Are you calling *me* a liar?" Cain demanded.

"No, sir. Not ever. But—"

Cain cut Wilson off. "I pride myself on being able to take the measure of anyone I meet. Li Dazhong is not the kind to panic. He would never fire wildly, not with so many of his own people around. You made it up because you knew how mad I would be at your lapse. Am I right?"

The sweat was pouring from Wilson, who had turned as white as a sheet.

"I didn't hear you?" Cain goaded. "Please don't insult me again by denying it."

"That's"—Wilson licked his lips and swallowed—"that's pretty much how it happened, I guess. But I swear I only glanced at her. I was thinking of how she reminded me of one of the girls at Whiskey Mill."

"Were you, indeed?" Tobias Cain said. From under his jacket he produced a short-barreled, nickel-plated, ivory-handled Smith and Wesson, and blew Wilson's brains out.

Nearly everyone jumped. The doctor came off his knee and put a shaking hand to his throat.

"Honestly, Mr. Cain! Was that necessary?"

"Something the matter?" Cain asked while replacing the spent cartridge. He did not give the dead man a second look.

"I must protest most vigorously. When you hired me, you never said anything about the conditions under which I had to work."

"I most certainly did. But you were so drunk the day I found you in that tavern, you don't remember. So shut your mouth, you sot, and do what I am paying you twice what you would earn anywhere else to do."

"I have a delicate constitution, I tell you."

"One more whine, Doctor," Cain said, "and I'll have Captain Jim give you a Modoc remedy for constitutions like yours. Would you like that?"

The doctor glanced at the swarthy, inscrutable warrior in the faded army jacket, and shuddered. "No, I don't believe I would."

"Didn't think so." Cain gestured at the Shote brothers. "Enough of this. Get cracking."

Shote and Vale dismounted and roved in ever widening circles. Now and again one or the other would run his fingers over the ground. Then Shote hunkered and grunted and his brother came over and squatted beside him.

Fargo knew what they were doing. Shote had found a set of tracks, both the right and left foot, imprinted in the dust, and the pair were memorizing them; the length, the width, the shape, the wear of the sole, the spacing between the prints. It was what he would do.

"We don't have all year," Tobias Cain said impatiently. "It will be dark soon, and that will slow us down."

The brothers climbed back on their horses. The trail led west toward the mountains. Cain beckoned to Twern and Kid Fontaine and issued instructions no one else heard. They reined toward an outbuilding.

The tracks were plain to follow. Li Dazhong had

made no attempt to hide his footprints. Perhaps because he believed that once darkness fell, they would not be able to trail him.

Fargo hoped Li was right, and Cain would call a halt and resume tracking at daybreak.

Then Merle Twern and Kid Fontaine came galloping up. They had been sent to fetch torches.

14

When it became too dark to see a hand at arm's length, Tobias Cain ordered the torches be given to Vale and Shote Viktor. The brothers tracked by the flickering light.

Fargo had done the same many times. Good trackers, competent trackers, could track almost as fast by torchlight as by day, and the Viktor brothers proved their reputations were not exaggerated. They tracked Li Dazhong at a pace that Fargo would have been hard-pressed to match.

Captain Jim was always at their side. When they dismounted, he dismounted. When they climbed back on their horses, so did he. Fargo did not know what to make of it. The brothers seemed to accept the Modoc's presence as a matter of course.

Night brought a welcome respite from the heat. A brisk breeze out of the northwest added to their relief.

Little was said. Tobias Cain was in a stormy mood and no one wanted to dare the thunder and lightning.

At one point Merle Twern proved brave enough to ask, "What will we do to him when we catch him, Mr. Cain?"

"I haven't decided yet. Anyone else, I'd bury him. But this one is worth more money than most."

They had left the Oasis behind and were pushing into the mountains. Li Dazhong had not stuck to the rutted track that linked the Oasis to Whiskey Mill. It soon became apparent that he was bearing to the northwest.

"Where does he think he's going?" Merle Twern wondered.

"Hell, that's simple," Cavendish said. "Chinamen can't tell direction worth a damn. He likely thinks he's still pointed toward Los Angeles."

"Could be," Twern said, but he did not sound convinced.

Since Cain had not told them to be quiet, Cavendish warmed to his subject. "Chinamen are downright pitiful when it comes to the wild. Why, they can't tell north and south and east from west when the sun is up. They gawk at rabbits and such like they've never set eyes on the critters before."

"Maybe they haven't," Hank said. "Some have spent their whole lives in the city."

"And others come from China, where things are bound to be different," Merle Twern commented.

"No matter where they are from," Cavendish scoffed, "the Chinese are next to worthless. Isn't that right, Mr. Cain?"

Tobias Cain did not reply.

"Were it up to me," Cavendish rambled on, "I would wipe out the whole race. What good are they? They don't look like us, they don't act like us, they don't think like us."

Fargo could not stay silent. "That's cause to exterminate them?"

"It's been cause enough to exterminate redskins, hasn't it?" Cavendish rebutted. "Get rid of the Chineses. Get rid of the Indians. Get rid of the blacks. The world would be a better place."

"Get rid of all of them?" Merle Twern said. "The women and the children, too?"

"Sure. Lice breed more lice, don't they? Am I right, Mr. Cain?"

Once again Tobias Cain did not comment.

"The Chinese are weak as well as worthless." Cavendish would not let it drop. "Look at how they let themselves be herded like sheep and told what to do. There isn't a one of them with any gumption."

"There's the one we're after," Merle Twern said.

"He's running, isn't he? That's not gumption where I come from. That's called being yellow. All Chinese are the same."

Tobias Cain broke his silence. "Mr. Cavendish?"

"Sir?"

"If you open that wretchedly ignorant mouth of yours one more time, you will join the recently departed Mr. Wilson in whatever special corner of hell is reserved for simpletons and jackasses."

Several chuckles greeted the threat. Cavendish took it seriously; he did not utter another word.

The tracks changed direction again, from northwest to north.

"Mighty strange," Krast said. "Maybe he's heading for Canada."

Evidently not, because soon the Viktor brothers bore to the northeast. A few minutes more and the tracks turned east.

"Why, the idiot is heading back to Death Valley," Hank said. "He can't make it across before daylight. He'll be fried alive once the sun comes up."

"He must figure it's the last thing we would expect," Merle Twern ventured. "And it is."

Soon the tracks changed direction once more.

"What the hell?" Krast said. "Now we're heading south!"

"He's led us in a circle," Hank declared.

Tobias Cain suddenly raised an arm, a signal for everyone to halt. The Viktor brothers did not notice, but Captain Jack did and said something. The brothers halted and turned.

"Anything wrong, Mr. Cain?" Shote asked.

"Don't you get it? Any of you?" Cain snapped. "Dazhong aimed to lead us in a circle all the time. He's not running away. He's attacking."

"One hombre against all of us?" Hank marveled. "He's loco."

"No, he's as crafty as a fox, this one," Cain said. "He wants to free the rest of the Chinese, and he's realized what our one weakness is. If he can destroy it, the Oasis is finished."

"The spring!" Krast exclaimed.

"The spring," Cain confirmed, and nearly stabbed his horse with his spurs. "Ride, you dunderheads! Ride!"

Ride they did, sweeping toward a distant spot of light that marked the shack under the gigantic slab. They had half a mile to cover when shots cracked, followed by strident shouts and cries.

To Fargo's bewilderment, Krast and a few of the others laughed or chortled or swapped broad grins.

"He may get past the guards but not Pink Eye!" Krast whooped. "I just wish I was there to see his face!"

The shooting stopped and the cries died out, and presently they came to a stop near the shack. The door was wide open and a rectangle of lamplight illumined the sprawled form of a dead guard who had been shot through the head.

Alighting, Cain led a rush toward boulders that bordered the spring. The spring itself was teardrop shaped, the narrow end of the teardrop at the base of the slab. The surface was as smooth as glass, the water as dark as the night except where it reflected the flickering torches held by the Viktor brothers. From the east end flowed the irrigation ditch that gave life to the Oasis.

Abruptly, the night erupted in a savage medley of

snarls and growls and barks, coming from deeper under the slab.

"Pink Eye has got him!" Kraft hollered.

Above them reared the monolith. Fargo tried not to think of what would result should it come crashing down while they were underneath.

Between two boulders lay another guard who had given his life in an attempt to stop Li Dazhong.

The snarling and barking rose to a crescendo and was punctuated by a yip. A few more yards and they found their quarry.

Impaled by the glare of the torches, his back to a boulder near the water's edge, stood Li Dazhong. He was caked with dust and dirt and streaked with blood. His shirt and pants were ripped. They had been torn by fangs and claws.

The animal responsible lay at Li's feet. It was an enormous dog, a mongrel with long, spindly legs, a barrel of a body covered with bristly red hair, and a mouth that bristled with glistening fangs. But the most notable feature about the dog was its left eye. For where the right eye was normal, the left eye was twice as big as the right and a bright pink. Hence the mongrel's name of Pink Eye.

Pink Eye was dead. A knife, evidently taken from one of the guards, had been buried to the hilt in Pink Eye's throat.

Cain's hard cases spread out, leveling weapons. Cain ignored Li Dazhong and squatted next to the dog. "Hell." He patted its head and neck and got blood on his fingers.

Fargo was surprised by the giant's tenderness. Cain was the last person he ever expected to become attached to a dog.

"I've had Pink Eye since he was a pup. Trained him myself. I had him here to help safeguard the spring."

Li Dahzong stared fearlessly at Cain. Blood seeped from a tear in his left sleeve. Large drops spattered at his feet. "I was so close," he said.

"What did you think you would do?" Tobias Cain demanded. "Plug the spring? Fill it with enough dirt and rocks to stop it up? All by your lonesome?"

Li Dazhong did not respond.

"Want me to shoot him for you, Mr. Cain?" Krast asked. "Not to kill, since he's so valuable to you. Maybe wing him in the knee or the foot?"

"In the shoulder," Tobias Cain said. "In the right shoulder. Aim high. I don't want him to bleed to death."

"Yes, sir, whatever you say."

Fargo took a step but there was nothing he could do, not with Captain Jim on one side of him and the Viktor brothers on the other, and Hank and Cavendish behind him.

Instead of using his rifle, Krast slicked his revolver in a cross draw and smoothly thumbed the hammer. The muzzle flashed smoke and lead.

Li Dazhong staggered and would have fallen had he not propped himself against the boulder. Gritting his teeth, he rasped defiantly, "You are dogs, not men!" He added a comment in Chinese, looking at Tobias Cain when he said it, and Cain rose and walked over to him and backhanded him across the mouth.

Dazhong folded like a house of cards.

"What did he say?" Krast asked.

"Learn Chinese and ask him," Cain said. Under his direction, Merle Twern and Kid Fontaine saw to binding Li Dazhong with his wrists behind him. No attempt was made to stanch Li's wounds or bandage his shoulder.

"I thought you didn't want him to bleed to death," Fargo remarked.

"He won't," Cain said confidently. "Besides, a little pain and blood are good for him. Maybe they will teach him to behave."

"Never!" Li spat.

At a command from Cain, they filed around the spring. The dead guards were carried to the shack. Two others, who had been wounded, were made comfortable while Merle Twern and Hank went to fetch the doctor.

Cain was in fine spirits now that the crisis was past, and talked and joked with his men. He had Krast open his saddlebags and pass around a bottle of red-eye.

Kid Fontaine was watching Li Dazhong and thirstily licking his thin lips. The Kid lit up like a candle when Fargo offered to watch the prisoner so the Kid could quench his thirst.

"You're a real pard. I'm obliged."

Dazhong was on his knees, his head bowed. He did not look up when Fargo leaned toward him and whispered.

"What *were* you trying to do?"

"If I did not tell the fiend you work for, it is foolish to expect me to tell you," Li said quietly.

Fargo made certain no one was in earshot before responding, "Things aren't as you think."

"You seek to deceive me but I will not be duped. Tell your employer he must try another way."

"I would like your trust," Fargo said.

"I would like to be in Los Angeles, but instead I am in the clutches of a madman. So you will forgive me if I do not care too much about what you would like."

Squatting, Fargo pretended to inspect the rope around Li's wrists. "I am not one of Cain's men."

"I saw you at Whiskey Mill, remember? Now you show up with the others to capture me." Li uttered a strangled snort. "I was shot in the shoulder, not the head."

118

"I'm only doing what I have to," Fargo whispered. "I've been hired to find a Chinese girl and take her back to San Francisco."

"Next you will say you *are* Chinese."

"Damn it, I'm offering my help."

"Sure you are. But your effort is commendable. You are an accomplished liar. Were I gullible I would believe you."

"Suit yourself. But you are making a mistake." Fargo stood and cradled the Henry. He had tried. Given the circumstances, he did not blame Dazhong for not trusting him.

"You have given up seeking to deceive me?" Li asked. "Too bad. Your antics took my mind off my pain."

"Just remember what I told you," Fargo said. He did not say anything more after that. He had too much to think about. As yet he had not had a chance to talk to May Ling. He must remedy that. Somehow he must get her alone, which might prove difficult given that no one was allowed near the mansion without Cain's consent.

Then there was May Ling herself. She appeared to revel in her role as Cain's bedmate. It was possible she did not want to be rescued, possible that once she found out who Fargo really was and why he was really there, she would run to her giant lover and let him know.

The savvy thing to do, Fargo reflected, was to forget May Ling. Forget the thousand dollars. Forget the hundreds of men and women forced to toil as slaves. Forget the families forced to pay to keep them alive. It was either that or go up against as vicious a pack of killers as ever drew breath.

"I must be loco," Fargo said into the wind.

15

For two days Fargo took part in the daily routine of the Oasis. He was up at dawn, ate breakfast with the men in the bunkhouse, and reported to the mansion by seven. Each morning the Chinese butler brought a slip of paper with Tobias Cain's instructions for the day.

Strange instructions they were.

The first day, Cain told him to ride a mile east of the Oasis and once there circle the Oasis to the north and look for tracks. Tracks of any kind. Including wildlife. He was to take note of every track he saw. Then he was to circle to the south and do the same thing. By sunset he was to report back to the mansion.

The temperature climbed to near 120 degrees. Fargo was nearly roasted alive. He had a canteen but the water did little to help. The Ovaro suffered worse and by sunset was plodding along with its head hung low.

Interestingly, the only tracks Fargo found were those of animals that came to the Oasis at night to drink and then slink away. And not many tracks, at that. Few creatures were hardy enough to survive in the merciless environment.

On the second day, the Chinese butler brought a note directing Fargo to ride to Whiskey Mill and tell Pardee that Miles Endor would be leaving the Oasis the next day. It seemed pointless to Fargo but he did as he was told. He took his time and arrived at Whiskey Mill about noon.

Pardee was at a table playing solitaire when Fargo strolled in. He did not act the least bit surprised.

"Cain always lets me know in advance when Endor is leaving. Endor likes to stay the night before pushing into the mountains, and I have to be sure I have enough liquor for his men and that Wen Po has the girls looking their best."

So that was it, Fargo reflected, and asked for a whiskey. He was in no hurry to get back. Pardee asked him for the latest news from the Oasis, and Fargo told him about Li Dazhong's attempt to stop up the spring.

"That stupid Chinese," Pardee laughed. "It would take a ton of dirt. The best way would be to bring that big old slab crashing down, but he'd need kegs of powder."

Fargo told him about Lu Wei.

Pardee's hand froze with a red seven over a black eight. "That's a shame. But she brought it on herself. No one pulls the wool over Tobias Cain's eyes. Not ever."

Fargo refrained from mentioning that he was doing quite nicely at it. "I met Cain's woman, May Ling."

"Isn't she something?" Pardee said. "When she first showed up, she screeched and screamed like they usually do about how Cain had no right to kidnap her, and she would be damned if she would do a lick of work. Cain took a liking to her. I could see that right off. She's prettier than most, and he has an eye for the pretty ones. So he had her brought to his mansion, and just like that, she stopped her squawking."

"She gave in easy, you're saying?"

"Hell, that girl has no more backbone than a bowl of oatmeal. All those luxuries, the servants, it took her breath away. The very next night, I hear, Cain bedded her, and she has been his sheet-warmer ever since. Little does she realize."

"Realize what?"

"May Ling has been putting on airs. Acting like Cain is her man and she is his woman. I hear she's even taken to calling him her husband."

"I heard it with my own ears," Fargo confirmed.

That tickled Pardee immensely. "The thing is, Cain goes through Chinese girls like you and I go through whiskey bottles. May Ling has lasted longer than most, but sooner or later I expect Cain will tire of her like he's tired of all the rest, and that will be that."

"What does he do to them?" Fargo thought that maybe Pardee knew more than Tilly, but he was wrong.

"They up and disappear."

"Cain has them killed?"

Pardee glanced at the front door and then whispered, "I hear he does them himself. Strangles them with his own hands. It's just a rumor, mind you, but it's fairly reliable, and it sure sounds like something Cain would do."

Fargo smothered a frown. Now, more than ever, he must get May Ling out of there. But how to go about it? That was the question.

"Listen, I don't suppose you would do me a favor?" Pardee unexpectedly asked.

"Depends," Fargo said.

"I don't get much time to myself. Not that there is a lot to do around this godforsaken place. But there are a few deer hereabouts, and whenever I can, I like to go hunting."

"You want me to go with you?"

"No. I want you to watch the saloon for me. If you wouldn't mind," Pardee said. He put down the deck. "You won't have to do anything. No one is due from the Oasis today. So you can sit and drink and play cards or whatever."

"I have to be back at the Oasis by nightfall," Fargo mentioned.

"I'll only be gone a couple of hours," Pardee promised. "That will give you plenty of time. What do you say?"

"So long as I don't have to pay for the whiskey."

In fifteen minutes Pardee was ready to go. He had traded his apron for a rifle, a pack, and a canteen. "I appreciate this," he said as he hiked off.

Fargo stood under the overhang until the brown vegetation swallowed Pardee, then went back in and took up the solitaire game where Pardee had left off. He was down to the final few cards when the front door creaked and in came Wen Po. He happened to see her face at the instant she saw him. Shock brought her to a stop, and she glanced anxiously about as if ready to flee.

"Something the matter?" Fargo asked.

"You! Here! What you do?"

"Cain sent me with a message for Pardee," Fargo explained. "Pardee is off hunting and I'm watching the place for him."

"Oh." Wen Po's wrinkled features relaxed. "Cain your friend now?" She tittered like a ten-year-old girl.

"I wouldn't go that far," Fargo said. He had no hankering to talk to her, but she lingered.

"Lu Wei? You maybe see her?"

Once again Fargo shared the news of the young woman's death.

"Silly girl. She come save sister, lose life. She try trick Mr. Cain. But no can trick him ever."

That made two people who seemed to believe Cain was invincible. "You don't admire her for trying to save her sister?" Fargo asked.

"Not admire stupid," Wen Po said, and giving him a pointed look, she laughed and went out.

Fargo liked the old woman less each time they met. Shrugging, he finished the solitaire and went behind the bar for a bottle. He chose the best Pardee had. As he was filling a glass, a shadow whisked in through the back and perfume wreathed him like a cloud. "I was wondering when you would show up."

"Wen Po just told me you were here," Tilly said gleefully. Throwing her arms around him, she passionately fused her mouth to his.

Fargo felt himself responding. She tasted nice, like the mint of evergreen sprigs, and the shapely contours of her body were enough to excite any man. Her full breasts against his chest reminded him of their last dalliance.

Breaking the kiss, Tilly grinned. "Before you say anything, I saw Pardee leave. We have plenty of time to ourselves."

Fargo grinned. "Has anyone every told you that you are a shameless hussy?"

"Just about everybody," Tilly said, giggling. "But don't hold that against me."

She caught herself and glanced sharply toward the front of the saloon. "That nosy Wen Po could be anywhere."

"Want to go to your house?" Fargo suggested. He had promised Pardee he would watch the saloon. He had not said anything about staying here.

Tilly's blond mane swayed as she shook her head. "And risk Wen Po spotting us? No. Let's do it right here."

"What if someone walks in?"

"Don't tell me a big, strapping hunk of hand-someness like you is skittish?" Tilly laughed. "But you have nothing to worry about. The girls never come in here unless told to. Wen Po might stray in looking for Pardee—"

"She knows he went hunting," Fargo enlightened her.

"In that case," the vivacious blonde said, "why are you standing there like a bump on a log when you could be using those hands of yours to treat me to what I like most in this world?"

"A back rub?" Fargo joked.

"So long as it involves my front and the rest of me, it will do nicely." Tilly pressed against him again, warm and willing and wanton.

Fargo cupped her breasts. She was wearing a blue dress, her mounds fit to burst out of the top. Slipping his hand down under, he pinched her right nipple and then her left. At each tweak she cooed and sighed and wriggled her hips.

"I like your touch. Some men are too rough. Some are too timid. But you are just right."

Fargo kissed her smooth neck, her ear, her soft earlobe. She was sensitive there. When he licked the lobe, she shivered, so he kept on licking until she was breathing with the heavy pant of a blacksmith's bellows. Her fuzzy mount ground against his hardening pole, making him as rigid as iron.

"You should charge women for the privilege," Tilly husked. "They would flock from miles around."

Fargo stopped licking to chuckle, then commenced undoing a row of tiny buttons and prying at tiny stays. "Why is it women always make it so damn hard to undress them?" he grumbled.

"Human nature," Tilly said. "People want something more if it's harder to get."

"This dress has more buttons than your other one," Fargo complained. "There must be thirty or forty."

"Poor baby." Tilly grinned. "I'll tell you what. While you are playing with them, I'll play with something else."

125

The pressure of her hand on his manhood sent a tingle through Fargo. She lightly stroked him, then cupped him lower down. "Yes, ma'am," he teased. "A hussy, if ever there was one."

"That makes two of us," Tilly said.

"You say the damnedest things."

After that neither said anything for the longest while. They couldn't, with their lips locked, and each taking turns sucking on the other's tongue.

Pressing her against the bar, Fargo finally freed her melons. They were wonderfully full and round, the nipples like tacks. He could not resist lowering his mouth to her right one and opening wide to inhale her. Her breast was a mouthful many times over. He pressed the tip of his tongue to the tip of her nipple and swirled it around and around.

"Ohhh. I like that."

Fargo gave her other melon the same attention. Her bosom was heaving when he pressed her against the bar and began running his hand up and down her legs, especially her inner thighs.

"I like that, too."

"Bet you do," Fargo said, and hitched at the lower half of her dress until he had it around her waist. Her undergarments posed a minor setback. Then his palm was on soft skin, and his fingers traveled an erotic path to the bushy junction of her legs. She groaned when he slid a finger where it would incite her the most.

"Yes! There!"

With the tip of his middle finger, Fargo parted her nether lips and lightly brushed her swollen knob. Tilly arched her back, her eyelids fluttering. As he began to slide his finger in, she held herself perfectly still except for her heavy breaths. Her hands rose to his shoulders. She rested her forehead on his chest.

Low mews filled the saloon.

Fargo inserted a second finger. Her hips began moving as her hands eagerly kneaded his broad shoulders and the tendons of his chest. She liked his muscles. His washboard stomach, especially.

Tilly gasped when Fargo suddenly thrust both fingers hard into her. At each stroke she gasped anew, and quivered. He pumped his fingers faster, then faster still, until she cried out and thrashed wildly. Eventually she subsided.

"Goodness, what you do to me."

"Ready for more?" Sliding his fingers out, Fargo aligned his pole. She groaned as he fed himself in, inch by gradual inch. Her legs rose and she wrapped them around his waist. Her arms hooked his neck. Tilly's skin was hot to the touch, her mouth the rim of a volcano.

Fargo took his time. He had been listening and heard nothing to indicate anyone was near.

Then came their mutual explosion. It was as intense as the last one, if not more so. Tilly moaned and gushed as Fargo drove up into her with the controlled power of a steam engine piston. Once over the pinnacle, they sagged against the bar and drifted down from the heights of bliss.

"A girl could get used to this," Tilly panted. "If you ever decide you want a sweetheart, let me know."

Fargo did not take the bait.

"You can do worse, you know."

Fargo hitched at his pants and glanced at the window, not really expecting to see anyone. But a face was pressed to the pane, watching them. The thing that surprised him was not the face, but who the face belonged to. Fargo had figured that if anyone spied on them it would be Wen Po. But Wen Po did not have stubble on her chin, or dark eyes that glittered like a weasel's, or a mop of brown hair.

It wasn't Wen Po at the window.

It was Hank.

16

In the time it took Fargo to pull his pants up, buckle his belt, and race outside, Hank had disappeared. Fargo sprinted past the frame house and heard a whinny. It came from behind the shacks.

Cavendish was astride a sorrel, waiting for Hank to mount. But Hank's horse, a buttermilk, was giving him problems. He had his foot in the stirrup and had hold of the saddle horn, but he could not mount because the buttermilk would not stop shying and prancing.

"What are you two doing here?" Fargo demanded.

Hank gave up trying to gain the saddle. Slipping his boot free, he turned and plastered a sheepish smile on his shifty features. "Sorry about back at the saloon. I looked in to see if Pardee was there."

"You haven't answered my question."

The burly Cavendish gigged his sorrel closer. "Who the hell do you think you are, talking to us like that? We work for Mr. Cain, the same as you."

A troubling suspicion bothered Fargo, and he voiced it aloud. "You followed me from the Oasis."

"That's loco." Hank laughed but the laugh was hollow. "Why would we trail you?"

"Because Cain told you to," Fargo said. And here he thought he had won Cain's confidence.

"That's loco, too," Hank declared. Averting his gaze, he explained. "Not that it's any of your business but we snuck away to visit the Chinawomen. Mr. Cain lets us come here twice a month, but that ain't anywhere near enough." He looked at Cavendish. "Isn't that right?"

"Why did you tell him?" Cavendish responded. "If he lets Mr. Cain know, Mr. Cain will come down on us like an avalanche."

They were either telling the truth, or they were good actors. Fargo could not decide which. "Now that you're here, you might as well do what you came for."

"We have to find Wen Po first," Hank said, "and bribe her into keeping quiet. Have you seen her?"

"Not in a while." Fargo turned to go back. He heard reins slap against a horse but did not think much of it. A mistake, as it turned out, because an instant later he was slammed into from behind. His boots left the ground and he was propelled like a pebble out of a slingshot into the rear of a shack. He got his arms up but they did little to cushion him. The world exploded in pain. He landed on his side, barely conscious.

"What the hell did you do that for?" Hank bawled.

"He didn't believe us," Cavendish said. "We'll have to hog-tie him and take him to Mr. Cain."

Fargo did not try to rise. He let them think he had been knocked out.

"Damn you," Hank griped. "If he's bad hurt, Mr. Cain will stomp you into the dirt. We're not supposed to act without orders."

A saddle creaked. Spurs jingled. Fargo, his eyes slitted, saw a shadow fall across him.

"My horse didn't hit him that hard," Cavendish said. "Give me your rope."

"Use your own. This was your brainstorm. I don't want any part of it," Hank replied.

"Deep down you're as yellow as the Chinese," Cavendish grumbled. "But have it your way. I'll use mine.

And I'll take the credit when Mr. Cain says we did the right thing."

"You hope," Hank spat. "Mr. Cain wants this one treated special, and what do you do? You damn near drive his head through a wall."

"Mr. Cain also likes for us to think for ourselves when we have to," Cavendish said.

A hand fell on Fargo's shoulder, and Cavendish began to roll him over. By then Fargo's senses had returned. He was ready. He contrived to keep his knees close to his chest, and as he was rolled onto his back, he drove both legs into Cavendish, catapulting him head over heels.

Hank squawked in alarm. Instead of resorting to his Remington, he swept toward Fargo, his fists flying, seeking to batter Fargo down before he could straighten. An uppercut landed. Then Fargo was braced, and when Hank cocked an arm, Fargo delivered an uppercut of his own. It rocked Hank on his heels. A punch to Hank's wind box, another to Hank's middle, and Hank lay stretched out in the dirt.

"Damn your hide!"

Fargo barely whirled in time. Cavendish had dismounted and drawn both bowies, and he came in swinging. Fargo ducked a streaking blade that knocked his hat from his head. He twisted, avoided a chest thrust, and backpedaled to give himself the split second he needed to draw his Colt. But as the Colt cleared leather, a bowie lanced at Fargo's wrist, hit the Colt's barrel with bone-jarring force and the Colt went flying.

Grinning confidently, Cavendish crouched. "So much for keeping you alive," he growled. "Mr. Cain will understand. He would do the same if he were me."

A gleaming blade whipped at Fargo's throat. He

dodged, shifted, dodged another stab at his gut. He glimpsed the Colt and sought to reach it, but Cavendish had seen it, too, and sprang in front of him.

"No, you don't!"

Fargo sprang back a good five feet. Before Cavendish could guess his intent, he had stooped, hiked his pant leg, and whipped his double-edged Arkansas toothpick from its ankle sheath.

Cavendish chortled and wagged his big blades. "That puny pigsticker against my bowies? You don't stand a prayer."

Fargo bought time to circle by saying, "It's not the size that counts."

"We'll see about that." Cavendish was confident. He was also uncommonly skilled. Showing off, he wove the twin bowies in a glittering pattern. "Still think you have a prayer?"

"Let's find out." Fargo was crouched low, the toothpick at his waist, his other hand almost brushing the ground.

Cavendish bared his teeth and pounced. He was in earnest now, and he speared the bowies in for the kill, one high, at Fargo's throat, the other low, at Fargo's belly. In a twinkling Fargo scooped up a handful of dirt and threw it at Cavendish's eyes. Usually the trick worked. But Cavendish whipped his blades in front of his face while simultaneously springing aside. Most of the dirt missed.

Fargo had been counting on that trick. A bowie sought his ribs, the other his legs. He pivoted, parried, was in the clear. But only for a moment.

Cavendish was determined not to give him a second's respite. The bowies became a steel whirlwind.

Fargo was in trouble. The toothpick was too small, the blade too thin. A solid blow from either bowie would break the blade. He had to rely on his wits and his agility. Unfortunately, Cavendish was almost as quick, almost as nimble. And Cavendish had those big bowies.

A glance showed Fargo his back was to the woods. He retreated toward the pinyon pines and junipers, always a whisker ahead of the blades thirsting for his lifeblood. Twice he flicked the toothpick at Cavendish's wrists and twice was thwarted by a darting bowie.

Suddenly Cavendish bounded in low, his blades sweeping in opposite arcs. He was going for Fargo's legs. Fargo threw himself back. The razor edges missed by the width of a hair.

Cavendish growled deep in his throat. Sidling to the left, he remarked, "They don't usually last this long."

Fargo stayed silent. He refused to be distracted. He considered throwing the toothpick at Cavendish's throat. Countless hours of practice had made him adept, but if he missed or Cavendish skipped aside he would be unarmed and Cavendish would still have those bowies. He decided not to try.

Cavendish unexpectedly stepped back. "There's something that's been bothering me, mister, and I guess now's as good a time as any to mention it since you won't be around much longer."

Wary of a trick, Fargo balanced on the balls of his feet, prepared to attack or defend as Cavendish's next move required.

"I don't think you are who you say you are."

Despite himself, Fargo froze.

"You told Mr. Cain your name was Bridger. But I saw a man who looks just like you, once. In St. Louis."

Fargo had been to St. Louis many a time. The doves were especially frisky, the whiskey as fine as anywhere.

"A friend said the man that looks like you was a famous scout like Kit Carson and Jim Bridger. The scout's name was Skye Fargo. Not an name easy to forget." Cavendish bared his teeth in a wolfish grin. "You lied to Mr. Cain, didn't you? You're not Kit Bridger. You're Fargo."

Fargo did not answer.

"All right. Don't say. But I know you are. The way you carry yourself, like a panther on the prowl, is just like the gent in St. Louis. You're too damned quick, too damned good with that pigsticker of yours to be anyone else." Cavendish lowered his bowies a little. "Pretty smart of me to figure that out, huh?"

"If you say so." Fargo broke his silence, and threw the Arkansas toothpick. They were only five feet apart. His knife was a blur. Then it became visible again, sunk in Cavendish's jugular.

Disbelief rooted Cavendish. Blood gouted from his throat and mouth. He dropped the bowies, grabbed the toothpick, and wrenched. In doing so he transformed himself into a scarlet geyser. Blood streamed from the wound in a fine mist. Cavendish staggered. He tried to talk, but all that came out were wet blubbery gurgles, like a baby with its mouth full of milk. He pressed his hands to his jugular in a futile bid to stanch the flow.

Fargo was careful to keep out of reach until the convulsing was over. Then he stepped forward to reclaim the toothpick. The metallic *click* of a gun hammer dissuaded him. That, and Hank's growl.

"Any sudden moves and I'll blow out your wick."

Hank was on one knee, his revolver in both hands, his face as grim as the death he had just witnessed. "I heard that last part. I know who you really are." Slowly unfurling, he backed off a couple of steps. "I should shoot you where you stand but Mr. Cain will want to deal with you his own self, I reckon."

"I'm not who Cavendish claimed," Fargo said, trying to confuse him.

"Sure you're not," Hank scoffed. "But whether you are or you aren't doesn't matter all that much, does it? You have to answer for killing Cavendish." He glanced at the horses.

Neither the buttermilk nor the sorrel had run off, although the buttermilk was still acting skittish.

"Get on Cavendish's horse."

"My own is at the saloon," Fargo said.

"And that's where it will stay." Hank took deliberate aim. "Get one thing clear. You are to do exactly as I say. You are to do it nice and slow. If you don't, or if you make any quick moves, I will gladly put a slug in you. Or a lot of slugs if I have to. So get on the damn sorrel or take lead."

A human turtle, Fargo did as he had been directed.

"Good. Now hold your arms out from your sides and keep them there."

Again Fargo complied.

Hank sidled to the buttermilk, which was only a few feet from the sorrel. He gripped the saddle horn and groped for the stirrup with his boot without taking his eyes off Fargo. Twice he missed but the third time his toe snagged the stirrup and he began to pull himself up, saying, "I can't wait to see what Mr. Cain does to you. Maybe he will snap your spine like I saw him do to a man once."

The buttermilk had been standing still. But suddenly it snorted and shied, throwing Hank off balance. His foot slipped out of the stirrup and he tottered on his boot heels.

Fargo launched himself from the sorrel. He slammed into Hank like a battering ram. His shoulder caught the weaselly man in the chest and they both went down. Hank sought to shove his revolver muzzle in Fargo's face and squeeze the trigger, but Fargo got a hand on the revolver and shoved the barrel aside. His left forefinger slipped under the hammer so that even if Hank squeezed the trigger, the gun would not go off.

Straining and heaving, each sought to wrest the Remington from the other. Hank was wiry and strong, and as they struggled he butted with his head and pumped his knees at Fargo's groin.

Fargo rolled to the left, his greater weight enabling him to pull Hank with him. He whipped to the right but could not throw Hank off. He drove his own knee up, but Hank clung to the Remington with the tenacity of a true weasel.

Fargo rose and Hank rose with him. Fargo swung his arms to one side and then the other, but he could not shake Hank off. Suddenly Hank acted more like a weasel than ever; he hissed and sank his teeth into Fargo's left hand. Agony exploded up Fargo's arm but he did not let go.

Hank tripped, and pulled Fargo down with him. The gleam of metal caught Fargo's eye. He dipped his right hand and brought it back up. The *thuck* of the bowie's big blade as it sheared through flesh was Hank's death knell. He expired without so much as a whimper.

Fargo was caked with sweat, and suddenly weary. Shaking it off, he rose. He had to dispose of the bodies and the horses before someone saw him. He had been lucky in that no shots had been fired. But his luck could change at any moment. He threw the bodies over the saddles, the buttermilk giving him a hard time, and stuffed their weapons in the saddlebags. Replacing the toothpick in his ankle sheath and the Colt in his holster, he hurriedly led the animals into the trees and wrapped the reins around handy limbs. He would come back later and take the bodies off somewhere and bury them, then strip the horses and give them swats on the rump.

Tilly was waiting in the saloon. She had put herself back together and brushed her hair. "There you are.

Where in blazes did you run off to? I looked out but didn't see you."

"I thought I saw someone looking in the window," Fargo said. He had slapped the dust from his buckskins and hat and adjusted his bandana. "I must have been mistaken."

"So everything is all right?"

"Never better," Fargo said.

17

It was dark when Fargo reached the Oasis. He stopped after descending the last hill and scanned the empty fields. All appeared quiet. He gigged the Ovaro and presently drew rein at the stable. A stoop-shouldered Chinese man in pigtails came out to take the reins. "I take off saddle. I feed horse," he said.

Fargo shucked the Henry and untied his bedroll. With the bedroll over his shoulder, he made for the bunkhouse. He was almost there when the door opened and light from within revealed him to the man who was emerging.

"Well, look who it is," Krast said with transparent dislike. "The boss has been looking for you."

"What for?" Fargo asked.

"How the hell would I know? He sent word that when you showed up, you were to report to him." Krast walked off toward the cookhouse.

Fargo wheeled and made for the mansion. Taking no chances, he had his left thumb on the Henry's hammer. His right thumb was hooked in his gun belt inches from the Colt. If he was walking into an ambush, if Cain had somehow found out about Hank and Cavendish, he would go down fighting.

The Chinese butler answered Fargo's knock. "Follow please," he said, and padded down the hall to an oak door. Opening it, he stepped aside. "Please be so kind as to wait here." He closed the door after him.

It was the parlor. Fargo sat in a settee and rested the Henry across his legs. The ticking of a clock on the mantel was the only sound. He was kept waiting for over five minutes.

The person who entered was not the person he was expecting.

May Ling seemed as surprised to see him as Fargo was to see her. "Oh!" she said, her hand rising to her throat. "I was unaware we had company."

"I'm waiting for Cain," Fargo explained, rising.

"Shouldn't that be *Mr.* Cain to you?" May Ling said archly. "He told me he was going to the stable. He should be back shortly."

Here was Fargo's chance to tell her why he was there. But he was unsure if he could trust her. He sat back down.

May Ling turned to go but changed her mind. "I am curious. Your name is Bridger, is it not?"

"That should be *Mr.* Bridger." Fargo gave her a dose of her own arrogant medicine.

"Why has my husband taken such an interest in you?" May Ling asked. "What about you is so special?"

"Why do you call him your husband when the two of you are not married?" Fargo rejoined. "What makes you think he cares for you?"

Indignation brought a flush to May Ling's exquisite features. "How dare you! When my husband gets back, I will tell him how rude you have been."

"Do you ever miss your family?"

May Ling's flush darkened. "Again you overstep yourself. What do you know of my life?"

Fargo took a gamble. "Only that your father misses you. He told me so himself in San Francisco."

Incredulous, May Ling came toward him but stopped midway. "You know my father? How can that be?"

"I met Shen a while back," Fargo hedged. "He told me you were missing. At the time I did not know about this place, or what had happened to you." That much was true.

May Ling glanced at the door, then came closer and lowered her voice. "Is he in good health, my father? What did he say about me?"

"He looks like someone who has had his heart ripped out," Fargo said, playing on her emotions. "He misses you. He said you are the only family he has left."

"That is true," May Ling said. "Then you did speak to him. You could find him again if you had to."

"Why would I want to?"

"To get word to him." May Ling glanced at the door again. "I will make it worth your while. I have been hiding money. It is not much. About two hundred dollars. But it is yours if you will do as I ask."

Fargo played his part. "I don't know. It's a long ride."

"If you will not do it for the money, do it for me," May Ling said. "I saw your face when Lu Wei was killed. You are not like these others."

"I saw your face, too," Fargo said. "You weren't very upset by it. Your exact words, as I recollect, were 'good riddance.'"

May Ling began wringing her slender hands. "We all have our parts to play. I must be true to mine or I will not be alive long."

Fargo digested that before he responded. "Are you saying that you're stringing Cain along? Then what's all that about him being your husband?"

Anxiety weighed heavily on May Ling's perfect

brow. She gazed toward the hallway and said, apparently to herself, "No. I must not. I would be a fool to trust you."

Fargo was off the settee so fast, he startled her. Bending, he whispered in her ear, "I'll go you one better than take word to your father. I'll take *you*."

"Why would you go to so much trouble for a woman you do not know?" May Ling asked suspiciously. "What do you hope to gain?"

On the brink of revealing his secret, Fargo froze when the front door slammed and a cavernous bellow boomed.

"May Ling! I'm back! Where are you?"

Panic seized May Ling. She motioned for Fargo to sit back down, then dashed over near the door, composed herself, and called out sweetly, "I am here, husband. There is someone to see you."

The giant's shadow preceded him. Tobias Cain filled the doorway, he was so huge. He smiled at May Ling and kissed her on the cheek. "Someone to see me, did you say?" She flicked a finger in the direction of the settee.

"Krast said you wanted to see me," Fargo said.

"Took you long enough to deliver that message to Pardee." Cain spoke casually but there was an edge to his tone that hinted he was not pleased.

"Pardee asked me to watch the saloon while he went hunting. Shouldn't I have?"

"Ah. That explains it." Cain smiled and draped an enormous arm across May Ling's shoulders. "You must be hungry so I won't keep you. Tomorrow Endor and his people head back. I'm riding along as far as Whiskey Mill. Krast and some of the others will go with me." Cain paused. "I want you to stay here and keep an eye on Li Dazhong."

"Why me?" Fargo wondered. There were any number of Cain's hired guns who could do it.

"Because I said so," Cain responded. "Because you work for me. Because he's a tricky devil and might try to escape again. Because I need someone I trust to make sure he doesn't." Cain chuckled. "Need any more reasons or are they enough?"

"More than enough," Fargo said, and touched his hat brim to May Ling. "I'll be getting along, then." His skin prickled as he walked past the giant so close that Cain could have reached out and crushed his neck. He suppressed a sigh of relief as he started down the hall.

"One more thing," Tobias Cain said.

Fargo stopped.

"You didn't see any sign of Hank or Cavendish today, did you? No one can seem to find them anywhere."

It was a good thing Fargo loved to play cards. His poker face served him in good stead. "Hank and Cavendish? Can't say as I did. Where could they have gotten to?"

"With those two there's no telling. Unless they snuck off to Whiskey Mill again. They are worse than elk in rut. They can't go a week without it."

The story Hank told was true, Fargo realized. The pair had gone to Whiskey Mill for the women. They were not following him.

Cain appeared unconcerned. "They'll show up before long," he predicted, and headed down the hall toward the dining room, his arm still around May Ling. "Be seeing you."

The Chinese butler let Fargo out. He went to the bunkhouse, dropped his bedroll on his bunk, and from there drifted to the cookhouse. Fully half of the forty cutthroats in Cain's employ were stuffing themselves with beef and potatoes. Krast was at a table with Vale and Shote Viktor and Captain Jim. At another table sat Merle Twern and Kid Fontaine.

141

The Kid grinned and tapped an empty chair next to his. "Have a seat, hoss. Where have you been all day?"

"Cain had me running an errand." Fargo slid the chair out with his boot. He poured himself a cup of coffee. It was so hot, it nearly scalded his mouth.

"Have you heard? We get to go to Whiskey Mill again tomorrow," Kid Fontaine said excitedly. "Twice in one week."

"I won't be going."

"Why not?" The Kid sounded genuinely disappointed.

Fargo told him about having to guard Li Dazhong. He did not share the seed of an idea that took root, but he thought about the seed for the rest of the evening and long into the night. He did not sleep much. He tried. But all he did was toss and turn.

Sunrise was half an hour shy of waking up the world when Fargo quietly stepped from the bunkhouse. The stable door was shut but not barred, so it was a simple matter to throw his saddle blanket and saddle on the Ovaro and tie his bedroll on the saddle. He went to the tack room and returned carrying a saddle and blanket for the horse in the next stall. One more trip, and he led three horses out the wide front doors and around to the cattle pens. On the side of the pens farthest from the mansion, he looped the reins around the top rail.

Next Fargo filled three water skins and hung one from the saddle horn of each saddle.

By then the new day had broken. Smoke puffed from the stone chimney on top of the cookhouse. Hired guns lined up at the washbasin. Over at the chicken coop a rooster crowed long and loud.

Fargo ate breakfast with the rest. Kid Fontaine sought him out and chatted about a woman he hoped to bed in Whiskey Mill.

"Sure, she's Chinese, but I've had her before and she rides smoother than a rocking chair. Maybe you've met her. Her name is Tu Shuzhen."

By seven the empty prison wagons were lined up in front of the mansion. Endor's men were in the seats, his riflemen at the front and the rear. Shortly thereafter, Miles Endor came strolling out of the mansion in the company of his host. Endor's big horse was brought and two men boosted him into the saddle.

Krast came clattering up at the head of Cain's underlings. Captain Jim, the Viktor brothers, the Kid, Merle Twern, and a dozen others were set to ride out.

Tobias Cain mounted and rode to the head of the column with Endor. At a wave of Cain's arm, whips cracked and the wagons lurched into motion.

Fargo watched from a corner of the bunkhouse where he could see without being seen. Not until the last of the riders was out of sight to the west did he stride into the open, making for the four long buildings with the barred windows and doors.

Chinese were filing out under the hard stares of overseers with whips. They would proceed to the cookhouse where each worker would be given a small bowl of rice and a glass of water. Then it was off to the fields for another blistering day of toil and despair.

After the last of the workers shuffled from the second building, Fargo went in. Beds lined both sides, crude box affairs with boards instead of mattresses to sleep on, and burlap bags for covers instead of quilts or blankets.

Li Dazhong was in bed, staring gloomily out a barred window. He was naked from the waist up. At his side, about to apply a change of bandages to Li's shoulder, was the doctor.

"How is he doing?"

The doctor's eyes were so bloodshot, they were more red than white. "Bridger, isn't it? I don't be-

143

lieve we have been introduced. I'm Brine. Andrew Brine." He pried at the old bandage and it slowly peeled off, the bottom red with dry blood. "To answer your question, the bullet went clean through. In a few days he will be back on his feet. In a week Cain will have him out in the fields." Brine said the last with disgust.

"You don't like what Cain is doing?" Fargo asked, thinking perhaps he had found an ally.

"I'm not being paid to approve or disapprove," Brine said while he worked. "I'm paid to keep these poor wretches alive so Cain can work them to death. The irony is quite marvelous, don't you think?"

"You can always leave."

Brine shook his head. "No, I cannot. I know too much, and I have a tendency to talk when I am in my cups, which is every day. Cain would bury me before he let me go."

Soon the doctor was done. He took a swig from his flask, picked up his black bag, and nodded at Fargo as he walked unsteadily out.

Li Dazhong had been silent the whole time. That changed. "You again. The one who does not work for the monster who runs this prison." He oozed sarcasm. "Why are you here?"

"I'm leaving in a while and I thought you might like to tag along," Fargo informed him. "I have horses saddled and waiting out by the cattle pens."

"Sure you do," Li said. "And will you also shoot me in the back when I am caught trying to flee?"

"It's your mistake to make," Fargo said. He did not have time to waste. He left. Since he would arouse more suspicion skulking about than moving openly, he walked straight to the mansion and knocked on the front door. He expected the Chinese butler to admit him.

The door slowly opened. Just inside stood May

Ling, a short-barreled revolver in her hand. With no warning whatsoever, she pointed it at his stomach. "I am told this will blow a hole in you the size of an apple."

18

Fargo never liked having a gun pointed at him. Acting on the assumption that if she really wanted to shoot him she would already have done so, he asked, "Have you thought about what we talked about?"

"Go away." Fear was in May Ling's voice, in her eyes. "This is a trick of some kind and I will not fall for it."

"I have horses waiting," Fargo said. "We can be gone in five minutes, in San Francisco by the end of the month."

"You do not listen worth a damn."

Fargo smiled. "And you have a decision to make. Do you want to see your father again or not? He hired me to find you, to bring you back. I can't tie you up and throw you over a horse. I'd never make it out of the Oasis. You must come willingly."

May Ling blanched. "Talking to you is like talking to a wall. How am I to believe you? Tobias might have put you up to this to test me. If I fail the test, he will do to me as he has done to all his other girls."

"So you know about them?"

"How could I not when he brags about killing them?" May Ling said. "I do not want to die. I would do anything to stay alive."

Fargo thought he saw the truth at last. "Does that

include sleeping with the man who kidnapped you? Does that include pretending to be in love with him?"

"I would do anything," May Ling reiterated. "You cannot imagine what it has been like. I was never so scared as when those men jumped me in San Francisco and tied and gagged me and threw a hood over my head. I thought they would do horrible things and then kill me. But they put me in a smelly, clammy room and kept me there for days. Then one night—I knew it was night because the city sounds are different at night than during the day—they threw me in a wagon and covered me with canvas. We traveled many miles before the wagon stopped for a few minutes. The canvas was removed. My hood and the ropes were taken off me. I saw I was in a wagon with bars, and I was not alone."

Fargo did not interrupt. She was letting out emotions she had bottled up since her abduction. It was good for her.

"Other Chinese were in the wagon, and in other wagons besides ours. We were brought here. The men who brought us told us what was in store. Either work the fields or work as whores. I refuse to sell my body, and the fields held no appeal. So I grasped at a straw."

"Cain," Fargo said.

"I could tell he was interested. Men have always been attracted to me. They praise my looks and want to touch me. Tobias Cain, after all, is just another man, with the same hungers. So I curried his favor, and won it. I—" May Ling suddenly stopped, aghast. "What have I done? I have just sealed my death."

"What will it take to get it through your thick head?" Fargo asked. "I am the only person here you can trust."

May Ling frowned. "I may never trust another human being for as long as I live. Again, how am I to believe you?"

Fargo remembered talking to her father, remembered Shen reminiscing about her as a little girl, how sweet she had been, and how much he missed her. "When you were seven your father brought home a kitten. You loved it so much, you would not let it out of your sight. One day you were playing with it in front of your house and it ran into the street and was run over by a carriage."

May Ling gasped.

"When you were ten, your father asked you if you wanted to live with his sister and her family. He said you needed a woman to teach you things only women know. But you said no."

"I had lost my mother. I would not lose him as well."

"When you were twelve you were at the docks with your father and saw a knife fight. One sailor slit another's throat. Some blood sprayed on you and you screamed and screamed. Your father said it took a week to calm you."

May Ling lowered the revolver. "You could not know all that unless you did indeed talk to him."

"Pack a small bag if you want," Fargo said. "We have to travel light."

May Ling gestured. "You need not wait out there. Come in and close the door."

Fargo did as he was bid and was taken aback when May Ling threw her arms around him and pressed her cheek to his chest.

"You cannot realize what this means. I had about given up hope."

She was warm and soft and smelled of lilacs, and it was all Fargo could do to pry her from him. "Time's wasting," he said more gruffly than he intended.

"Oh. Yes. I am sorry. But I am so glad." Beaming happily, May Ling whirled and hastened down the hall. She disappeared up a flight of stairs.

Fargo paced. The sooner they left, the more of a lead they would have on Cain and the rest after Cain returned, found her missing, and figured out who was to blame. They must put as many miles behind them as they could before the Viktor brothers and Captain Jim were put on their trail.

The minutes dragged. Fargo opened the door a crack and peered out. Chinese were working the fields. An overseer cracked a whip. Several more were over by the cookhouse, talking. Everything appeared normal. He closed the door, and suddenly sensed he was not alone. "Ready to go?"

He thought it was May Ling.

The Chinese butler was slinking toward him with a curved dagger upraised. The instant after Fargo turned, the butler sprang. Fargo got an arm up and blocked a descending wrist.

Springing back, the butler hissed, "You not take her! Wong not let you. Maybe so, Cain kill Wong!"

The dagger slashed with the speed of a striking sidewinder. Fargo threw himself back against the door and was spared.

Wong was nearly beside himself. "You not hear? You take missy, Cain be very mad. Maybe he kill Wong."

"Tell him I took you by surprise and knocked you out," Fargo said.

A crafty smile lit the pigtailed man's features. "Or Wong kill you. Maybe so, Cain be happy."

"Listen to me," Fargo began, but got no further. Wong darted in. The dagger flashed low. Fargo twisted, brought his right fist up. His knuckles connected with Wong's chin and the butler landed on his back. "Now to find something to tie you with."

But Wong was still conscious. He still had fight left in him. Springing up, he wagged the dagger. "Maybe so you die now, Fargo!"

A gunshot would have brought Cain's hired guns on the run. Fargo had to end it quietly, and quickly. He started to dip his hand toward his ankle sheath. Abruptly, he realized what Wong had just called him. "You know who I am?"

Wong did not answer. He slid in close. Fargo had no time to draw the Arkansas toothpick. The dagger lanced at his neck, but Fargo grabbed Wong's wrist and slammed Wong against the door. The little man was a lot tougher than he looked. He shrugged it off and came in again.

Fargo feinted left. Wong thrust, overextending himself. In a heartbeat Fargo had his Colt out and brought the barrel crashing down on the crown of Wong's head. For most that was enough, and the butler was no exception. "You should have listened," Fargo said to the bundle at his feet.

May Ling came hurrying down the hall, a leather bag slung over her shoulder. At the sight of Wong, she stopped and gasped.

"He tried to stop me from taking you," Fargo explained.

"I am not surprised. He is a vile little man. I often catch him spying on me, and suspect he reports what I do to Tobias."

"Tie him while I fetch the horses," Fargo directed. "I'll bring them around back." He walked out into the harsh glare of the sun. The morning had grown uncomfortably warm and would soon be scorching hot.

No one paid particular attention to him. Fargo knit his brow, pondering. It troubled him, Wong knowing his real name. Cavendish had known it, too, but Cavendish had seen him before. He supposed Wong might have seen him somewhere, but the prospect was so unlikely there had to be another explanation. The only one he could think of caused him to glance sharply to the west, but he did not spot any riders.

Fargo came to the cattle pens. He got his next surprise of the day when he saw who was waiting beside the three horses. "What's this?"

"I changed my mind," Li Dazhong said. He was fully dressed, a bulge on his shoulder under his shirt.

"Why?" It seemed too sudden to Fargo.

"I thought over what you said," Li replied. "I decided I might be wrong about you."

Fargo untied the Ovaro and one of the other horses, and forked leather. "The last one is yours. Can you ride?"

"Not especially well, no. But I will do what I must." Li grinned and unwound the reins. He used his good arm to pull himself into the saddle. His feet barely reached the stirrups.

"Keep your head down so no one gets a good look at you until we're in the clear," Fargo cautioned. To most of the hired guns, one Chinese tended to look pretty much like any other, as a few had commented several times since he arrived.

Fargo clucked to the Ovaro. He did not make for the mansion but instead rode toward a shed to the east of it. When he was almost there, he abruptly changed directions and came up behind the mansion.

"Why are we here?" Li Dazhong asked uneasily.

His answer came in the form of May Ling. The back door opened and she swiftly slipped out and ran to the horse Fargo was holding for her. She accepted the reins, then stiffened in surprise.

"You did not tell me someone was coming with us."

"He wants out of here just as much as you do."

"I do not know," May Ling said.

"That makes two of us," Li Dazhong declared. "She is Cain's woman. Why should she want to give all this up?"

"I suggest you two hash it out later," Fargo advised. He gigged the pinto.

Acres of tilled fields stretched before them to the north. Beyond lay the formidable desert. Fargo followed a winding track, holding to a walk although his nerves screamed for him to fan the wind.

"Shouldn't we head west?" May Ling asked.

"Toward Whiskey Mill and your husband?" Fargo said. "We'll swing west later on."

The Chinese workers did not look up from their toil. They feared the sting of the whip. But several overseers wore puzzled expressions, and one barred their way.

"What's this, mister? Where are you taking these two?"

May Ling answered before Fargo could. "I am going for a ride. My husband has assigned this man to guard me."

"What about that one?" the hard case asked, with a jerk of his thumb at Li Dazhong. "He's that trouble-maker who was shot the other night."

"The doctor says he must have air and exercise if he is to heal," May Ling said. "Now out of our way or you will answer to Tobias Cain!"

The man was suspicious but he stepped to the side so they could pass.

Fargo flicked his reins. He had gone ten feet, if that, when a shrill cry wafted across the fields. He reined around. A window on the second floor of the mansion was open. Leaning out, his hands cupped to his mouth, was Wong.

"Stop them! Stop them! They try escape!"

"I knew it!" the overseer exclaimed, and went for his revolver.

Fargo was faster. His shot cored the man's head. "Ride!" he bawled, and snapped a shot to discourage several others.

Confusion spread. Many of the Chinese flattened to avoid taking a stray slug. Overseers were shouting, demanding to know what was going on. Wong continued his shrill yelling.

As soon as May Ling and Li Dazhong galloped past, Fargo used his spurs. He was ready to shoot anyone who tried to stop him. Suddenly there was a *crack*, and something wrapped tight about his neck. He clawed at the whip and tried to rein up, but the next moment he was wrenched bodily from the saddle and tumbled to the earth. His shoulder took the brunt. He began to rise as boots pounded. The handle of a whip smashed against his temple.

Hooves drummed. May Ling slammed her mount into the overseer holding the whip, and he lost his grip and buckled.

Fingers flying, Fargo unwound the lash and was back in the saddle before anyone else could reach them. "Thanks," he said.

May Ling smiled.

Li Dazhong had slowed to wait for them. Pistols cracked, but only a few. Most of Cain's men were too far off. Those that did shoot were firing on the run and their aim suffered.

At a gallop Fargo raced toward the north end of the Oasis. May Ling was on his left, bent low. Li Dazhong was on his right, doing his best to stay in the saddle. A few final whines of lead and they left the Oasis behind and were riding pell-mell across the valley floor.

Almost instantly, withering heat enveloped them, and the air became so hot it was hard to breathe.

The Oasis was in an uproar. Men were running for horses. Wong was still shrieking from the upstairs window.

Ahead lay the parched expanse of Death Valley. Not a spot of green anywhere, only the baked brown of dead land. Not a trace of animal life, either. It was as if they were fleeing headlong into hell.

Worry etching her flawless features, May Ling glanced grimly at Fargo. "I hope you know what you are doing."

"As do I," Li Dazhong echoed.

"That makes three of us," Fargo said. But he said it to himself.

19

The heat was awful. It sapped the vitality. It brought sweat from every pore. It made metal hot to the touch. It seeped into the marrow, so that within an hour of leaving the Oasis, Skye Fargo felt like he was being roasted alive. Every breath seared his lungs with fiery discomfort. He craved water, lots and lots of water, but he steeled himself against the craving and kept rimming his parched lips with a tongue that was almost as dry.

To Fargo's surprise, no one gave chase. They had slowed from a gallop to a walk to spare the horses, but from the way the three mounts hung their heads and plodded on leaden hooves, the animals were already exhausted.

"Oh my," May Ling said for what had to be the tenth time. "I knew it would be bad but not *this* bad. We must change directions soon and head west or we will perish."

"Not until I say so," Fargo said. From here on out the cat and mouse was in earnest, and he must rely on all his skill as a scout to stay alive.

May Ling squinted up at the blazing orb responsible for the earthly Hades. "I should have brought a hat. I have never been so hot."

"Stop thinking about how hot it is and you won't feel it as much," Fargo suggested.

"I could shut it from my mind completely and still feel the heat," May Ling disagreed, mopping at a stray wisp of hair that drooped over her forehead. "This valley is an oven."

"I have never known such heat," Li Dazhong threw in. He looked considerably paler.

"If you need to, drink some water," Fargo said. "But only a few sips at a time. We have to make it last."

"I can wait," Li said, with a longing glance at the water skin hanging from his saddle horn. The skins held a lot more than a canteen, which was why Fargo had brought them. They were also a lot heavier, but May Ling and Li did not weigh as much as an average man, so the added weight was not an extra burden for their mounts.

They had to go easy with the horses. Without their mounts, it was doubtful Fargo and the others would make it out of Death Valley alive. Not that Fargo intended to remain there much longer.

By Fargo's reckoning it was close to ten o'clock when he drew rein and announced, "This is far enough. We'll swing toward the mountains. By tonight we'll be up in the high country where it will be cool."

"I can hardly wait," May Ling said, mopping at her perspiring face with a sleeve. "Summer is no longer my favorite time of year."

Grinning, Fargo lifted his reins.

"What is that?" Li Dazhong asked. He had twisted in the saddle and was staring in the direction of the Oasis.

Fargo swore under his breath. A dust cloud was rising to the cloudless sky. "They're after us."

Li pointed to the southwest. "There is another."

Sure enough, to Fargo's consternation, a second dust cloud was being raised. The second cloud was close to the hills and moving faster than the first. The reason spiked alarm in Fargo. "They are trying to head us off."

As much as Fargo did not want to, he brought the Ovaro to a gallop. But it was soon apparent they could not reach the black hills ahead of the second band of pursuers. He came to a stop, and swore some more.

"What now?" May Ling asked.

They couldn't go back. They couldn't reach the mountains to the west. Their best bet now was the mountains to the east.

"This way," Fargo said, and reined around.

May Ling followed his example and promptly blurted, "Oh my!"

"This is not good," Li said.

A *third* dust cloud was visible to the southeast. This one, like the second, was out ahead of the riders coming down the center of the valley.

"Tell me you expected this," May Ling said. "Tell me we can still get away."

"We can still get away," Fargo assured her. But he had *not* expected Cain's men to split into three groups. With south, west, and east no longer open to them, they were left with north. North, into the fiery heart of Death Valley. "Stay close," he said, and wheeled the pinto.

Half an hour later their pursuers had not gained any. Neither had they slowed or given up.

"There must be a lot of them," Li Dazhong remarked.

Fargo had been thinking the same thing. Based on the amount of dust raised, he was willing to wager that the groups to the east and the west were made up of six to ten riders. The cloud to the south was larger. No less than a dozen were involved. Which meant twenty men or more were after them, and there had barely been that many left at the Oasis. The rest were supposed to be off with Tobias Cain.

Fargo wondered. He still could not get over the fact that Wong knew who he was. And what that hinted at. If he was right, he had been played for a fool from the day he arrived in Whiskey Mill. He would like to think that was not the case, that he had not been tricked so easily.

Noon came. Directly overhead, the circle of flame that was the sun shone with unrelenting intensity. The air was sweltering, the ground practically sizzled. An egg, cracked open and poured onto a flat rock, would fry within seconds.

"I can't take much more of this," May Ling said. Her movements were wooden, her eyelids hooded. Her cheeks, her brow, her neck were red and turning redder. Her hair, so luxurious when they started out, hung in limp defeat.

Li Dazhong had not said much all morning. Now he gingerly touched his shoulder, and winced. "I feel weak. The two of you should go on without me."

"We are in this together," Fargo said. "I talked you into it, so I will stay with you until it is over."

"You are an honorable man, Bridger or Fargo or whatever your name is," Li said. "But you should save yourself if you can."

Fargo thought of his fondness for cards and women and whiskey, not necessarily in that order, and replied, "I'm no more honorable than anyone else."

May Ling looked back, then slumped in her saddle. "We are deceiving ourselves. Escape is impossible."

"Not if we can stay ahead of them until nightfall," Fargo said, to bolster her spirits. "Once it is dark we will try to reach the mountains to the west."

But night was hours off.

The valley floor became more broken. Along about two in the afternoon they entered a dry wash with high banks and Fargo halted in a patch of feeble shade. "The horses need to rest."

"So do I," May Ling said, and wearily climbed down. She tugged at the water skin but could not slip the straps over the saddle horn.

Fargo did it for her. He opened the water skin and held it so she could drink. She drank more than she should have, but he did not stop her.

Li Dazhong had poured a little water into his palm and was running his hand over his face and neck. "I will never take water for granted again." He undid his shirt partway and pulled on his left sleeve to expose his shoulder. The wound had been bleeding and the bandage was stained.

Fargo began to regret asking Li to come. If the wound became infected, Li's life was in jeopardy.

May Ling sank against the bank with a slight grin. "I almost feel alive again. But what I wouldn't give for a bath."

Fargo limited himself to a swallow. He took off his hat, poured some water into the crown, and held the hat so the Ovaro could drink. In turn, he gave the other horses water, too. As he was hanging the water skin over his saddle horn, he caught May Ling studying him. "What?"

"You puzzle me."

Fargo had nothing to say to that.

"You risk your life for two strangers," May Ling said. "You risk your life for two people others would look down their noses at simply because we are Chinese and not white."

"Your father is paying me a thousand dollars."

"That is the only reason you are doing this? For the money?" May Ling sounded skeptical.

"Can you think of a better one?" Her prying made Fargo uncomfortable. To prevent more questions he climbed the bank and gazed to the south. The dust clouds were still rising, and they were closer. "We can't stay here much longer."

Li Dazhong squatted with his back to the bank. He looked worse than ever. "I suggest you leave me when you ride on."

"We have already been through that," Fargo reminded him.

"I feel weaker. My shoulder throbs. I do not know if I can even ride," Li informed them.

"Then I'll throw you over your horse and tie you down," Fargo said. "But you are coming whether you want to or not."

"You are stubborn," Li said.

"He is male," May Ling remarked with a grin.

They rode on. The brief rest had refreshed them and their animals, but within five minutes they were as hot as ever and their horses plodded tiredly.

"Are there other springs in this part of Death Valley?" May Ling asked.

Not that Fargo knew of. There were a few watering holes, but the water was bad, unfit for man and beast.

"This is a terrible place," May Ling said. "The worst on earth."

Fargo would not go that far. Just to the south lay the Mojave Desert, which was as inhospitable as Death Valley. Once, apparently, the Mojave had been lush and green, because dry lake beds were scattered across its length and width. So were a few extinct volcanoes.

Death Valley had its own geologic oddities. North of them were stark mud hills, some sculpted in the shape of pyramids. Scattered craters pockmarked the valley floor. The dry washes suggested that at one time, ages ago, Death Valley had been as green as the Mojave Desert.

But now it was dry and barren and hot, and getting hotter. The worst of the afternoon was upon them. When Fargo breathed, he would swear he was breathing fire. Li Dazhong's bay began to wheeze, its lungs laboring.

"We will not get away," May Ling said. "I should not have let you talk me into coming."

"You give up too easy."

"Perhaps. Or perhaps it is that I know Cain will soon send the Viktor brothers and Captain Jim after us, if he has not done so already, and no one has ever escaped them. Ever."

"I hear tell there is a first time for everything," Fargo mentioned. But he was not as confident as he sounded. He had seen with his own eyes that the brothers were seasoned trackers, and the Modoc was a two-legged wolverine. They were not to be taken lightly.

Li Dazhong's bay fell slightly behind. Fargo slowed so it could come up alongside the Ovaro.

Li himself was a portrait of frailty and weakness. The blistering heat and the movement had aggravated the wound worse than they had anticipated.

"If you need to rest again, just say so," Fargo said.

"I refuse to slow you down. My life is of some value to Cain, so long as my father pays him the money he requires. The same with May Ling. But you have no such value. If they catch us they will kill you."

"They will try."

"You can ride off and leave us," Li proposed. "Increase your chances of getting away."

"Cows can fly, too."

A lopsided smirk curled Li's lips. "I saw one fly the other day and made the mistake of standing under it."

Fargo chuckled. He swiveled in the saddle. The dust clouds were not any closer. That puzzled him. He suspected their pursuers were content to trail them until the heat took its inevitable toll. Then they could be captured without a fight.

"I would imagine my days as Cain's favorite are numbered," May Ling remarked. "He will replace me with someone younger and prettier."

"That's not possible," Fargo said.

"What?"

"There is no one prettier."

May Ling was as susceptible to flattery as most any female. "Thank you for that." She coughed and fiddled with her hair. "A different time, a different place, and it would have been nice to get to know you better."

It became too hot to talk, too hot for anything but staying upright in the saddle. Several times Fargo permitted them to drink water, but it did not help much.

Eventually the sun sank to the west. The shadows of the mountains lengthened, and the slightest of breezes brought the promise of a stronger breeze later, and welcome relief from the inferno.

"As soon as it is dark enough we will swing west," Fargo said. He turned in the saddle again. The dust was far enough away that he felt justified in saying, "Hold up. We'll rest a spell."

Li nearly fell dismounting. He sat down heavily. He did not object when Fargo knelt and examined the bullet hole. The edges were discolored. It was becoming infected. Cauterizing would help, but there was no wood or brush for a fire.

"Look!" May Ling exclaimed, pointing.

Three riders had appeared. They were ahead of the main party. At that distance they were little more than stick figures, but Fargo had more than a fair inkling who they were.

Vale and Shote Viktor, and Captain Jim had been sent ahead after them.

"What do we do?" May Ling cried.

The only thing they could. "Ride like hell," Fargo said.

20

The sun had dipped below the mountains half an hour ago. Twilight was giving way to the ink of night. Stars had blossomed.

Fargo had been pushing hard to the north to gain more of a lead on the trackers and the Modoc. May Ling was doing fine now that the terrific heat of the day was rapidly fading to the welcome cool of evening. Li Dazhong, however, was not doing well. He was so weak he could barely sit his saddle. His infected shoulder was to blame. Fargo had used some of their precious water to wash the wound thoroughly, but it did little good. They needed to boil the water, but they could not take the time to light a fire even if they had the fuel to do so. They needed to reach the mountains. Once there, Fargo could treat the wound properly.

Soon Fargo drew rein and the other two followed his example. It was dark enough now. He listened but heard only the sigh of the breeze and the distant yip of a coyote. Dismounting, he untied his bedroll and spread out his blankets. May Ling and Li watched with interest as he drew the Arkansas toothpick and cut a blanket into large enough squares for what he had in mind. Working rapidly, he cut whangs from his buckskins and tied them together until they were long enough. He had to cut a lot of whangs. He needed twelve bindings. Then he slid a square of blanket over each of the Ovaro's hooves and tied them with the whangs.

"What are you doing?" May Ling asked in bewilderment.

Fargo would have thought it was obvious. "To muffle the sound we'll make." He tied squares to the hooves of her mount and then moved to Li's. The bay did not like it and tried to kick him, but a smack on the flank made it behave.

At a cautious walk they rode on, bent low over their saddles to shrink their silhouettes.

Fargo let the other two go ahead so he could watch behind them. Now that night had fallen, the Viktor brothers and Captain Jim would come on swiftly to overtake them.

They had gone several hundred yards when Fargo whispered for May Ling and Li to stop. Faint to his ears came the thud of hooves. A few moments later the darkling silhouettes of three riders appeared, trotting from south to north. The human bloodhounds were soon swallowed by the night.

Fargo grinned. His ruse had worked. He gigged the Ovaro past May Ling and Li and assumed the lead. A quarter of a mile fell behind them. Half a mile. A mile. They still had a ways to go.

May Ling brought her horse up next to the Ovaro. Her teeth flashed in the darkness. "You did it!" she whispered. "You saved us!"

No sooner were the words out of her mouth than a man called out not more than a hundred yards in front of them.

"Did you hear something?"

To the south, maybe another hundred yards, a man answered. "No! What did it sound like?"

"Horses," the first man said.

To the north a third man snarled, "Not another peep out of either of you or I'll damn well come over there and beat on your noggins with a rock!" The voice was familiar; it was Krast.

Instantly, Fargo drew rein. He remembered the dust cloud to the southwest. Krast and other hired guns had spread out in a long line. They were there for one reason, to keep him and the others from reaching the mountains.

Fargo did some quick thinking. He could go north or south and try to swing around them, but he did not know how far the line extended. Or he could try to slip through there. He whispered for May Ling and Li to come closer and shared his reasoning, ending with, "I'll leave it up to you. The more moving about we do, the greater the chance we'll be spotted. I'm for trying to break through here, but it might be safer if we try to swing around."

"That would take hours," May Ling whispered. "I am with you. I say we try right here."

"I say the same," Li whispered. "My shoulder is worse. I do not know how much longer I can keep going."

"Then here it is." Fargo palmed his Colt. "Stay next to me. If I tell you to, ride like hell."

Their horses abreast, they advanced. May Ling and Li hugged their saddles, but Fargo was only slightly bent so he could spot trouble before it spotted them. He intended to pass through the skirmish line between the first rider who had called out and the other to the south.

Fargo spotted the first one. Mount and man were indistinct shapes. Fargo could not be sure, but the rider appeared to be staring to the northeast. Maybe the man had caught a glimpse of the Viktor brothers and Captain Jim.

Somewhere to the south a horse nickered. Farther off, someone growled, "Keep that nag quiet, damn it!"

Every nerve raw, Fargo came within twenty feet of

where he would slip through. May Ling was smiling, thinking they were almost in the clear. Li Dazhong had dropped a dozen feet back. Fargo twisted to see if Li was all right. He was a second too late.

Uttering a loud groan, Li pitched from the saddle. He landed with a thud. His horse shied and whinnied.

"Over here! They're here!" the rider to the north bawled. "I can see them!" Apparently he could, too, because he reined his mount toward them and flourished a six-shooter.

Scattered yells erupted, the hired guns demanding to know exactly where Fargo and his companions were. Hooves thundered as riders converged.

Reining the Ovaro around, Fargo swung down to help Li. He slid his arm under Li's shoulder and started to lift, but Li pushed against his chest.

"No! Save yourselves. I would slow you down."

May Ling screamed.

Dirt geysers spewed as Fargo straightened and whirled. His Colt at his waist, he snapped off a shot. Forty feet out, the rider to the north clutched at his head and was flung backward off his mount. He smashed to the ground face-first and did not move.

From the south came another rider, firing on the gallop.

In two long strides Fargo was at the Ovaro. Reluctantly, he vaulted into the saddle. He was tensing his legs to dig in his spurs and race to the west when more riders acquired shape and substance.

"Damn!" Fargo snapped lead, then reined east. It was the only way open to them. May Ling galloped at his side, her long hair flying. They were a mutual study in grimness.

From out of the northeast galloped three riders. Shote and Vale and Captain Jim, Fargo guessed.

From the southeast came more.

Fargo and May Ling were in the center of a swiftly

tightening circle. A noose, Fargo now knew beyond any shade of doubt, cleverly spread to ensnare them. And he had waltzed right into it, leading May Ling and Li into the trap. He was furious with himself. But his fury had to be set aside. If he was to stay alive, he needed a clear head.

Rifles and pistols banged. Slugs sizzled in the night air. It did not occur to Fargo until later that while the slugs came close, the shots were either wide or high. The men shooting at them were deliberately missing.

A gully opened almost under the noses of their mounts. Fargo went down the incline in a spray of dirt and rocks. At the bottom he hauled on the reins and was out of the saddle before the Ovaro came to a stop. Shucking the Henry from the saddle scabbard, he scrambled to the top.

Cain's men were sweeping toward the gully from all sides. In their eagerness they were careless.

Fargo shoved the Colt into his holster and tucked the Henry's hardwood stock to his shoulder. He fired three times as rapidly as he could work the lever. Riders to the north, west, and east toppled. The rest were quick to scatter and seek cover.

Gravel crunched as May Ling hunkered by Fargo. Her hand found his arm and lightly squeezed. "Thank you for trying."

"We're not caught yet," Fargo said, but he was not fooling anyone, least of all himself.

Commands were being barked. Not by Krast, but by the deviously cruel mastermind who had orchestrated the trap. Hooves stopped thudding and spurs stopped jangling and an unnatural silence fell. But only for a minute.

"Why not make it easy on yourselves and give up?" came a rumbling request from out of the dark to the south.

"Go to hell, Cain!" Fargo hollered. It was childish but he was mad, damned mad. At himself.

Tobias Cain laughed. "I didn't take you for a sore loser, Fargo. I outfoxed you. Accept it." Cain's voice came from a different point than before. He was moving as he talked.

Fargo had to ask. "How long have you been on to me?" He had to know how big a fool he had been.

"From the day you showed up in Whiskey Mill," Cain answered. "After you and I traded punches, Cavendish came up to me in the saloon. He told me he had seen you once. That your real name was Skye Fargo."

Fargo placed the Henry's stock on the ground, gripped the barrel with both hands, and bowed his head. "Damn me to hell."

"I wasn't quite convinced, though," Cain rumbled on. "Not until Wen Po told me she overheard Lu Wei and you talking."

"The whole damn time," Fargo said.

"I wanted to find out what you were up to. To do that, I needed to gain your trust, and keep an eye on you at the same time. That's why I invited you to supper and had you report to the mansion each morning. Did it work?"

"Bastard."

Cain heard him, and laughed. "I sure pulled the wool over your eyes, didn't I? I figured you would show your hand sooner or later and I was right. So it was May Ling you were after all along."

May Ling gave Fargo a sorrowful look, then leaped to her feet. "It is not what you think, Tobias!" she cried. "He forced me to come with him!"

"Sure he did," Cain said.

"I would never leave you!" May Ling said. "You have given me more than I ever dreamed I could have! I want to be with you always."

"You almost sound like you mean it."

May Ling took a few steps. "I do! I have never felt

for any man as I feel for you, Tobias. What must I do to prove how much I care?"

Strangely, Cain was silent awhile. Then he said, "We have you surrounded. If I give the order to throw lead, my men will blast you to bits. Be smart and come out with your hands up."

Sinking back down, May Ling gripped Fargo's wrist. "We should do as he wants. It is not wise to make him madder than he already is."

"Give up if you want," Fargo said. Cain might let her live. But Cain would never spare him.

"We should surrender together," May Ling advised. "I will plead with him on your behalf."

"Fat lot of good that will do," Fargo bluntly responded. "I know too much. He can never let me leave Death Valley alive."

"He might not kill you right away," May Ling said. "He likes to play with his victims like a snake plays with a rodent."

"Is that supposed to be good news?"

"You misunderstand," May Ling replied. "We will give up, and at the first opportunity, I will find a way to help you as you have tried to help me."

"No."

"Why not?" May Ling wrung her hands, glancing anxiously out at the darkness. "They will shoot you otherwise. There are too many for you to overcome. Be sensible. Live a little longer."

"No," Fargo said again. Her insistence mystified him. She had to know her idea stood about as much chance of working as her jumping over the moon. "You go to him if you want, but I'm staying put."

Tobias Cain had moved closer but not so near that they could see him. "What is all the whispering about? You don't stand a chance. Throw your guns out while you still can."

"Not now, not ever." Fargo yearned for a clear shot.

169

Just one. But try as he might to penetrate the murk, he could not spot the giant. He rose a little higher to see over a boulder a few feet away. Then it hit him. The boulder had not been there when they sought cover in the gully. He started to bring up the Henry.

In the blink of an eye, Captain Jim unfolded and sprang. An arm lashed out at the exact split second that Fargo squeezed the trigger, swatting the muzzle down. The slug meant for the Modoc dug a furrow in the ground. Almost in the same motion, Captain Jim threw himself at Fargo to tackle him, but Fargo side-stepped and Captain Jim plunged into the gully.

The patter of footsteps brought Fargo around in a crouch. He was a hair too slow. Vale and Shote Viktor piled onto him, one high, the other low. Fargo was bowled off his feet. He sent Vale tumbling with a boot to the midriff. Shote got hold of the Henry and tried to wrest it loose. A fist to the jaw buckled his knees, but he clung to the barrel.

Belatedly, Fargo realized they were not using weapons. They wanted him alive. That was their mistake. He let go of the Henry and drew his Colt. Or tried to. His head exploded in pain and blinding cartwheels of light. All the strength went out of his limbs and he fell to his knees, confused until he saw May Ling standing at arm's length with a melon-sized rock in her hands. A rock spattered with his blood.

"I am sorry," she said. "You should have listened."

Captain Jim reared, his knife in his hand. Grinning, he reached for Fargo's throat.

Then Fargo was in a bottomless well, falling, falling, falling.

21

A buzzing in Fargo's ears roused him from the depths of a black pit. At first he thought the buzzing was made by insects. Then pain spiked through him, kicked his senses to full life, and he became aware of the sun on his face and chest and arms. He was naked from the waist up. The buzzing became words.

"—good and tight. I don't want him getting loose. That would defeat the whole purpose," Tobias Cain rumbled.

"Why not shoot him and be done with it?" May Ling asked.

"Shooting would be too quick, too painless," Cain said. "You should know me well enough by now, my dear, to know that anyone who defies me must suffer before they die. My only regret is that I can not stay to see his finish." He paused. "I saw your eyelids flutter, Fargo. I know you have revived. Open your eyes, if you please."

It was pointless to continue shamming. Fargo opened them, and winced in new pain. The sun was high in the sky and he had inadvertently looked right at it. He went to move and couldn't. Twisting his neck revealed why. His wrists and ankles were tied to stakes firmly imbedded in the ground. Exactly how firmly became apparent when he strained against them.

"That will do you no good," Tobias Cain said. "But

feel free to fight your fate all you want. I have never believed in going meekly into the hereafter."

"Makes two of us," Fargo croaked, his half-parched throat and mouth not cooperating as they should. On his right squatted Cain. On his left stood May Ling. Waiting on horseback were seventeen or eighteen others, among them the Viktor brothers, Captain Jim, Krast, Merle Twern, and Kid Fontaine. Li Dazhong had been thrown on a horse with another man and was slumped over, his eyes closed.

Fargo licked his dry lips. "Is Li—" he began.

"Dead?" Cain finished. "No. But he is damn close to it, which is why I can't stay. He is too valuable to me. I must get him to Dr. Brine and have that next-to-worthless sawbones earn his keep." Cain rose.

Fargo looked at May Ling and she averted her gaze.

At that, Tobias Cain laughed. "You never expected her to betray you, did you? It never occurred to you that she might be stringing you along?" Cain held out a giant arm and May Ling came to him and embraced him warmly. They kissed. "Your mistake was in thinking everyone else thinks as you do."

Fargo did not reply. He couldn't quite believe she had duped him. Maybe she was being cosy with Cain again to keep him from killing her.

"You have a soft spot for women," the giant remarked. "It has proven to be your undoing."

"Are you fixing to talk me to death?" Fargo asked.

"Not at all. I never gloat over a fallen foe. But I would like you to look around. We are miles from where you were knocked out."

For as far as Fargo could see, the ground was littered with boulders and slabs of rock.

"Not very remarkable, is it?" Cain said. "Except in one respect." Stooping, he picked up a stone and threw it. The stone bounced off a boulder and clattered to the ground. At the noise, a buzzing sounded, a different sort of buzzing than Fargo had heard when he revived. "Know what that is?"

Fargo nodded.

"Many people think Death Valley is a lifeless wasteland," Tobias Cain said, "but they are mistaken. Some hardy forms of life not only live in the valley, they flourish. Rattlesnakes, for instance. They are all over the place. They do most of their hunting at night. But like snakes everywhere, they like to come out during the day and warm themselves." Cain grinned. "In some areas they are particularly thick. Nesting areas, I suppose." He gestured. "This happens to be one of them."

Fargo detected movement at the shadowed base of the boulder Cain had hit with the stone.

"A lot of rattlers were sunning themselves when we rode up, but they scattered and hid," Cain related. "As soon as we leave they will come out again. They can't help but notice you. It should be interesting, don't you think?"

"I aim to kill you before this is done," Fargo declared.

Tobias Cain snorted. "Admirable bluster, but that's all it is. You are a scout. You are familiar with what these snakes will do." He took May Ling by the hand and ushered her to her horse, then climbed on his own.

Fargo shut his eyes against the stabbing glare of the sun. His pulse had started to race, but he willed himself to stay calm. So long as he was alive, there was hope. He opened his eyes again.

"Any parting words or insults?" Tobias Cain asked.

"The law will get on your trail eventually."

"Perhaps," Cain conceded. "But by then I will have taken my leave of Death Valley and be living in luxury where they can never find me. I will remember to drink a toast in your memory." He raised his reins.

"Time I was going. I'll send someone to cover your remains. I'll give you that courtesy, at least."

Fargo glanced at May Ling, but she still would not look at him. Then Cain barked a command and the entire bunch trotted off to the south, raising a large cloud of dust in their wake.

Fargo watched the dust settle back to earth. Where his skin was exposed, he felt like he was burning up. But that was not his worst problem.

A soft sound bore home the fact Fargo was not alone. The rattlers were stirring. Sinuous forms slowly slithered from out of the shade. Only a few at first, then more and more. They were all around him, too many to count. Big rattlers, middling rattlers, little rattlers. Some were darker in color than others. Some had different markings. All had several things in common: forked tongues, curved fangs, and the rattles that gave them their name.

Fargo's skin crawled. He had never been so close to so many rattlesnakes at one time. Many were lying still and soaking up the sun. Others were more active, crawling every which way, seemingly unable to lie still if they wanted to. They were constantly crawling over one another. The hissing went on without cease. Occasionally a snake would rear and bare its fangs at another.

Fargo strained against the stakes, but they would not budge. He tried to twist his wrists, but the ropes were too tight. He was as helpless as a man could be.

Several rattlers drifted in his direction. They did not seem to be aware he was there, as yet.

Gritting his teeth, Fargo twisted harder. The rope dug into his flesh, but he closed his mind to the torment. He had one chance and one chance only. But whoever tied him had done a good job.

The scrape of scales caused Fargo to glance to his left. His blood chilled. A large rattler was within an arm's length. Suddenly it stopped and its blunt triangular head rose off the ground. Over and over its forked tongue flicked out. Its eyes, with their unsettling vertical slits, were fixed on him.

Fargo kept twisting his forearms. He told himself he must not stop no matter what the rattler did, but when the snake reared higher and its tail buzzed, he froze.

The rattler coiled.

The serpent was not close enough for Fargo to try the desperate gambit he had used on the mountain. Not that he would if he could. This snake was five times as big, five times as thick. Even if he could bite deep enough to inflict a mortal wound, he might not be able to hold on to it. It would strike back, biting him, and that would be that.

The snake reared higher still.

Fargo braced for the inevitable, for the searing pain of its fangs and the burning of venom in his veins. He would not die right away. Some men lasted minutes.

He felt no fear. Only fury. Fury at the man who had done this to him. Fury that he could not avenge his death.

The notion that Tobias Cain would get away with murdering him ate at him like acid.

Then the rattler sank down, its tail quieted, and the big snake lay still.

Just in time, Fargo stopped himself from exhaling in relief. Any movement might provoke the snake into coiling again. He watched it, hoping it would crawl off. A few seconds more and the snake did start to crawl, not away from him but toward him.

Fargo had to lie motionless and helpless as the big rattler crawled up onto his chest, and stopped.

Fargo went rigid. The feel of the thing's scales, the proximity of its hideous head and those chilling eyes, frayed his nerves to ribbons. It took every ounce of

175

willpower he possessed not to cry out or buck his body. He waited for the snake to crawl off, but it showed no inclination to go anywhere.

Shouting at snakes often drove them away, but Fargo was not about to try it with the rattler lying there on top of him. He told himself that surely the rattler was not going to do what he thought it was going to do. But it did. It stretched out to sun itself.

Fargo closed his eyes. Part of his mind insisted this could not be happening. He had the silly idea that if he pinched himself, he would wake up. But the next sensation he felt was not a pinch.

Another rattler was crawling onto his legs.

Fargo opened his eyes but he could not see the second snake. It was down near his ankles, and he dared not lift his head to peer over the big rattler on his chest. He swallowed, or tried to. His mouth was completely dry.

Fargo thought his plight could not get any worse. He was wrong. A couple of minutes dragged by, and suddenly he nearly gave a start. Something had brushed his neck, ever so lightly. It happened again, and yet a third time. He wondered if it was a rattler's tongue, and had his hunch confirmed when a rattlesnake crawled up across his throat, and stopped.

The snakes liked the warmth his body gave off. To them, it was the same as the heat given off by a flat rock.

Fargo held himself still. He breathed shallow so his chest would not rise and fall too drastically. He supposed he should be grateful. The rattlers had not bitten him. So far.

The sun inched across the sky with the most terrible slowness imaginable.

Sweat oozed from Fargo's every pore. He grew hotter than he had ever been, so hot he was half convinced he was on fire, so hot he would swear his brain was being boiled. His lungs were aflame. He had bouts of light-headedness, periods of nausea.

It did not help Fargo's state of mind that all around him rattlers slithered and hissed and rattled. He lost count of the number of times a serpent brushed against him. Once, a rattler crawled up under his right arm and coiled there, resting. At the contact, goose bumps spread all over him.

The snake under his arm was the first to crawl away. By then, judging by the sun, it was past three, and so hot even some of the rattlers were seeking shade. They would lie up until nightfall and then prowl for prey.

What with Fargo's senses swimming in and out, he did not notice the distant drumming at first. He was jarred from his daze by the vibration of the ground.

Horses were approaching. Horses meant riders. Riders might mean Tobias Cain had sent some men to make sure Fargo was dead, and if not, to carry out what the rattlesnakes had failed to do.

Nearly all the snakes were moving now. They sensed the horses. Most scurried to seek cover. The rattler on Fargo's legs crawled off. The rattler on his neck was next. That left the big rattler on his chest, which was content to stay where it was.

The hoofbeats rose to thunder, and stopped. A horse nickered. Saddle leather creaked and spurs jingled.

"You've been lying out here this whole time with just that one measly snake? Dang. If I had known that, I wouldn't have worried near as much."

Kid Fontaine's pockmarked face floated into view, his derby pushed back on his head.

"I hope you appreciate I've ridden like hell to get here. I figured I would find you dead."

"The snake," Fargo whispered. He did not want to talk too loudly or it might stir up the big rattler, which, oddly enough, had not moved.

The Kid cocked an ear. "What was that? I can't hear you when you mumble."

Fargo shifted his eyes toward his chest, not once but several times.

"Are you having a fit?" Kid Fontaine asked. "Am I too late and you were already bit?"

"Get it off," Fargo whispered.

"Oh. Sure." Kid Fontaine drew back a foot, and kicked. His toe caught the rattler in the side but not squarely enough.

Instead of sailing off Fargo's chest, the snake rolled across Fargo's stomach and came to rest on his groin.

"Damn. I didn't mean for that to happen," the Kid remarked.

The rattler coiled and reared.

Fargo felt himself shrivel.

"Don't move." Kid Fontaine stepped back, his hands dropping to his black-handled Remingtons.

"Don't!" Fargo squeaked. He envisioned the Kid missing, and shriveled even more.

"Why the hell not? Make up your mind. First you want it off, and then you don't. I don't mind telling you, you can be downright peculiar." The Kid's hands flashed but only his right Remington boomed, and at the blast, the rattlersnake's head exploded in a spray of gore. One of its eyes splatted onto Fargo's chest and lay staring up at him.

The Kid blew smoke from the Remington's barrel, and chuckled. "That was slick if I say so my own self."

Fargo had to cough before his vocal cords would work. "I don't suppose you could stop patting yourself on the back long enough to cut me loose?"

"I didn't hear any thanks come out of your mouth." The Kid began to replace the spent cartridge, taking his leisurely time. "Until I do, my ears aren't working."

Fargo wished that he could stand up—and that he had a club.

22

Kid Fontaine had a lot in common with a chipmunk. Not only did he have the face of a chipmunk and the teeth of a chipmunk; he did not know when to stop chattering. Hooking his thumbs in his gun belt, he puffed out his chest and declared, "Yes, sir. I am as good as my word. I told you I wouldn't forget the good turn you did me. You saved my hide. Now I've saved yours."

Fargo was stretching and bending to restore circulation. His wrists and ankles hurt abominably. No more so than his head. "And you are willing to swear Cain doesn't know you slipped away?"

The Kid nodded. "Mr. Cain sent Merle and me and four others to Whiskey Mill to look for Hank and Cavendish. But I had loosened one of the shoes on my horse so it was about ready to fall off. When it took to limping, I climbed down and ran my hands up and down its leg. I told them I was worried it was going lame, and for them to go on without me and I would get another horse and catch up when I could." The Kid grinned at his cleverness. "I went to the stable, put the shoe back on, got your pinto and water skins, and here I am."

"Did you bring my revolver and rifle?" Fargo gingerly pulled his right sleeve over his wrist where the skin had scraped off.

"Sorry. Captain Jim laid claim to your Colt, and I

wasn't about to try and steal it back. Not from that Modoc, I wasn't. He's meaner than a rabid dog and will kill anyone as soon as spit on them."

"My Henry?"

"Shote Viktor thinks it's the prettiest thing this side of a naked woman. I reckon it's how all that brass shines in the sun. He asked Mr. Cain if he could have it." The Kid walked to his sorrel and opened a saddlebag. "I did bring you these, though."

Into Fargo's hands were placed a pair of Reynolds nickel-plated revolvers, along with ammunition.

"I stole them from the cook," Kid Fontaine boasted. "He keeps them in a trunk at the foot of his bed and hardly ever takes them out, so it should be days before he notices they are missing."

Fargo was grateful but he had never fired a Reynolds. Never handled one, for that matter. While it was similar to the Colt 1860 Army, it was not identical. It had a different heft, a different balance. He twirled them a few times to test the feel.

"So which way are we heading?" Kid Fontaine asked.

Fargo gazed across Death Valley. He had been unconscious when they brought him there, and needed to get his bearings. "The Oasis is to the southwest, I take it?" He deduced that from the fact he was closer to the mountain range that bordered Death Valley to the east than the range to the west.

"About four miles," the Kid confirmed.

"Then that's the direction I'm heading." Fargo hunkered and commenced loading the revolvers.

"Are you loco? Mr. Cain wants you dead. His curly wolves will put holes in you on sight."

"You don't need to come with me." Fargo had noticed tendrils of dust to the southwest, too far off to have been raised by the Ovaro and the sorrel.

"That's good, because I sure as hell ain't!" the Kid

exclaimed. "It would be the same as slitting my wrists. Why in hell do you want to stick your head back in the bear's mouth when you are free to light a shuck?"

"The Chinese," Fargo said.

Kid Fontaine scratched his pimply chin. "What do they have to do with anything? Don't tell me you're going back for their sake? What are they to you? May Ling, I can maybe savvy. But the rest?"

The mention prompted Fargo to ask, "What about May Ling? Is she still alive?"

"As far as I know. Mr. Cain took her into the mansion. For a while there was some yelling and screaming but it quieted down." The Kid folded his arms. "Why? Have you taken a shine to her?"

"She is in trouble. She needs help." The tendrils of dust, Fargo observed, were nearer.

"You *do* know she was the one who conked you on the noggin?" the Kid asked. "On account of her, you just spent most of the day cuddling with rattle-snakes. Seems to me you should want to stick one down her dress, not save her."

"I have another reason."

"Make it a good one. I'm startin' to suspect you spent too much time under the sun."

"Tobias Cain," Fargo said.

"What about him? Other than he has a small army, which you don't seem to reckon is worth a shucks or you wouldn't be so all-fired eager to get yourself killed."

"He has to be stopped."

Kid Fontaine laughed. "And you have picked yourself to do the job. Damned decent of you. But we both know that's just part of it. Tell me the rest. Tell me the whole truth."

Fargo stopped loading. "No one does what he did to me." Some might call him childish, but there it was.

"That's more like it, friend," the Kid said. "Hate, I

can savvy. Revenge, I can savvy. But that other stuff is for Bible-thumpers and those who walk around with their noses in the air."

"I understand why you don't want to lend a hand," Fargo said.

"I'm good but I'm not *that* good. Neither are you. We would be outnumbered ten to one."

"Twenty to one." Fargo wedged the pair of Reynolds revolvers under his belt and held out his hand. "Fan the breeze. If we ever see each other again, the first drinks are on me."

The Kid looked at the hand as if it were a rattler about to strike. "I thought we were pards."

When it was obvious the Kid was not going to shake, Fargo shrugged and stepped to the Ovaro. He did not climb on. Taking the reins, he made for a cluster of boulders, some of which were larger than the pinto.

"Hold on," Kid Fontaine bleated. "Where are you off to?"

"Whoever followed you will be here soon," Fargo said. "We should be well hid before then."

"Whoever followed—" the Kid repeated, and spun. A string of oaths escaped him. "It can't be! No one saw me leave!" He hitched at his gun belt as if eager for a fight, then grabbed the reins to his mount and hurried to catch up. "How can you be sure it's just one hombre?"

"If there was more than one, there would be more dust."

"You believe me, don't you, about me sneaking off?" the Kid asked. "It's not a trick of any kind."

"I believe you," Fargo assured him. "It would be just like Cain to want to be sure. He's not the kind to take anything for granted. And he did promise to send someone to bury me."

"Leave whoever it is to me. I'm itching to plant

someone." Kid Fontaine grinned. "I can whip any of Cain's lunkheads without half trying."

"Does that include Captain Jim?"

The Kid's bluster evaporated like water would in that blistering heat. "What makes you think it's him?"

"That's who I would send." Fargo was alert for rattlers, but the commotion had driven them into hiding. Other than buzzing from under a few boulders, the reptiles stayed out of sight.

The dust grew closer. It was as if the wind were raising a dust devil, only there was no wind, and instead of swirling, as dust devils do, the dust rose straight into the sky.

In the heart of the dust a stick figure appeared. Soon Fargo could tell that the stick figure was a horse and rider. After a while, the rider was near enough for them to see the faded army coat.

"You were right," Kid Fontaine whispered. He did not sound happy about it.

Fargo sought to put the Kid at ease. "Cain has done us a favor."

"You wouldn't say that if you've seen some of the things I've seen that Modoc do. Sometimes I think he's not quite human." Kid Fontaine indulged in his habit of nipping his lower lip with his buckteeth, then went on. "He can go without food and water for more days than anyone else, and still live. The heat never bothers him. He soaks it in like a sponge. He's almost as good a tracker as Shote and Vale. But the thing he's best at, the thing he likes the most, is killing. He does it for the pleasure. I've seen him snatch flies out of the air, pull their wings off, then drop them and crush them under his moccasin while grinning like a cat."

"He's a man, nothing more."

"A spooky man," the Kid said. "A deadly man. Deadlier than me by a long shot, I am not ashamed to admit."

"Why was he cast out of his tribe?" Fargo asked.

"What makes you think he was?"

"The Modocs keep to themselves," Fargo said. "They don't like whites that much." One day in the future, he suspected, the tribe would rise up against the invaders.

"Captain Jim keeps to himself, too," the Kid said. "The only one he hardly ever talks to is Tobias Cain. He thinks Cain is some kind of god."

Fargo took his eyes from the approaching warrior. "How's that again?"

"Something to do with Modoc beliefs about the old days," Kid Fontaine responded. "I heard Cain and Captain Jim talking once. The Modocs think that way back when the world was young, giants roamed this neck of the woods. The Modocs were afraid of them, and they are usually not afraid of anybody. So to Captain Jim, that makes Cain special somehow. Maybe not a god, exactly, but close to it."

"When Captain Jim gets here, let me handle him," Fargo suggested.

The Kid snickered. "I reckon if you twist my arm, I might let you." Fontaine looked at him. "Aren't you the least bit scared of him?"

"He can die just like anyone else," Fargo said, and put his hands on the Reynolds revolvers.

"So can you," the Kid reminded him.

After that, they were quiet.

The Modoc and his bay were only fifty yards out. He had not shucked his rifle from its scabbard or drawn Fargo's Colt. He rode with the wary ease of a man supremely confident in his own ability. His dark eyes flicked everywhere, seeing everything, missing nothing.

"Why do I feel like a rabbit all of a sudden?" Kid Fontaine whispered.

Captain Jim came to the exact spot where the Kid had reined up—and drew rein. He did not dismount but hooked his leg around the saddle horn and stared at the stakes and the ropes. No surprise registered. Rather, a slow smile curled his lips. He gazed at the cluster of boulders and said, "You can come out, white man."

Fargo stepped from behind the large boulder.

Captain Jim was as calm as if they were long lost friends. "The pup freed you, I see. Can he hear me?"

"He can hear you," Fargo said.

"Stay out of this, boy. I will take you back to the giant one. He can decide what to do with you."

"You're getting a little ahead of yourself, aren't you?" Fargo asked while sidling to the left. "I might not be that easy."

"You are better than most," Captain Jim said.

Fargo was surprised by the compliment. "You should not have knifed Lu Wei," he remarked.

"What was she to you?"

"She was defenseless." Fargo would never forget the look on her face as her life faded.

Captain Jim shrugged. "The giant one wanted it done."

"And you lick his boots for him."

Captain Jim did a strange thing; he smiled. "You can not make me mad. I will not lose my head."

"Why did you come in this close? You knew the Kid was here. You knew I would be free."

"I do not like to kill from far away," Captain Jim replied. "I like to see their eyes. I like to see their fear."

"One last question, then," Fargo said. "Is May Ling still alive?"

The Modoc answered the question with a question of his own. "Do you know her or is it money?"

"Her father hired me."

"She was alive when I left. But she might not be

for long. The giant one intends for her to suffer. He likes to see their fear, too."

Fargo was watching the Modoc's hands. When it happened, they would be his only warning, if any.

Then Kid Fontaine came from behind the boulder. He was smiling that cocky smile of his. "Remember me?"

Fargo quickly whispered, "Stay out of this."

"What kind of pard would I be if I did?" the Kid said, making no attempt to lower his voice.

The Modoc shifted in his saddle. "I am not here for you, boy. Leave now and you will live."

"But not for long," Kid Fontaine replied. "Only until Cain gets those big hands of his on me."

Captain Jim glanced at Fargo. "Talk to him. He is your friend."

"He's a grown man. He can do as he pleases."

The renegade did not like it. Whatever slight edge he felt he had was no longer a factor. Not with two against one. His brow furrowed. He was debating, adjusting, accepting.

The Kid moved slowly to the right, saying, "I've always wanted to kill me an Injun. Maybe I'll scalp you and show off your hair at every saloon I visit."

"You are both going to die," Captain Jim said, and made his move.

23

When Fargo first came West after the deaths of his parents, he came to St. Louis. It was the stepping-off point for those bound for the untamed frontier beyond the mighty Mississippi River. He was young. The bustling city, with its riotous mix of humanity, fascinated him. He stayed ten days. He earned money sweeping a store. Nights he spent at a saloon called the *Gristle Pit*. The strange name drew him in. He stayed for the whiskey, and the women.

Fargo had never touched a drop of liquor before his parents were murdered, but he soon developed a lasting fondness for coffin varnish, as some called it. Whiskey warmed his gut and tempered his mood. He also developed a lasting fondness for the doves who served it.

It was on a Friday night that Fargo learned one of the most important lessons of his life. He had sat in on a poker game, another habit he was to become quite fond of. Four other players were at the table, among them a tall, handsome gambler called Mississippi Dan. Also in the game was a river rat named Haskell. A third player, the one to Fargo's right, was an old man with skin like leather but the friendliest disposition that side of a missionary. His name was Charlie.

The game had been under way for about an hour. Fargo played cautiously, not wanting to lose much money. The others were patient with him, since he had remarked it was his first time. All except Haskell, who kept complaining that Fargo was taking too long to make up his mind when he had to decide how many cards to lay down.

Mississippi Dan, dressed completely in black except for a white shirt, had been as friendly as Charlie, at first. But then he grew quiet, and Fargo wondered if maybe he was to blame. He wasn't. He soon noticed that Mississippi Dan was watching Haskell with the penetrating eyes of an eagle, yet doing so in such a way that Haskell did not catch on.

It was Fargo's first game but he wasn't stupid. He knew Mississippi Dan must suspect Haskell of being up to no good. The very next hand, the pot rose to near five hundred dollars. Fargo had to bow out. So did Charlie and the other player. That left the gambler and the river rat.

Mississippi Dan raised. Haskell called. Haskell was leaning forward with his elbows on the table. He wore a smirk as he said, "Let's see what you have, fancy pants."

The gambler had a full house.

Crowing gleefully, Haskell laid down four jacks. "I beat you!" he whooped, and went to rake in the pot.

Mississippi Dan's hand rose, palm out. "Ordinarily, I do not mind losing," he said suavely. "That is, when the play is honest."

"Are you accusing me of cheating?" Haskell angrily demanded.

"Lift your right sleeve, if you please," Mississippi Dan said politely. "I would like to see what you have up there."

"See this!" Haskell snarled, and in the blink of an

eye he had a dirk in his hand and was lunging across the table. He was fast, amazingly fast, and by rights the gambler should have died.

But then Fargo witnessed the incredible. Mississippi Dan hardly seemed to move, except for his right arm. A derringer materialized in his fingers as if out of thin air. At the *crack*, a hole appeared in the middle of Haskell's forehead and he collapsed on top of the pot. Casually, almost delicately, Mississippi Dan reached across and hiked the river rat's sleeve, exposing, for all to see, the rig the river rat had used to cheat.

Later, sharing drinks at the bar with old Charlie, Fargo had remarked how he thought the gambler was a dead man when the river rat sprang at him. "Haskell was fast as could be."

Charlie had tittered and arched a gray eyebrow. "Fast is good, quick is better."

"There's a difference?" Fargo had asked.

"There sure as hell is, boy. Fast is a spooked antelope. Fast is a bobcat when it pounces on a rabbit. Fast is a horse that wins race after race. But quick is a cottonmouth when it strikes. Quick is a bee in flight. Quick is lightning. And quick will beat fast every time. If you have to be one or the other, be quick."

"It's up to me?"

"Who else?" Charlie had rejoined.

"But how does someone go about being quick?" Fargo had wanted to know.

"They practice at it. They practice until they are slicker than axle grease. Until their reflexes are as sharp as a razor."

Fargo never forgot the old man's words. He applied them. He became quick himself. He met others who were quick, too, but none, ever, as quick as the man called Captain Jim.

*   *   *

The Modoc's right arm flashed even as his powerful form hurled itself at the ground.

Kid Fontaine went for his Remingtons, his hands twin streaks. But he had barely gripped them when he cried out. Staggering, he gaped at the steel sliver imbedded to the hilt in his left shoulder. The next instant his legs buckled.

Simultaneous with the Modoc's throw, Fargo drew. He had the Reynolds revolvers out in less than the blink of an eye, thumbing back the hammers as he cleared his belt. He instinctively pointed the muzzles at Captain Jim, and fired. But Captain Jim had left the saddle. At a range of less than twenty feet, Fargo did something he had not done in so long, he could not remember the last time he did it; he missed.

Fargo pivoted as the Modoc hit the ground, curling his thumbs. He fired again. His slugs kicked up dirt where Captain Jim had been.

Scuttling with astonishing speed, the warrior reached a waist-high boulder and darted behind it.

Backpedaling, Fargo squeezed off two shots to keep the Modoc pinned down while he gained the shelter of the large boulder. He succeeded.

Captain Jim did the last thing Fargo expected. He laughed. "Now we see who is best, eh?"

Fargo risked a peek. Kid Fontaine was on his side, motionless. Fargo could not see the knife. The Kid's back was to him. "Damn," he said softly. He had liked the boy. Given a few more years, the Kid might have turned out all right. Fargo glanced past the sprawled form at the boulder the Modoc had ducked behind. Captain Jim did not show himself.

Again instinct took a hand. Fargo crouched, went around the horses, and angled past several other boulders until he came to one no larger than a chair. Kneeling behind it, he removed his hat and rose just high enough to peer over. The way he had it figured, Captain Jim would work around to a vantage point near the big boulder in the belief he was still behind it, too. But the warrior was in for an unwelcome surprise.

The sun burned mercilessly down as the seconds became minutes and the minutes became a quarter of an hour.

Fargo didn't move. Beads of sweat trickled down his forehead and into his eyes, stinging terribly, but he did not blink. The slightest twitch would give him away. The Modoc's senses were as keen as his own, if not keener.

Fargo was so intent on spotting Captain Jim that he did not see the scorpion until it was a few inches from his arm. The slight *scritching* sound the scorpion made as it climbed the boulder alerted him. He looked down, and the sweat caking his body went from hot to cold. He was surprised on two counts. First, scorpions usually came out at night. Second, it wasn't just any scorpion, but one of the giant desert variety. About six inches long, the thing had yellow pincers, legs, and tail, but the body was black. Its tail was curled high above the body, the stinger segment about the size of Fargo's thumbnail. The stinger curved outward for deeper penetration.

Fargo had barely enough time to move his arm, but if he moved, Captain Jim might spot him. He remained perfectly still. The giant scorpion came to his arm and crawled up on it.

Suddenly the scorpion stopped. Its pinchers opened and closed and its tail unfurled. Fargo tensed, thinking it was about to strike. He did not know if his sleeve was thick enough to protect him.

The scorpion lowered its tail. It started to crawl off Fargo's arm, then abruptly changed directions and started *up* his arm toward his neck and face.

Fargo scoured the boulders but did not spot Captain

Jim. He went to shake his arm and fling the scorpion off, when, without warning, the scorpion scuttled twice as swiftly along his biceps to his shoulder, and poised there.

The poison of a giant desert scorpion was rarely fatal. It did leave victims swollen and sick. It was also swift-acting, especially when the stinger struck the neck or face.

Again Fargo started to shift so he could swat it off. But the scorpion moved yet again, crawling up close to his neck, so close that he could only see part of it. Something brushed his skin. The tip of a pincer, he imagined.

Fargo stayed calm. After having rattlers crawl all over him, he was not as alarmed about the scorpion as he might have been. But he was by the sound of a revolver being cocked.

"I would tell you not to move but there is no need."

Fargo had been careless. He had been so preoccupied with the scorpion, he had let the Modoc slip up on him.

"Drop the revolvers," Captain Jim said.

Fargo did so. They clattered noisily.

"Stand."

Dreading what the scorpion might do, Fargo slowly straightened. He had been right to dread. The giant desert scorpion ran in a circle on his shoulder, its pincers waving. When he stopped moving, so did the scorpion.

"You made it too easy," Captain Jim remarked. "Raise your hands and turn around."

Keeping his upper arms rigid, Fargo raised his hands as high as his shoulders. He turned as slow as molasses. Death stared him in the face, death in the guise of the mildly amused Modoc.

"Snakes and a scorpion," Captain Jim said. "As whites would say, you are not having a good day."

"I've had better," Fargo conceded. He was puzzled as to why the warrior had not shot him already, and said so.

"I told you. I like to see the eyes," Captain Jim said. "I want to see yours when you die." He raised the Colt and took deliberate aim.

Fargo was desperate. In another few moments the Colt would spit lead and smoke. He could try to rush the Modoc even though he would not live to reach him, and as soon as he moved, the scorpion might use its stinger. *The scorpion.* Grasping at a straw, Fargo asked, "What if I beg for my life? Would that do any good?" He tried to sound suitably scared.

The Modoc's usually expressionless face quirked in perplexity. "A man like you? Beg?"

"If you'll let me."

A sadistic smile hinted at the answer. "Maybe I will," Captain Jim said. "Maybe, if you cry and moan."

"Thank you!" Fargo said while inwardly girding himself for what he had to do. He clasped his hands and started to sink to his knees, one eye always on the scorpion. "A few minutes more is all I ask. Just a few more minutes." As he begged, his right hand flew to his shoulder. At that instant, being quick counted for everything. Being quick enabled him to pinch the scorpion's tail just below the stinger before the scorpion could strike. Being quick enabled him to fling the scorpion at Captain Jim's swarthy face before Captain Jim could squeeze the trigger.

As he threw the scorpion, Fargo dived. The Colt went off but the slug *spanged* off the boulder instead of ripping through his body.

But being quick did not keep Fargo from making a mistake. Flat on his stomach, he rolled toward the revolvers he had dropped. But he did not reach them. He slowed, riveted by what he had caused. Because luck had been with him. The scorpion had not only struck Captain Jim's face, it was clinging to him with its pincers and segmented legs and stabbing with its stinger, again and again and again.

For all of five seconds Captain Jim was too stunned to react. Then he dropped the Colt, swooped both hands to his face, and tore the scorpion from him. Casting it to the ground, he brought his right heel smashing down.

Fargo rose on an elbow and reached out for a revolver. A blow to his ribs knocked the breath out of him. He was flipped onto his back. A knee rammed into the pit of his stomach. Iron fingers clamped onto his throat.

"Now you die!" Captain Jim hissed. He held a gleaming knife, identical to the knife sticking in Kid Fontaine. He drove the blade at Fargo's chest, but Fargo seized the Modoc's wrist and held the knife at bay.

Locked together, they struggled. Captain Jim could not bury the knife. Fargo could not throw him off. For a few seconds they stopped thrashing and glared, eye to eye. Fargo saw that the Modoc's cheeks and one eyebrow were starting to swell. A dozen tiny prick marks were bleeding. One cheek was torn open where a pincer had sliced deep.

"You will die slow for this," Captain Jim hissed.

Fargo arced his knee at the Modoc's groin, but the warrior twisted and deflected the knee with his thigh. Before Fargo could straighten, Captain Jim's own knee connected where it hurt any man the most. It hurt Fargo. Agony exploded through him, and it was all he could do to hold on to the Modoc's knife arm. His vision swam, and he lost his grip. A sharp jab in the neck turned him to stone.

Captain Jim rose on one knee, the tip of his knife pressed to Fargo's jugular. His facial muscles were twitching spasmodically. "I have never wanted to kill any man as much as I want to kill you."

"I know the feeling," said a youthful voice.

Captain Jim glanced up. Shock slowed him. He went to rise but a revolver banged and he was smashed back by a slug that cored his sternum and ruptured out his spine. Again the revolver banged, and a third time, and what was left of the Modoc's forehead when he slumped to the ground would not fill a coffee cup.

Kid Fontaine shuffled over, his left shoulder hunched, a hand over the wound. In his other hand was a smoking Remington. He was grinning. "Damn, that felt good," he said.

Fargo slowly sat up. "That makes twice you've saved me."

"Now you owe me," the Kid said, and collapsed.

24

The mantle of night lay over the Panamint Mountains.

Lights glowed in Whiskey Mill. The saloon door was propped open to admit the cool air, and from inside came the tinkle of poker chips, the clink of glasses and bottles, and the murmur of conversation.

Fargo circled and approached from the north. He drew rein at the water trough and moved on foot to the rear of the saloon and along it until he came to the back of the frame house. The door was not locked. Palming his Colt, he cautiously entered and moved through the kitchen and down the hall to the parlor. Lamps glowed in several rooms, but there was no trace of Tilly.

Opening the front door, Fargo peered out. Five horses were at the hitch rail in front of the saloon. Light rimmed the doors of the eight shacks, and from within two of them came the sounds of human lust. He slipped out and turned right. At the corner of the saloon he slowed and edged to the window.

Pardee was behind the bar, wiping glasses. Merle Twern and two hard cases were playing poker at a table in the middle of the room. Tilly was at the far end of the bar, nursing a drink and looking bored.

Fargo holstered the Colt, squared his shoulders, and strolled on in. The result was almost comical.

Pardee saw him first. Pardee's head snapped up and

he fumbled with a glass and nearly dropped it. Tilly froze with her drink halfway to her luscious mouth. Merle Twern's face was contorted in an astounded O. The other two hired guns did not try to hide their own surprise.

Making for the bar, Fargo smiled at Pardee. "A bottle of red-eye. The best you have."

"C-c-coming r-r-right up," Pardee stuttered. He ranged along the shelf, selected a bottle, and gingerly brought it over and set it on the bar as if afraid it would be shot out of his hand.

Fargo opened it and chugged. After the ordeal he had been through earlier, the whiskey was a tonic for his tired body. He downed a third of the whiskey, gave a contented sigh, and wiped his mouth with the back of his hand. Then he turned so his back was to the bar, rested his elbows on the edge, and asked, "Mind if I sit in?"

Merle Twern's mouth was still agape. Snapping it shut, he nodded, then said in more of a squeak than his normal tone, "Pull out a chair."

Fargo moved around the table and chose a chair where he could watch Pardee and the front door. Pardee gaped. Tilly had lowered her drink and appeared tremendously confused.

Setting the bottle on the table with a loud *thunk*, Fargo folded his arms and regarded Twern and the other two. They were as confused as Tilly and not sure what to say or do. "Five card stud?"

Merle Twern nodded. He gathered in the cards and clumsily shuffled. He had to try twice to speak. "I'm sort of surprised to see you here."

"Why is that?" Fargo asked, lowering his left arm to the table and his right arm to his lap.

"It's just that, well, the last time I saw you, you were staked out half naked and left to die."

"Oh, that," Fargo said. "I didn't."

"Didn't what?" Merle Twern asked, his confusion dulling his wits.

"I didn't die." Fargo used his left and chugged more whiskey. It would take a lot of time to blunt the memory of the rattlesnakes and the scorpion so he could make it through the night without waking up in a cold sweat.

A man with the face of a goat and dirty fingernails laughed nervously. "Hell, we can see that for our own selves. What happened? Did Mr. Cain change his mind about killing you?"

"Tobias Cain can go to hell," Fargo said. "As soon as I'm done here, I aim to send him there to join the Modoc."

"Captain Jim?" Merle Twern said. "What about him?"

"The rattlesnakes will be crawling in his blood tonight."

Merle Twern and the other two were speechless with astonishment. Finally Twern resumed shuffling. Cards slipped between his fingers and he awkwardly gathered them up. "Captain Jim is dead?"

"That's what I just said." Fargo leaned back. Pardee was glancing at the front door and the window as if he expected someone else to walk in. Tilly had set down her glass and was sidling along the bar, acting uncertain whether to come over.

"I never reckoned anyone could kill that redskin," the man with the goat face said. "Not with how he used those knives of his."

The last cardplayer, a short man with fuzzy blond stubble on his chin, nodded. "That there was the deadliest Injun ever born. How did you do in that devil? Back-shoot him?"

"I sicced a scorpion on him," Fargo said, and tilted the bottle. But he only took a swallow. He had to keep his wits and senses sharp for what was to come.

"A scorpion?" the short man repeated, and scratched his fuzzy stubble. "What in hell are you talking about?"

"A desert scorpion. About as long as my hands. I wouldn't recommend one for a pet, though."

"The sun has baked this jasper's brains," the short man said to Merle Twern and the other.

"No," Merle Twern said, his brow puckered. He was shrewder than they, and possibly beginning to suspect.

The man with the goat face was perplexed about something else. "How did you get here, mister? How did you get loose, I mean?"

"You should be more concerned about something else," Fargo said.

Merle Twern began to deal the cards. He did so slowly, methodically, pausing between each card. When he had dealt five to each of them, he picked his hand up but did not look at it. "What did you mean by after you are done here?"

"After I burn Whiskey Mill to the ground." Fargo picked up his cards with his left hand.

Tilly was still sidling along the bar. A few more steps and she would be between Fargo and Pardee.

Pardee was knotting and unknotting his fists.

"You plan to burn down the saloon?" the goat-faced man asked.

"The whole place," Fargo said. "I need a lot of smoke. Enough to be seen from the Oasis."

"Why are you telling us this?" quizzed the man with the fuzzy chin.

"So you can make up your minds whether it's worth it," Fargo said.

"What is worth what?"

"Whether this place is worth dying for. Whether Tobias Cain is worth dying for. You might want to go on living."

"So that's it," Merle Twern said.

"Ride out while you can."

Twern placed his cards on the table. "You have sand. I'll grant you that. But you are the one who should ride out."

The goat-faced man was looking from one to the other. "I don't savvy any of this."

"The important thing," Fargo said, "is that you have a decision to make. Do you go or do you die?"

"You are that sure of yourself?" Merle Twern marveled. "There are seven of us and only one of you." He added offhandedly, "Tilly and the Chinese girls don't count."

Fargo noted the number. Seven. Not the five Tobias Cain had sent to find Hank and Cavendish. Not six, if you counted Pardee. But seven. "I have it to do."

Tilly had stopped and was listening. She was in front of Pardee, blocking Fargo's view. But Fargo's ears worked just fine, and his hearing, honed by years of life in the wild, was better than most. The scrape of an object being slid from under the bar and the twin clicks were as plain as Tilly's startled bleat when he heaved to his feet and pointed his Colt at her. "Get down!"

Tilly dropped.

Pardee had a scattergun almost level. He was alight with devious glee. He thought he was being clever.

Fargo shot him through the head.

Staggering back, Pardee crashed against the shelves. Bottles toppled and smashed to bits on the floor. The scattergun went off into the plank that served as a bar.

Merle Twern thought he saw his chance. He shoved his chair back and rose, his hands slapping his revolver with considerable speed. The other two followed his lead.

Fargo kicked the table, upending it at the man with

201

the goat face and the short one with the fuzzy chin. At the same instant, he triggered two quick shots into Merle Twern's chest. A swift bound carried him clear of the chairs just as the other two untangled themselves and pointed pistols at the spot where he had just been. The Colt's next slug caught fuzzy-chin in the ear. The last shot made a scarlet mess of goat-face's mouth.

Gurgling and flopping about, goat-face was a while dying.

Fargo bent over Merle Twern and probed a wrist for a pulse. There was none. He immediately began reloading. "You can get up now. It's over." Or it almost was. He had two to deal with yet. He finished reloading and turned toward the bar, and shriveled inside.

Tilly was on her side, eyes wide in shock, her arms and legs twitching. A wet crimson sheen spread from under her.

"No!" Fargo ran to her and hunkered. A jagged hole in the plank accounted for her condition. The buckshot had blown through the wood as if it were tissue paper and caught Tilly full in the back.

"Tilly?" Fargo clasped her hand. He started to roll her over to see how bad it was, then stopped. The glimpse had been enough.

Tilly blinked, and swallowed. "I'm a goner, aren't I?"

Fargo's eyes said what he could not.

"Don't blame yourself," Tilly said gently. "It was a fluke. Pardee would never have shot me on purpose."

"Is there anything I can get you?" Fargo's tongue felt thick and stiff. "Water? Whiskey? Anything?"

"Just don't leave me," Tilly said. She was not twitching as much, but she was as white as paper and growing whiter.

"I'm sorry."

"Cut that out. How were you to know? Crystal balls are make-believe." Tilly clutched his hand tighter. "I was so sad. They told me you were dead."

Fargo could not reply for the tightness in his throat. He liked her, liked her a lot. Women who accepted themselves and others for what they were and enjoyed snuggling under the sheets as much as he did were the sort of women who appealed to him the most.

Incredibly, Tilly managed a weak grin. "And here I was, thinking I'd never get shed of this place." A lone tear formed at the corner of her left eye and trickled down over her nose and cheek. "Someone up there doesn't like me."

"You shouldn't talk."

"Why not? To save my strength? I don't have any." Tilly smiled at him. "Talking is all I can do. Which is too bad. I was looking forward to you and me spending a week or two together. The nights would be—" Her green eyes widened. "Look out!"

Fargo whirled.

It was Wen Po. Fury contorted her wrinkled face. In her bony right hand was a knife with a double-edged blade in the shape of an S. The long handle was etched ivory. Uttering a piercing shriek, she threw herself at him, stabbing viciously.

Fargo got a forearm up and blocked the blow. But he was off-balance, his weight on the balls of his feet. Although she was smaller and lighter, he was knocked against the bar. He attempted to draw the Colt.

Another screech, and Wen Po was on him. For someone so old and frail-seeming, she possessed remarkable agility.

The blade lanced at Fargo's neck. He jerked aside and the steel thunked against a barrel. Wen Po whipped back the knife to try again. Fargo had no hope of grabbing her arm, so he did the only thing he could. He kicked her, hard. For most, that would have been enough to send them tottering. All Wen Po did was howl like a she-wolf and come at him anew.

Fargo kicked her again, with both boots this time, full in the stomach. She flew back against a table, braced her hand on it, and launched herself at him a third time, a frenzied female whirlwind who would not be denied.

Fargo was making it hard for himself. He had no desire to kill her. He would rather disarm her and send her back to whatever cranny of San Francisco's Chinatown she crawled out of. But she was beside herself. Maybe she liked lording it over the girls. Maybe she wanted to go on doing it.

The strange knife grazed Fargo's arm. Not deep, but enough to sting and draw blood. He caught hold of her wrist, but it was liking trying to hold on to a writhing eel. She slipped free and skipped back and crouched.

His eyes on her knife, Fargo slowly rose. She did not notice him palm the Arkansas toothpick. "Why are you doing this?"

"You not spoil things!" Wen Po hissed.

Holding the toothpick against his leg, Fargo said, "I'll give you one chance. Leave. Now."

Wen Po sneered. "Fool!" she said, and sprang. A squeal was torn from her throat as she impaled herself. Incredulous, she flopped at his feet, stared up at the dripping toothpick, said something in Chinese, and was gone.

Fargo turned and bent over Tilly. "Thanks for the—" He did not finish. There was no need. Gently, he closed her eyes, eased her onto her back, and folded her arms across her bosom. Touching her golden locks, he said simply, "Damn."

Absorbed in regret, Fargo forgot that Merle Twern had mentioned there were seven of them. He forgot he had only accounted for five. Forgot there were two left, and they were bound to hear the shots and come on the run.

The next moment, Fargo was reminded of them.

He was shot.

25

Luckily for Fargo the gunman did not aim but snapped the shot from his hip as he barreled into the saloon halfdressed.

The slug creased Fargo's side, barely breaking the skin. Diving, he drew and squeezed off an answer. Hot lead brought his would-be slayer to a stop. The man gawked at the new hole in his chest, then melted.

Fargo kept the Colt trained on the doorway. The last of the five men Cain had sent was unaccounted for. But the man did not appear. Nor did he show at the window. Swinging around on his belly, Fargo crawled past Wen Po and Tilly to the end of the bar. Once he was safe behind it, he rose and cat-footed through the kitchen to the back door. Opening the door just wide enough to slip out, he glided along the wall to the south corner.

Whiskey Mill was deathly still.

Staying low, Fargo ran to the frame house. He went in the back door. The kitchen smelled of coffee. He went through and on to the front. The latch rasped slightly when he worked it. Careful not to show himself, he surveyed the dusty excuse for a street. He saw no one. He opened the door wider to step out and nearly had the top of his head blown off. A heavy-caliber slug cored the jamb a hand's width from his ear. He ducked back as the boom of the rifle echoed.

The last man was being canny.

Fargo had not glimpsed the muzzle flash, but he suspected the man was on a slope that rose to the southwest. It took a skilled marksman to come as close as the man had to blowing out Fargo's wick.

Fargo hurried down the hall to a bedroom. The closet was in a corner. Tilly had not owned shirts or britches, so he settled for a dress. He sat on the edge of the bed, stuffed two pillows into the dress, wrapped the sleeves around the pillows and knotted them, then wrapped and tied off the bottom. Up close it did not look anything like him, but the rifleman was not up close.

Fargo returned to the front of the house. Keeping well back, he nudged the door with his toe. Immediately there came a sharp retort. Slivers flew from a hole above him. Shoving the door open, he flung the mock-up out the door to the right, toward the saloon. The rifleman took the bait and rapidly fired three shots.

Fargo went out the door to the left, toward the shacks. He ran a dozen feet. Dropping flat, he rolled until he was deep in darkness close to the first shack. He heard the *spang* of the rifle, but the shots were nowhere near him.

Silence descended once more.

The rifleman knew he had been tricked and would move to a new position. Fargo used the time to dash to the rear of the shack and from there raced the length of the entire row until he came to the last one. Sinking onto his belly, he wormed along the base of the wall until he was at the front corner. He was now a hundred yards from the slope, much too far for a reliable pistol shot at night. He wished he had the Henry.

Extending the Colt, Fargo steadied his right wrist with his left hand. Now all he could do was wait and hope impatience caused the rifleman to make a mistake. He strained his ears for the telltale snap of a twig or the crunch of dry vegetation. But in that he was thwarted by an unexpected source.

The Chinese women began talking back and forth through the walls of their shacks. They did not talk loud, but it was loud enough that Fargo could not hear any sounds from the slope. But he stayed where he was. To move now, after the rifleman had lost sight of him, was worse than reckless. It would be stupid.

Once again the minutes dragged. Fargo's right arm ached and his shoulders protested, but he did not move a muscle. He might only get one shot. He must make it count.

Down the street a shack door opened. A woman poked her head out. She spoke excitedly and the next woman farther down opened her door to answer. Pretty soon five of the eight doors were open. Tongues wagged excitedly. But none of the Chinese women ventured from their shacks. Fargo thought he heard the name Wen Po a view times. That might have something to do with it.

Then a dark shape detached itself from the greater darkness of the night and stalked parallel with the street. The rifleman was searching for Fargo. Moving away from him, not toward him.

Fargo centered the Colt's sights on the middle of the man's back. He still did not have a good enough shot. Which was just as well. Then coincidence lent a hand. The woman in the third shack opened her door just as the man with the rifle came abreast of it. Bathed in the rectangle of light that spilled out, the man whirled toward her.

Fargo had his clear shot but it was a long one. He elevated the barrel, mentally crossed his fingers, and fired.

A heartbeat elapsed. The rifleman flung out both

arms and did a pirouette, much like he would if he were dancing at a church social. He did not quite make it all the way around. His legs gave out, his head flopped, and once he was prone he did not move.

The door to the third shack slammed shut and the women became as quiet as terrified mice.

Fargo did not take his Colt off the man until he verified he was dead. Reloading, he went into the saloon, chose a new bottle, and sat at a table. He had hours to spare. His stomach growled but he had gone so long without food that it could wait.

It wasn't ten minutes before faces appeared at the window. Scared faces, worried faces. Their eyes widened at the carnage, and the faces hastily disappeared. But in ten minutes they were back. Quietly, nervously, they filed into the saloon, their hands clasped in front of them, their heads bowed. They sank to their knees before his table and dipped their foreheads to the floor.

"So sorry, sir, to disturb you," said one of the Oriental flowers.

Between the half bottle he had drunk earlier and the half bottle he had just helped himself to, Fargo was feeling quite fine. "What can I do for you ladies?" He noticed that Tu Shuzhen was not one of the eight.

"We are most confused," the flower said. She was extraordinarily pretty, with rose petal lips and delicate eyebrows.

"Enough of this," Fargo said, tapping the bottle, "and I'll be so confused I can't walk straight."

The flower motioned at the littered bodies. "We are confused about them. What does it mean?"

"It means they are dead."

"No. I am sorry. I—" She stopped because Fargo had held up his hand.

"What's your name, girl?"

"Mr. Pardee says I am to call myself Juicy Lucy." She paused. "So sorry, but what is juicy?"

"You can forget what Mr. Pardee wants," Fargo told her. "Right about now he's wetting his pants in hell. What is your real name? Your Chinese name?"

"Ni Ting, honorable sir."

Fargo chuckled.

"Sorry?"

"Never mind. I'm not honorable and I'm not a sir. Get up, all of you." Fargo waited until they had done so, then continued. "The human fruit"—and he pointed at several of the deceased—"means you and your friends are free. Take the horses outside. Fill as many water skins as you can find, pack all the food the horses can carry, and head west."

"You want us to leave on horseback?" Ni Ting sounded horrified.

"That's the general notion," Fargo confirmed. "But let me guess. Not one of you has ever sat a saddle."

"That is right. How did you know?"

"It has been one of those days." Fargo sighed. "I'll leave it up to you, then. I can find a spot where you can hide until this is over, or you can wait here for Tobias Cain and take your chances with him."

"So sorry again, but I still do not understand. Until what is over? Take what chances?"

"By an hour after sunrise you will understand. Until then, gather up everything of yours you want to keep. Then get some rest. Things will start to happen about dawn."

"Happen?"

Fargo wagged his fingers. "Go pack your things. I'll wake you at dawn."

They wore their confusion like a shroud as they filed out. The last woman, a slip of a girl, paused at the door, and bowed.

"Would you care for company, sir?"

It took a few moments for Fargo to take her meaning. He smiled. "No, thanks. I'd be up most of the night and I can't afford to lose the sleep." The girl, appearing disappointed, turned to go, when he thought of something. "Wait. There was a woman in the first shack when I was here last. Tu Shuzhen. What happened to her?"

"Pardee learned she had talked to you, and was mad. He hit her. She said all she did was talk about her friend, Lu Wei. But they took her to the Oasis to work." The girl cast a glance at Wen Po, and left.

Fargo tilted the bottle but after a quick swig put it down again. The whiskey tasted flat. He had reached the point where if he drank any more, it would impair his senses. He couldn't have that. He went into the kitchen and helped himself to a slab of cold beef, bread and butter, and a pie Tilly must have baked shortly before he arrived because it was fresh and warm.

Fargo ate in the saloon, surrounded by the bodies, and as he ate he worked out how he would go about bringing the little empire of the Death Valley despot crashing down around Tobias Cain's ears.

The first step was sleep. Fargo was worn out from his ordeal under the sun and the long ride to Whiskey Mill. He stretched out right there on the floor. In the house next door was a comfortable bed, the bed Tilly had slept in, a bed that would still bear her scent. He would rather not be reminded of their lovemaking. With a glance at her body, which he had covered with a blanket, he drew his Colt, rested his head on his arm, and went to sleep.

Fargo had an added reason for sleeping in the saloon. If more of Cain's hired guns showed up, they would mistake him for one of the dead and be considerably surprised when he rose from the afterworld to treat them to lead.

For as long as Fargo could remember, he had the habit of waking up at the crack of dawn. This day was no exception. The sun had not yet risen when he was up and fixing coffee. He got the stove going, using wood from a nearby box, filled the pot with water, added the grounds from a can in the cupboard, and while the brew came to a boil, he went about the saloon splashing whale oil from the lamps on the walls and floor and furniture.

The place reeked when he was done but Fargo didn't mind. He sat and drank five piping hot cups of black coffee. He was in no hurry. He would give the women time to get up and get organized.

Feeling refreshed and raring to start his campaign, Fargo emptied the wood from the wood box and filled it with food. He carried the box outside and set it by the hitch rail.

A golden crown emblazoned the sky with vivid streaks of pink.

Fargo went back in. Water was brought from the Oasis twice a week in water skins. They always hung in the kitchen. He made several trips, placing them with the wooden box. Lastly, he ranged along the shelf behind the bar, found the most expensive bottle of whiskey, and put it in his saddlebags.

Next Fargo led the Ovaro around to the front, left it at the hitch rail with the other horses, and entered the frame house. It was the work of minutes to pour more whale oil.

When Fargo came out, the women were astir. Shack doors were open and their personal effects were outside.

Fargo gave a holler and heads poked out. He bellowed for them to come and give a listen, and they did. They were as timid as last night, and listened quietly as he explained what he was about to do.

"Mr. Cain will be very mad," Ni Ting remarked.

"I hope so," Fargo said. "I hope he's so mad, he doesn't think straight." He was counting on that. "I'm also worried about what he might do to you."

"We will not be to blame," Ni Ting said.

"Cain might still take his anger out on you. I would feel better if you hide until I come for you." Fargo pointed at the water skins and the box of food. "That will tide you over until I do. Talk it over."

They did. They huddled in a circle and whispered back and forth. Presently, they faced him, all of them smiling.

Ni Ting bowed. "We have decided, honorable sir, to hide out, as you call it."

Fargo already had the spot picked. He had noticed it when he initially rode into Whiskey Mill. To the northwest, only five hundred yards away, was a bowl-shaped depression about as wide as a Conestoga was long. A rise west of it blocked much of the sun for most of the day.

The women brought their belongings. Fargo hung the water skins from his saddle, shouldered the box of food, and led a curious procession from Whiskey Mill to the bowl. The women chattered in Chinese. They smiled and laughed a lot.

"Don't let anyone see you," Fargo advised when they were settled in. "The wind is blowing away from you so you won't have to worry about the smoke." He went to climb on the Ovaro.

Ni Ting grasped his hand. "You are the only man who ever helped us. We are grateful. Very grateful," she stressed.

"That's nice." Fargo went to turn but she did not let go.

"If you will let us, we want to thank you when you come back," Ni Ting said. "You may have your pick."

"My pick of what?" Fargo asked, and felt like a jackass when he saw their beaming upturned faces. "I'll keep it in mind."

The sun crowned the eastern horizon. Fargo had to hurry. A burning brand from the kitchen stove sufficed to set the saloon on fire. As the flames sprang to life, he backed out, then ran to the house and soon had it ablaze. In short order he did the same with the shacks.

Fargo did not linger to admire his handiwork. Mounting, he galloped east along the trail to the Oasis. Gray tendrils were wafting into the sky, but it would be half an hour or more, he reckoned, before the smoke was thick enough to be seen from the mansion.

Fargo smiled grimly. Tobias Cain was about to have the worst day of his life. If things went as planned, it would also, coincidentally enough, be the last day of Cain's life.

Either that, Fargo reflected, or the last day of his own.

26

It took longer than Fargo expected. He had been hidden in a wash near the trail that linked Whiskey Mill to the Oasis for two hours when hooves thundered and close to twenty riders roared past in a thick cloud of dust, Tobias Cain in front, Krast and the Viktor brothers flanking him.

The dust hid Fargo as he gigged the Ovaro out of the wash and reined east. He recalled being told that Cain had about forty hired guns. He had accounted for at least ten. Since twenty were with Cain, that left ten or so still at the Oasis, either working as overseers or guarding the spring.

Fargo reined to the south and then east in a wide loop that brought him to the garden of hell at a point only a few hundred yards from the buildings. Again luck smiled on him. The Chinese were toiling in fields to the west and north. He reached the stable without an outcry being given and reined up in the shade along the south wall. He crept inside. No one was there. On a hook near the stalls hung an old slicker. He shrugged into it and made for the mansion.

If anyone saw him, they might think it strange, a man wearing a slicker, as hot as it was. But the slicker covered his buckskins. With his hat pulled low, no one would recognize him. Or so he hoped.

Fargo did not go to the front door. He walked

around back and tried the door that opened into the kitchen. The latch was well oiled. Which was just as well, because the moment he inched the door open, he heard someone talking in Chinese.

The butler, Wong, was placing a cup of tea on a tray next to a bowl of noodles and a plate of small rolls.

No one else was in the kitchen. The butler was talking to himself.

Fargo stayed where he was. Wong picked up the tray, smiling and humming, and headed down the hall. Fargo slipped inside and followed. Wong went up the stairs to the second floor. At the top Wong bore to the right.

Fargo imagined that Wong was taking the food to May Ling. He went slowly, placing each foot with care so as not to jangle his spurs. He did not know if Cain had other servants.

Wong's voice drew Fargo to a bedroom. The door was open. Wong was seated in a plush chair beside a small table. On the table was the tray. As Fargo looked on, Wong sipped some of the tea and noisily smacked his lips. Then Wong placed the bowl of noodles in his lap and began eating, using chopsticks. Grinning broadly, he talked as he ate. Clearly, he was enjoying himself.

The door blocked Fargo's view of whoever Wong was talking to. But by putting an eye to the crack between the door and the jamb, Fargo received a shock.

Wong was talking to May Ling. But she could not answer. A gag prevented her from doing more than making angry sounds. She had reason to be angry. She was flat on her back on a four-poster bed, her wrists and ankles bound to the posts, her body stark naked.

Under different circumstances her flawless body would have stirred Fargo, down low. But the terrible things that had been done to her filled him with icy fury, not lust.

May Ling had been tortured. Someone had pressed the lit end of a cigar to her soft flesh so many times, the burn marks dotted her skin like large black measles. Her tormentor had taken particular delight in pressing the cigar to her thighs and breasts. Black and blue marks from a severe beating were mixed with the burns. Her lips were swollen, her right cheek split. A knot as big as a hen's egg deformed her right temple. Struggling against the ropes, May Ling snarled through her gag. It sounded like she said, "Bastard!"

Perhaps that was why Wong abruptly switched from Chinese to English. Cackling merrily, he said, "Why mad at me? I not hurt you. The giant one kill you slow, not me."

May Ling snarled more but was muffled by the gag.

Rising, Wong moved to the front of the bed. He pried at the gag, wary not to let his fingers too near her teeth, until the gag slid over her lower lip.

"You bastard! You dog! You pig! Cut me loose!"

Wong returned to his chair.

"Didn't you hear me? Release me this instant!" May Ling raged. "I am your mistress and you must do as I say."

"You mistress no more," Wong said. "You nothing now. You try trick giant one. Giant one say Wong not listen to you."

May Ling visibly struggled to control her temper. "How can you sit there gloating? We are both Chinese. We should work together. Free me and we can get away."

Wong spoke with his mouth full of noodles. "We both Chinese, yes. But you American Chinese. Wong China Chinese."

"What difference does that make?"

"In China Wong very poor. Have no house. Never much food. Come to America, to San Francisco. Meet giant one. Him bring Wong here. Him give Wong clothes. Him feed Wong good food. Let Wong live in great house."

May Ling raised her head off the bed. "Are you saying you were not kidnapped like the rest of us? That you work for Cain because you like it here?"

"Like very much, yes," Wong said, and popped a noodle into his mouth. "Wong want stay long time."

"You don't mind that your own people are being enslaved for money?" May Ling asked.

"Wong not slave. Wong happy. Wong want stay long time."

"All you care about is yourself," May Ling snapped. "You don't give a damn about anyone else."

"No damn," Wong said, and smiled.

"Then why did you come upstairs? Why are you sitting there eating and staring at me?"

"Wong like see tits."

May Ling surged up off the bed like a tigress, but the ropes brought her down. Shaking with fury, she clawed her fingers at empty air. "If only I were loose! I would scratch your eyes out."

The little man laughed in sadistic delight.

Suddenly May Ling stopped raging. Smiling sweetly, she said, "We all get what we deserve in the end."

"You lie to giant one," Wong said. "You deserve be punished."

"I wasn't talking about him. I was talking about you. I hope he splits your skull open, you miserable worm."

"Eh?"

By then Fargo was next to the chair. Wong glanced up just as he brought the barrel of the Colt slashing down. He did not use enough force to kill, as much as he wanted to. Wong was unarmed. But he did crush Wong's nose and pulp his mouth and leave the little slug in a crumpled heap on the floor.

"You are alive!" May Ling exclaimed as Fargo attacked the ropes with the Arkansas toothpick. "Tobias told me you were dead! He said Captain Jim was due back any time with your body."

"The Modoc is buzzard food." Fargo cut the last rope and she melted into his arms and clung to him as someone who was drowning might cling to a log.

"I am sorry I hit you. I was afraid they would shoot you, and I knew Tobias would not kill you outright. I thought I could somehow help you escape later. You believe me, don't you?"

Fargo assumed a poker face. "I believe you."

"I tried to convince Tobias you made me go with you. But he wouldn't listen. He did this to me. Then someone saw smoke off in the direction of Whiskey Mill, and Tobias rushed out. But he promised to do worse when he gets back."

"You have to be strong. I have a lot to do. But first we must make sure you are safe. Get dressed."

"Where will we go?"

"You'll find out soon enough," Fargo said.

Wong weighed no more than a sack of potatoes. Or so it seemed as Fargo dragged him down the hall to the stairs. He rolled Wong to the edge of the top step and pushed with the toe of his boot. The little man bounced rather nicely.

Fargo went into each of the bedrooms and emptied lamps over beds and rugs and curtains. Soon a pungent odor filled the air.

As Fargo was coming out of the next to last bedroom, he nearly collided with May Ling. She wore a Chinese-style long top and pants that made her look mannish, quite a feat given her natural beauty.

"What are you doing? What is that smell?"

"Pack whatever you hold dear," Fargo said. "I'm getting you out of here before I light the match."

"Match?" May Ling repeated. Understanding dawned, and she hastened to her room.

Fargo went downstairs. Wong was groaning and stirring. "We can't have that," Fargo said. Palming the Colt, he slugged him across the temple. Not once but twice. The groaning and the stirring ceased.

Tobias Cain liked a lot of light at night. Fargo had plenty of lamps to spill over whatever would burn best. By the time he was done the whole mansion stunk.

The kitchen stove was still warm from Wong's meal. Fargo kindled the red coals and soon had a fire.

May Ling had not one, not two, but three bags, each big enough to stick a calf in. She staggered as she set them down at the foot of the stairs. Accidentally, perhaps, she set one on Wong's face.

"You want to take all that?" Fargo gripped the straps to the nearest bag and lifted. He thought it would be as light as Wong. It was as heavy as the Ovaro, or damn near. "What the hell is in these?" He opened the bag and nearly choked.

Everything of value May Ling could find, from brass candlesticks to a silver tray to a gold watch that must belong to Tobias Cain, had been stuffed into the bag, along with blankets, sheets, a quilt. But that was not enough to account for the weight. Fargo bent and moved the top layer aside. He nearly choked a second time.

The bottom half of the bag contained coins: gold dollars, gold eagles, double eagles, half eagles, some quarter eagles, silver dollars, and more. At a rough guess, Fargo pegged the tally at thousands of dollars. He hefted the other two bags. They weren't as heavy. They were heavier.

"Where did you get all this?"

"From Cain's bedroom," May Ling revealed. "He has a secret compartment under the floor. He does not suspect I know about it. I spied on him one night when he thought I was asleep."

"Is there more?"

"Much more," May Ling said. "But this was all I could carry. There is a wagon in the stable. If you bring it, we can deprive Tobias of every cent he has hoarded. What do you say?"

Fargo did not have to think about it. "No."

"But it is a fortune!" May Ling exclaimed. "Enough for both of us to live like Cain is living now for the rest of our lives."

"We can't take any of it," Fargo said. "Not even these."

May Ling had been stabbed in the gut, or that was the impression she gave. "What kind of man are you that you do not care about money?"

"The kind who wants to go on breathing," Fargo said. "You can't take the bags because we will be riding double."

"But it is so much *money*!" May Ling exclaimed, a new sort of gleam in her lovely eyes. "Why leave it for Tobias? He does not deserve it."

"The money should go to the people working the fields," Fargo reminded her. "It came from their families."

"We can be rich!" May Ling persisted. "I insist you fetch the wagon and load these bags while I fill more."

Fargo began to wonder if the comments she made the first time he saw her had been an act or were her true feelings. "Insist all you want." Taking hold of her wrist, he started toward the kitchen.

May Ling tugged and dug in her heels. "Stop! What are you doing? I refuse to leave without the money."

"We don't have time for this," Fargo warned. He had no way of predicting how soon Cain would return. It might be two hours. It might be ten. Pulling harder, he hauled May Ling as far as the kitchen doorway. There, she gripped the jamb with her free hand and would not let go.

"This is silly," Fargo said. His patience has been stretched as far as he would allow. "Let's go."

May Ling spat angrily in Chinese, then said in English, "You can not make me if I do not want to."

"Guess again," Fargo said, and slugged her. He pulled his punch, but he clipped her on the jaw as neatly as could be, a swift sock that had the desired effect of causing her to collapse in his arms.

On the way through the kitchen Fargo yanked a towel off the counter.

The sun was as bright as ever. Fargo stayed close to the house until he came to the northeast corner. Setting May Ling down, he waved the towel over his head. He waved it for several minutes, until a horse and rider came out of the haze and the heat at a trot. The rider was leading another mount by the reins. His derby and clothes were caked thick with dust.

"What happened to her?" Kid Fontaine asked as he drew rein. He had a bulge under his shirt on his left shoulder, the result of the bandage Fargo had applied.

"The heat got to her." Fargo, none too gently, slung May Ling over the back of Captain Jim's horse, and tied her on. "Do you remember what I told you?"

The Kid nodded. "I'm to keep her with me and wait out there until you come say it's safe. But I don't like it much. Leaving you to face them by your lonesome just ain't right."

"You have a clipped wing," Fargo said. But that was not the real reason he wanted the Kid to sit the bloodshed out.

"I ain't helpless. I can shoot with my other hand,

you know." Kid Fontaine patted the Remington on his right hip.

"Just keep your eyes peeled."

"That's easy to do with this," the Kid said, and drew from a pocket a small folding telescope they had found in Captain Jim's saddlebags. "Imagine. That tricky redskin having a spyglass."

To the west, workers were pulling weeds in a field of potatoes. Their overseer was staring toward the mansion.

"Light a shuck," Fargo directed. "And be careful."

The Kid snickered. "You're the David about to tangle with Goliath. Seems to me you're the hombre who should walk on eggs."

Fargo did not move until they were swallowed by the haze. Then he rubbed his hands in anticipation and turned.

Time to sling the next stone.

Fargo had set the upper floor on fire and was coming down the stairs when a slug came as close as a cat's whisker to taking off his head. He dropping the burning brand he had taken from the stove and had his Colt in his hand as he leaped the last six steps. His would-be slayer's revolver crashed again but missed. Then Fargo was at the bottom. His answering shot found its mark, the overseer who had been staring at the mansion a while ago.

Stepping over the body, Fargo went to the kitchen for another brand. The walls were thick enough to muffle the shots, but he hurried as he went from room to room, setting Tobias Cain's den of luxury so completely ablaze that even if Cain and all his men showed up, they could not put out the flames. He was opening the back door when he remembered something he had forgotten. The rising heat was almost unbearable as he dragged Wong outside and left him in the dirt a dozen yards from the mansion.

Fargo's next stop was the long coolie building where Li Dazhong had been. Li was there again, in the same bed, asleep.

In a chair beside the bed, sipping on a silver flask, sat Dr. Brine. Brine gave a start when Fargo came up. "I say! Am I seeing ghosts now?"

"Find a horse and ride," Fargo said.

Brine nervously upended the flask and gulped before saying, "How's that? I can't leave. Cain would throttle me."

"A lot of blood is about to be spilled. If you don't leave, some of it might be yours." Fargo bent over Li. "How is he?"

"Holding his own, which is a miracle considering what he has been through. I've done all that's humanly possible. The rest is up to Providence." Brine capped the flask and slid it into an inside pocket. "Now then, about riding off—"

"On second thought," Fargo interrupted, "help me carry him to the stable."

"Whatever for? In his condition that could kill him."

"Help me," Fargo repeated. "Be quick about it. And bring your black bag."

Something in his tone silenced the protest Dr. Brine was about to make. Brine's eyes about popped from his head when he saw wisps of smoke rising from the mansion and flames visible through the windows.

"My word. What have you done?"

"You've heard about Cain staking me out for the rattlers?" Fargo scanned the fields, but no one else had noticed the smoke yet.

Brine nodded. "He is most inventive when it comes to disposing of those he no longer has any use for."

"They say that one good turn deserves another," Fargo said, and nodded at the burning mansion.

"Cain will be furious."

"I imagine he already is. I burned Whiskey Mill to the ground this morning."

Brine was speechless.

"Now do you see why you have to get out of here and take Li with you?" Fargo asked.

Nodding, Dr. Brine glanced longingly at the pocket that contained his flask. "You have unleashed hell on earth. I hope you know what you are doing. If not, by tonight there won't be enough left of you to fill a gunnysack."

They placed Li Dazhong in the wagon. As Fargo hitched a team, shouts broke out in the fields. He was handing the reins up to Dr. Brine when overseers came running up to the mansion, driving workers ahead of them with their whips.

"Swing around to the back of the stable, then head northeast. You'll find Kid Fontaine. Stay with him until this is over."

"Out in the desert? The heat will fry us."

"He has water skins and jerky, and you can take shelter in the shade under the wagon." Fargo slapped one of the horses, and the wagon rattled into motion.

Flames were shooting from the mansion roof. More Chinese and their guards rushed up, and a lot of confused yelling resulted. An overseer was bellowing for buckets of water to be brought. It would do no good.

No one paid any attention to Fargo in the slicker. He went back into the stable, lit a lantern, and dashed it into the hayloft. Then he ran from stall to stall, releasing the horses and giving each a swat on the hind end. The last trotted to safety and he was backing through the double doors when a pair of Cain's cutthroats appeared.

"What in hell are you doing?" a beanpole demanded.

Fargo pointed at smoke rising from the loft door. "The stable is on fire. I didn't want the horses to burn."

The second man angrily shook his whip. "What in God's name is going on? Who is doing this?"

"I am," Fargo said.

Bewilderment slowed their efforts to unlimber their hardware. Fargo shot the beanpole through the head and the other through the heart. He darted around the corner before anyone near the mansion could spot him.

Once on the Ovaro, Fargo reined toward the cookhouse. That was where the food was stored.

The cook had come out and was watching the mansion burn. "Hell in a basket!" he blurted as Fargo swung down. "I wonder how that got started. Mr. Cain will be fit to be tied."

"I hope you're right. I wouldn't want to think I went to all that trouble for nothing."

The cook looked at him. The man's double chins quivered and he threw up his arms. "I'm not wearing a gun."

"Is your stove hot?"

"It sure is. I'm baking bread for tonight. Why do you ask?" The cook glanced at the mansion, and the answer hit him. "Oh God. Look, I have my things in the back. Can I get them?"

"You're not fixing to try anything, are you?" Fargo asked, his hand on the Colt.

"I'm no gun shark, mister. I'm a grease belly, nothing more. I feed folks. I don't swap lead. You let me get my things and I promise I will slink away like a mouse and you will never set eyes on me again."

"You have five minutes to start slinking." Fargo followed the cook in. Half a dozen loaves of bread had already been baked and set aside to cool. He poked a finger into one, ripped off a piece. It was delicious. Taking a seat where he could watch the front door and the door to the cook's quarters, he proceeded to devour half the loaf with enthusiasm. He was famished.

The cook came out carrying a battered bag. "How was the bread?"

"If I had the time I'd eat the other half," Fargo said honestly.

The cook jabbed a thumb at the storeroom. "If you

destroy that, everyone here will starve. Do you want that on your conscience?"

"If you hurry you might catch a horse," Fargo suggested. The cook bustled out, and Fargo walked to the doorway.

Half the mansion was a sheet of flame. The other half soon would be. The guards were as mesmerized as their charges. No one had noticed the stable roof was dotted with tiny flames rapidly growing larger.

Setting the cookhouse on fire was easy. Fargo kicked the stove over. But only after he poured himself a cup of coffee. He led the Ovaro a safe distance and stood sipping and watching until flames gouted from the cookhouse windows. Next would be the bunkhouse and then the coolie buildings.

Fargo reached for the saddle horn. His gaze drifted to the west and a scowl creased his beard. He had hoped to have more time.

Tobias Cain swept across the Oasis like an avenging god. He was off his big horse before it stopped moving and plowed through the Chinese like they were chaff. They tried to get out of his way, but they were not fast enough. He left thirty or forty doubled over and groaning.

Cain halted a dozen steps from the mansion. He could get no closer. The inferno was too intense. Shielding his face from the flesh-devouring heat, he clutched at empty air as if it were a throat he was strangling. A spurt of flame drove him back. He reeled as if drunk, then threw his huge arms wide, raised his contorted face to the sky, and roared like the primeval animal he had become.

Cain raked the Chinese and his own men with eyes that burned as bright as the mansion. "Who did this? *Who the hell did this?*"

An overseer, bolder than the others, stepped forward. "We don't know. Charlie said he thought he saw something suspicious and came for a look-see. He never came back. It wasn't long after that we first saw the flames."

"Wong might know," Tobias Cain bellowed. "Where is he?"

"Dead," a man said.

Fargo, listening from the shadow of a coolie building, perked his ears. He was sure he had dragged the little butler far enough from the mansion.

"Dead how?" Cain demanded.

"I saw him lying out back," the man reported. "Everyone was shouting and running around, and he jumped up, took one look, and ran into the mansion, screaming in Chinese. That was the last we saw of him."

"Maybe he went in after May Ling," someone suggested.

At the mention of her name, Tobias Cain turned toward the conflagration and smiled. "I hope to heaven she was in there. It would serve the bitch right for betraying me."

At that juncture a keen-eyed gunnie shouted, "Look! The stable and the cookhouse are on fire too!"

Cain roared commands, directing attempts to save both structures. The overseers cracked whips mercilessly. Every last Chinese scrambled for buckets and shovels.

For the moment Fargo had done all he could. He rode east until he came to where the tilled land ended and the desert began. He headed north. Cain and company would be busy for hours. He could see to the safety of the others.

Fargo was surprised the Kid did not show himself as he neared the gully. The wagon was there, as it was supposed to be, and the Kid's horse, but not Captain Jim's. Figures were in the shade underneath.

Descending, Fargo dismounted. "Did the Modoc's horse run off?"

The head that poked out was Dr. Brine's. He was red and sweaty and holding his flask like it was the Holy Grail. "Thank God you've come! I am afraid he will not last much longer."

"Li Dazhong is dying?"

"No. He is improving. It's Kid Fontaine. The knife went deep. He lost too much blood before I got here."

Only then did Fargo see the broad dark stain near the gully rim. He had ridden right past it. Squatting, he eased under the wagon. Li Dazhong was lying between the rear wheels, peacefully sleeping. Kid Fontaine was on his back under the front of the wagon, a blanket covering him to his chin. His skin was pasty white and he was shivering as if it were thirty below. His grin was more of a grimace.

"Every time I turn around lately, I get stabbed."

"Who did it?" Fargo asked, although he already knew.

"That Chinese gal. When she came to, she went on and on about going back. Pestered me fierce. I told her we were doing like you said and staying put until we heard from you." The Kid coughed and red drops dribbled from the corners of his mouth. "I was lying up there looking through the telescope when she came and lay next to me. She was talking sweet-like, about how she didn't mean to raise a fuss, and how it was kind of me to watch over her. Then there was this pain in my back and I passed out. When I came to, the doc was bending over me."

"I've done all I could for him," Dr. Brine said.

"Where did May Ling go?" Fargo asked.

The doctor answered, "I saw her as I was leaving the Oasis. She was coming out of the mansion, lugging a bag so heavy she could hardly carry it. She had a couple of others near her horse."

Fargo swore.

"When last I looked back, she was riding west."

"That gal is plumb poison," Kid Fontaine said. "She can smile out one side of her mouth while lying out the other side. Don't you trust her."

"I won't make the same mistake again," Fargo vowed.

"So how did you do?" the Kid inquired. "I'm not dying for nothing, am I? Is that son of a bitch dead yet?"

"Cain will get his soon enough," Fargo said. He described setting the three buildings on fire. "They'll be ashes by sunset."

"That's something, at least." Kid Fontaine closed his eyes, and sighed. "This is a hell of a note. I always reckoned on dying from too much lead in my system, not a pretty girl with a knife."

"May Ling won't get away with it," Fargo vowed.

The Kid licked a drop of blood from his lips. "Do me a favor, will you?"

"Name it."

"I have a sister in St. Louis. Got a letter from her in my saddlebags. It has where she lives. Would you send her my things and tell her I fell off my horse and broke my fool neck? Or maybe that I was bit by a rattler? The truth is too embarrassing."

"I'll get word to her."

"Thanks. I've said it before, I'll say it again. You're a good pard. Too bad we didn't meet sooner." The Kid smiled and the smile froze on his face. His eyes abruptly glazed and his chest stopped rising.

"Damn her." Fargo searched the Kid's pockets, then crawled from under the wagon. He was on the Ovaro and raising the reins when the doctor stuck his head out again.

"I take it you want me to stay here?"

"Until sunset," Fargo said. "If I'm not back by then I won't be coming back. Head due west. You'll come to a small settlement in about ten days. Use the water sparingly, and you'll make it." He pricked the pinto with his spurs.

"Good luck!" Dr. Brine called out.

Fargo would need it.

28

That May Ling reached the Panamint Mountains was not remarkable. Captain Jim liked horses with endurance, and his bay possessed more than a common amount. That accounted for how May Ling made it over the first high ridge. But the weltering temperature and the three heavy bags May Ling had managed to tie on the saddle took their toll.

The bay flagged. May Ling did not have much experience with horses. To her mind, when an animal did not do as she wanted it to do, the animal had to be encouraged. She encouraged the bay by slapping it with the reins and pummeling it with her legs, and when that did not motivate the horse to move faster, she climbed down, found a suitable stick, climbed back on, and belabored its neck and head.

The bay snorted and went faster. May Ling smiled, pleased with herself. But her smile was premature. The bay went up the next slope at a trot, but halfway to the top it floundered, teetered, and fell.

May Ling shrieked and tried to throw herself clear. Her legs were too short to reach the stirrups, so she had not bothered to use them. Leaping clear should have been easy. But when she leaped, she had the stick between her legs. The stick snagged on the saddle horn and she snagged on the stick. It broke under her weight, but it slowed her just enough that the bay came down on top of her right foot. May Ling screamed. The horse slid off her and kept on sliding. By throwing out her hands, May Ling stopped herself from following it down. She clutched her foot and promptly let go. Another scream rose to the few vagrant clouds.

Amid a flurry of stones and dust, the bay slid to the bottom. It tried to stand but its left front leg gave out.

Midway between May Ling and the horse lay one of the bags. On spotting it, May Ling forgot about her foot. She slithered to the bag and flung her arms around it as if it were a lover. Then she slid toward the bay, pulling the bag after her.

Fargo watched it all through the telescope he had taken from Kid Fontaine. Now, folding the spyglass, he shoved it into his saddlebags, forked leather, and rode from his place of concealment on the second ridge. He had circled on ahead of her half an hour ago.

Frantically untying the two bags still attached to the saddle, May Ling did not realize he was there until a loose stone clattered from under the Ovaro, bounced a couple of times, and struck her on the elbow.

A bolt of lightning could not have jolted May Ling more. "You!" she cried. Amazingly, she regained her composure in a blink of her beautiful eyes, and added, "I am glad to see you!"

"Same here," Fargo said, reining up ten feet from the bay. Close enough, but not too close.

"Help me! I think my horse broke its leg." May Ling tugged at the bag, but it was partially pinned.

"That's your horse?" Fargo said dryly. "Mighty strange. It looks a lot like Captain Jim's."

"His. Mine. What difference does it make? Climb down and give me a hand with these." Despite the futility, May Ling continued to tug.

"Aren't those the bags with the money?" Fargo asked.

"What do you think?" May Ling suddenly cried out and stared aghast at her left hand. A fingernail had ripped off and her finger was bleeding.

"The bags I told you to leave at the mansion?"

About to stick the finger in her mouth, May Ling looked up sharply. "Yes, the very same. What about it? You didn't expect me to, did you?"

"Money means a lot to you," Fargo observed.

"If I had more time, I would have brought Tobias's entire fortune," May Ling declared. She caressed one of the bags. "Only a fool would pass up a chance like this, and I am not a fool."

"Money means more to you than anything," Fargo amended. "More than your freedom."

"Why do you think I put up with Tobias panting after me? Why do you think I tried to persuade him to take me for his wife?"

"Suppose you tell me."

"Are you stupid? You saw his mansion. You saw how he lived. The fine furniture. The clothes. That wretched Wong to wait on him hand and foot. He lived as regally as the emperor of China. In his cache in the bedroom he had more money than most banks, and more poured in all the time." May Ling glowed with greed. "Who wouldn't want that?"

"What about the women and men in the coolie buildings?"

May Ling seemed genuinely puzzled. "What about them?"

Fargo nodded at the bags. "Their blood, their sweat, their lives, filled those bags with the money you love so much."

"So? They are not my family. They are not my friends. Why should I care if they suffer?"

"Speaking of family," Fargo said, "your own father has been paying ransom to keep you alive."

"All of which I will repay him." May Ling patted the bags. "You see? Money is the answer to everything."

"One last question," Fargo said.

"If you must," Ming Ling retorted. "But then climb down and help me. We will tie the bags on your horse." Again she tugged at the one that was stuck. Sitting back, she moped her brow with her sleeve. "What is your question?"

"Did you think Kid Fontaine was dead when you left him with that knife in his back?"

May Ling did not bat an eyelid. "I have no idea what you are talking about. When I left him he was alive and well."

"You killed him and rode to the mansion and dragged out those bags while I was setting the stable and the cookhouse on fire," Fargo said. "You are a bitch, May Ling. A conniving, vicious, shifty, bloodthirsty, lying bitch. But I guess I can't hold the lying against you. I told a lie, myself. That wasn't my last question. I have one more. How do you intend to get from there"—he pointed at the exhausted bay—"to San Francisco?"

Startled, May Ling stood, winced in pain, and sat back down. She clasped her ankle and remarked through clenched teeth, "I think my foot is broken."

Fargo stared at the shattered sliver of bone that protruded from the bay's front leg. "I call that fair." He started to rein the Ovaro around.

Fleeting fear touched May Ling. "Wait! What are you doing? You can't leave me here like this."

"Care to bet one of those bags on it?"

May Ling thought she understood. "Of course you can have one of the bags. The other two are enough for me." She smiled her most ravishing smile. "I look forward to the nights together on the trail."

"You are worse than those rattlers." Fargo had had enough. She had brought it on herself, and he would be damned if he would waste more time on her. He raised a finger to his hat brim. "Adios, lady."

"Wait!" May Ling pleaded. "How can you ride off and abandon me? What kind of man are you?"

"You're right," Fargo said. "I am forgetting something." Drawing his Colt, he kneed the Ovaro.

"No! You wouldn't!" May Ling recoiled, her arms over her head. "I am sorry I killed the boy. Truly and really sorry."

"Like hell you are." Fargo aimed to be sure, and fired.

At the blast, May Ling shrieked. She flung herself flat, her arms over her head. Fearfully, she peered up at him and the smoking Colt. Then, realizing she had not been shot, she slowly sat up and stared at the bullet hole in the unfortunate bay. "Did you have to do that?"

Fargo replaced the cartridge. He never liked putting a horse out of its misery, but it had to be done. Otherwise the animal would linger for days in the most terrible torment. Sliding the Colt into his holster, he reined east. "So long."

"Wait!" May Ling squawked. "Where are you going?"

"I'm not done with Tobias Cain," Fargo informed her.

"What about me?"

"I'll come back with packhorses for the money later," Fargo said. Three or four with sturdy packs should suffice.

May Ling thought she understood. "Bring water and food for me, will you? I am so thirsty. My mouth is parched."

Fargo squinted at the sun. "You should last out the day. Maybe tomorrow too. I don't give you much more than that."

"You are really going to ride off and leave me?"

"Yes." Fargo expected screams, shrieks, curses. She did not so much as whimper. At the top of the rise he looked back. May Ling was still trying to free the pinned bag. Some people had no more sense than a tree stump.

Fargo headed for the spring. It was the key. Without water, the Oasis would wither. Without the Oasis, Cain's scheme would fall apart. He would not have the food to keep his captives alive. If he could not prove they were alive, he could not demand money from their families.

The spring was the key. Destroy it, and Fargo destroyed the whole enterprise. But how to go about it? That was the question Fargo could not answer. He thought another look at the spring might help him come up with a brainstorm. So, leaving the Ovaro in the shade of a hill a quarter of a mile to the north, he crept on foot as close as he dared.

Tobias Cain was many things, many of them the worst traits humankind possessed, but one thing he was not was stupid. He had sent seven extra men to the spring to help stand guard.

Fargo saw them clearly through the spyglass. He saw Krast snap orders and the men spread out around the spring, making it impossible for anyone to approach undetected. Then Krast went into the shack.

The guards did not concern Fargo much. He would deal with them when the time came. What did concern him was the answer to his question. Because, for the life of him, he could not figure out how to permanently stop the flow. A few kegs of black powder would bring the slab crashing down, but he did not have a single keg. Poisoning the water would do it, but he did not have poison. Filling the spring with dirt and rocks would work but would take weeks, and Cain's men would have something to say about it in leaden undertones.

Fargo was stumped. He toyed with ideas, everything from throwing a dead animal or three into the spring to taking the powder from a thousand cartridges to fashion a bomb. But the former was not practical and the latter would take as long as filling the spring with dirt and rocks.

Closing the spyglass and placing it in a pocket, Fargo worked to the west until he was sure the guards could not see him and came up on the gigantic slab from the rear. He stood at the base and stared up at the tremendously huge rectangle of solid rock. If only he had a way to bring it down. The slab weighed tons. The task seemed impossible. But Fargo had to come up with something or he might as well light a shuck for some other part of the country. Give up, forget the Chinese, let Cain go on collecting ransoms until he was as rich as Midas.

"Like hell," Fargo gritted aloud. There *had* to be a way. He moved along the base and discovered a groove about as wide as his shoulders. The groove went from near the bottom to near the top. Climbing onto the slab, he straightened. The steep angle made footing precarious. He had gone ten feet or so when he came on a crack. He did not pay it much attention since it was only a foot long and barely a hairline wide. But then he came to another, and a third, each larger than the crack before it. Forty feet up was a crack as long as he was tall, and as wide as his hand. Beyond, he saw more. The slab's weight was to blame.

Gravity wanted the slab to crash down as much as he did. An idea percolated like coffee in a coffeepot. He ran a hand over the big crack, stuck his fingers in to see how deep it was. Elation filled him. "It should work!" he said aloud, and then wanted to kick himself. Uncurling, he listened, but apparently none of the guards had heard.

Fargo's elation was short-lived. As he stood there contemplating the network of cracks, the idea lost some of its luster. It would take a lot of wood. He could go up into the Panamint Mountains and gather brush and chop down trees, but hauling everything to the slab would take days even if he had a means to haul it, which he didn't.

Then there was the little matter of the smoke his idea would raise. Enough to be seen for miles during the day and smelled from a long way off at night. Someone was bound to investigate.

Fargo was loath to give up. He pondered deeply as he retraced his steps to the Ovaro, and he was still pondering as he neared the dry wash where he had left Dr. Brine and Li Dazhong.

The sun was its usual pitiless presence. Fargo would swear his insides were as baked as that bread.

The wagon and team were as he had left them. Underneath, stretched out in the shade, were the physician and Li.

Fargo assumed they were asleep. He rode into the wash and dismounted. Stretching to relieve a cramp, he sank to his knees. He reached out to give Brine a shake. "How is your patient, Doctor?"

It took a few moments for the slit throat and the blood seeping into the ground to register.

Then a voice came from behind him in a distinct Southern drawl.

"So much as twitch and you are worm food, mister."

"Let me be the one to shoot him," a different voice said to one side.

"Why you?"

"Why not?"

"How about if we both do it? Share and share alike, Ma always said. I reckon that goes for killing as much as food."

"Ma would be so proud of us. Both it is, then."

A gun hammer clicked.

29

Fargo was not quite sure which brother had snuck up behind him until he was told to raise his arms and turn around and saw his Henry in the other's hands. "Shote."

"None other." Shote Viktor grinned. "And where you find me, you always find my brother."

Vale Viktor held a revolver. He went around a bend and returned leading three horses. One was Kid Fontaine's. Over it had been thrown Li Dazhong's unconscious form. "Pretty slick how we let you walk into our trap, wasn't it?"

"Why did you kill Brine?" Fargo asked. He yearned to go for his Colt, but the muzzle of his own rifle dissuaded him.

"Orders," Shote responded. "Mr. Cain wants you, that little Chinese fella, and May Ling brought back alive. But he was mad as hell that the sawbones ran out on him, and said we could do to him as we pleased."

Fargo regretted having brought Brine along. It had cost the alcoholic physician his life.

"Where is May Ling, anyhow?" Vale asked. "We saw where she lit out and you went after her."

Shote nodded. "We reckoned you would bring her back." He pressed the Henry against Fargo's chest. "Hold real still."

Vale came around behind Fargo and relieved him of the Colt. "I didn't hear you answer my brother."

"May Ling headed west but she didn't get far," Fargo revealed. "Her horse broke a leg."

Shote stepped back, his eyes narrowing. "You up and left her? Is that what you want us to believe?"

"Why would you do a thing like that?" Vale asked. "After you helped her to escape?"

"I gave her all the help I was going to," Fargo said.

Vale indicated Fontaine. "Why stab the Kid in the back? We know it was him saved you from the snakes. We followed his tracks."

"Someone else stabbed him," was all Fargo would say.

Scratching his chin, Shote Viktor said, "Something doesn't add up here, brother. What say we fetch the woman like Mr. Cain wants, then take all three of them back to the Oasis?"

"Fine with me," Vale said. He went to his saddlebags and removed short lengths of rope. "I always keep these handy." He smirked at Fargo. "Never know when they might come in handy."

"Handy." Shote snickered. "That's a good one, brother."

Fargo had to submit to his wrists being bound. Vale tied them in front of him so he could ride. Neither brother checked him for other weapons. They made him take the lead, Shote right behind with the Henry, Vale leading the spare horse with Li Dazhong tied to the saddle.

"You're not going to bury Brine?" Fargo asked as they rode up out of the wash.

"The coyotes and buzzards hereabouts don't get enough to eat as it is," Shote said.

Once more Fargo had to endure the blistering sun, the withering heat. "Mind if I have some water?" he asked when they were halfway to the hills.

"Not at all," Shote said, "if you don't mind me blowing your spine in half when you reach for a water skin."

Fargo licked his dry lips and thought of the Arkansas toothpick in its ankle sheath.

Shote was in a talkative mood. "I've never seen Mr. Cain so riled," he commented a while later. "You burning his mansion down about made him loco. You should have heard him. The things he wants to do to you about curled my toes."

Vale snickered and said, "You sure didn't do the Chinese any favors by burning down those buildings."

"I didn't?" Fargo said.

"Hell no. Mr. Cain is going to put them to work rebuilding everything. They'll work in the fields during the day and work on the buildings at night."

"He'll work them to death," Shote said, "and it's all your fault, mister. When they start dropping like flies, they'll have you to thank."

At the top of the rise Fargo reined up. The brothers came up on either side of him and stared at the dead horse below.

"That was Captain Jim's," Shote said.

"Where's May Ling?" Vale wanted to know.

Fargo was wondering the same thing. They descended. A glittering ribbon provided a clue, but he did not say anything.

"What's this, brother?" Shoe drew rein and slid down. He walked to the ribbon, swore, and scooped up a gold coin. "Where in blazes did this come from?"

Vale dismounted too. He pried at one of the bags still hooked over the dead animal's saddle. Sliding a hand in, he drew out a handful of gleaming eagles and double eagles. "Sweet Jesus!"

Shote drew his long knife and chopped at the handles. Within moments he and his brother were each dipping their arms in a bag and gaping at the coins that cascaded from their fingers.

"Mr. Cain never said anything about these!"

"Maybe he doesn't know."

Shote and Vale glanced at one another and then at Fargo. "You didn't answer me," Shote said. "Where did these come from? And get down from that pinto before I blow you out of the saddle."

Fargo told them. Lying was pointless, and the truth might save his hide. "There were three bags," he finished. "She must have the last one."

"Stay with these money bags," Shote said to Vale, "and keep an eye on the scout. I won't be long." He swung onto his mount and followed the trail of coins off into the junipers and pinyons.

Vale palmed his revolver and stepped back. "I don't understand you, mister. Why in God's name did you leave May Ling with all this money? There's enough here to set you up as a king."

"I knew she wouldn't get very far," Fargo said.

"So you planned to come back after she keeled over and help yourself? Is that it?" Vale chuckled. "Damned sneaky." Vale sat on the dead horse and swatted at several flies that took exception.

"How about if we strike a deal?" Fargo proposed. "Your brother and you take all the money and go, and leave me alive."

"What do you take us for? Jackasses? I can drill you any time I want. Why should we let you live?"

"Tobias Cain."

Vale considered before answering. "He would wonder what happened to us, wouldn't he? That is, if Shote and me were dumb enough to ride off with the money like you want. But I have a better idea. How about if my brother and me bury the money where no one is likely to find it? Then we shoot May Ling and gut you, and tell Mr. Cain the two of you jumped us and we didn't have any choice. How would that be?"

"Cain wants her alive. Isn't that what you told me?"

Vale Viktor shrugged. "For this much money Shote and me can take a few chances. We'll stick around another six months or so, so as not to make Mr. Cain suspicious. Then we'll head for parts unknown and set ourselves up in grand style."

"You have it all worked out," Fargo complimented him. He squatted so his left side was to the dead horse and placed his bound hands on the ground in front of him.

"I have to talk it over with Shote first. We never do anything without the other's say-so."

Fargo casually gazed to the west. The other brother was out of sight. From under his hat brim he focused on Vale, who was pointing his revolver at the ground. Fargo edged his bound hands toward his boots.

Vale flipped and caught a gold coin. He held it so it caught the sun just right. Laughing in delight, he flipped it and caught it a dozen more times.

As slow as a snail, Fargo hiked up his pant leg. It was impossible to guess how long Shote would be gone, so he had to act quickly yet do so with the utmost care. He eased his fingers under his boot and gripped the toothpick's hilt. Sliding it between his hands, he lowered them to the ground again. Now all he needed was some way to distract Vale Viktor.

Not ten seconds later Li Dazhong groaned and stirred. He was hanging over the saddle on his stomach and tried to move, but he was bound fast. Muttering in Chinese, he raised his head. "Untie me."

"Ask real nice," Vale Viktor said.

"Please untie me. I do not feel well and this is making me feel worse."

"That's not nice enough."

Li reddened but controlled his temper. "What would you have me say? Will you *please* let me off this horse? I would be very grateful."

Vale tittered. "Chinamen are so stupid. You could ask nice from now until the cows come home and I wouldn't cut you loose."

"Cain wants Li alive, too," Fargo mentioned.

"He can flap his gums so I suspect he's still breathing," Vale quipped. But he stopped flipping the coin, and sighed. "Still, I reckon it wouldn't do to have him get sick. The stink is bad enough without that."

"I do not have an odor," Li said indignantly.

"Trade noses with me and then say that. All you Chinese smell the same. Like leather that has been out in the rain."

"When was the last time you took a bath?" Fargo asked.

Vale stood and pocketed the coin he had been flipping. "Last year sometime. Why? I sure as hell don't smell like any Chinese."

"No, you smell more like the north end of a buffalo heading south," Fargo said. "Women must gag when they get close to you."

Amazement rooted Vale. "What did you just say?"

"Are you hard of hearing? You and your brother reek to high heaven. On hot days like this it's worse. I hold my breath whenever you're upwind."

"Is that a fact?" Anger chiseled Vale's features as he hefted his revolver and advanced. "Maybe I can help. Maybe if you don't have a nose, you won't have anything to complain about." He stopped and raised the revolver. "Some people just don't know when they are well off."

"I've noticed that, too," Fargo said, and drove the Arkansas toothpick into Vale's groin. Vale bleated and instinctively jerked back. It was the wrong thing to do. Blood gushed in a deluge. The pain had to be terrible but Vale Viktor did not crumble. Snarling, he shoved the muzzle of his revolver against Fargo and squeezed the trigger.

At the selfsame instant, Fargo lashed out with both legs. The revolver boomed but missed and Vale crashed onto his back. Howling like a gut-shot wolf, Vale twisted and thrust his revolver at Fargo's face.

Fargo buried the toothpick in Vale's right eye.

After the quaking stopped, Fargo wiped his knife clean on Vale's clothes. He cut Li Dazhong free and the little man in black voiced his thanks. Li tried to dismount, but his arms and legs would not work as they should. Fargo had to help him. He placed a hand on Li's forehead. The fever had broken. Whatever Dr. Brine did had Li on the mend.

"Forget about me. The other brother will return soon."

Fargo went to Vale's horse. He had seen Vale shove his Colt in a saddlebag. Confirming it was loaded, Fargo twirled it into his holster. Now all he needed was his Henry.

"I thought I heard something," Li Dazhong said.

Fargo heard it too. The clomp of hooves. Shote was on his way back. Moving swiftly, Fargo dragged Vale to the dead horse and propped him against it. From a distance it might fool his brother.

"What are you doing?" Li blurted as Fargo scooped him up and swung him over to Kid Fontaine's horse.

"Act like you are still tied," Fargo directed, and slid Li belly-down over the saddle. Then Fargo sat where he had been sitting when Shote left, stuck the Colt between his legs, and held his hands close together to give the impression they were still tied.

Shote took his sweet time. The clomp of hooves grew steadily but slowly louder. But it was May Ling who lurched into sight first, weaving and staggering, teetering on the brink of collapse. She was a mess.

Her hair, her face, her clothes were pale with dust, her lips cracked, her eyes dull.

The Henry's stock resting on one leg, the third bag of money hooked over his saddle horn, Shote Viktor stared hard at his brother. "I heard a shot but I reckon everything is all right."

"He was putting me in my place," Fargo said to distract Shote from Vale.

"Too bad he didn't shoot you," Shote said. He gigged his zebra dun so that its shoulder bumped May Ling, and she very nearly pitched off her feet. Laughing, Shote called out, "She's not putting on airs anymore, is she, Vale?"

"She's sure not," Fargo said. "Knock her down, why don't you? Break a few bones."

"I wasn't talking to you," Shote snapped. But he clucked to the zebra dun and bumped into May Ling once more. She tripped and fell to one knee. Cackling merrily, Shote glanced at his brother, apparently expecting Vale to find it as comical as he did. When Vale did not share in the glee, he rose in the stirrups. "Why are you just sitting there like that?"

"Because he's dead," Fargo said, and shot Shote through the head. He was on his feet before the body thudded to earth. The Henry came first. He ran past May Ling, but she did not acknowledge him. Her dull eyes gazed blankly ahead.

Li Dazhong awkwardly climbed down. He was slowly regaining his strength. "Two less we must deal with," he remarked.

Fargo nodded. "Only twenty-five or so to go, give or take a few."

30

A pall of smoke hung over the Oasis. Under it, the green acreage was scarred by the charred black skeletons of the mansion, the stable, and the cookhouse.

The day after the fire, Tobias Cain put a third of the Chinese to work sifting through the smoldering remains of the mansion. It was not hard for Fargo, watching through the spyglass, to guess what they were searching for. Cain personally oversaw the search. Hired guns ringed the mansion, but at a distance, so they could not see what the Chinese recovered.

Krast had charge of the rest of the Chinese. Only a handful were sent to the fields. The rest had the job of clearing away what was left of the stable and the cookhouse so new buildings could be constructed.

Fargo deemed it strange that no one was sent to hunt for the Viktor brothers. Then again, Cain was obsessed with finding every ounce of gold from his cache in the mansion. The fire had fused many of the coins into melted yellow lumps. Big lumps, little lumps, of all different shapes, composed mostly of gold streaked with silver although a few were of silver streaked with gold.

Fargo decided to do Tobias Cain a favor.

It was between noon and one. The workers were

permitted to rest and eat meager portions. An overseer was the first to notice the plodding figure and the horse, and gave a shout.

Cain and Krast came running.

May Ling's head was bowed, her hands bound behind her. A rope was looped around her waist, the other end leading the horse over which the bodies of Shote and Vale Viktor had been thrown.

In one sense Cain was predictable. He raged about, bellowing commands that the bodies be buried. Then he seized May Ling and viciously slapped her but stopped when all she did was stare blankly up at him.

But in another sense Cain was not predictable. He did not send any of his cutthroats out to find Fargo. Cain kept them at the Oasis, except for the nine guarding the spring.

Fargo flattered himself that he understood why. Tobias Cain was afraid of losing more of his underlings. Cain had barely enough to continue to hold sway over the Chinese. Too few, and the captives might be tempted to revolt.

That was where Fargo came in. He conspired to help the revolt along. That night, abetted by a moonless sky, he crept in close to the barred coolie buildings. He did not go alone. Li Dazhong was beside him.

Through the barred windows, open to admit the night breeze, Li whispered to those inside the buildings. The message was always the same. Their hour of deliverance was at hand. Spread the word.

The next day was a repeat of the one before. Except that the Chinese did not work as hard, even when urged on by the overseers. A sullen, silent defiance was evident, and more widespread as the day waned.

May Ling worked shoulder to shoulder with the rest. Her special status as Cain's bed partner was over. She was no longer exempt from toil.

The girls from Whiskey Mill also took part. Tu Shuzhen and Ni Ting were assigned to work the cook pots set up near where the cookhouse had been.

Fargo did not show his hand until after sunset. Twilight had descended. He crawled in close, waited until there was barely enough light to see by, and shot one of Cain's men through the shoulder. As others came on the run, he hollered, "Desert Cain or die!" Then he faded into the gathering night.

The next morning, the sun was not yet up when a guard posted near the coolie buildings was shot through the leg. Again Fargo's voice rang across the Oasis. "Desert Cain or die!" He was gone by the time Krast organized a search party.

That day the Chinese were more sullen and uncooperative than ever. The overseers were a nervous bunch, and often Fargo would see two or three secretly talking and casting hard looks at the tyrant who lorded it over them.

Unrest was spreading, and not just among the captives.

That night, three hired guns slunk off to the west. Fargo did not try to stop them.

He was counting on them to inspire others, and they did. The night after, three more snuck away.

That night, too, Fargo and Li Dazhong slipped past the guards and Li whispered more words through more barred windows.

Later, back in the wash, not far from the graves Fargo had dug for Kid Fontaine and Dr. Brine, Fargo asked the crucial question. "Do you think they will do it?"

"They are not as afraid as they once were," Li Dazhong said. He was lying on a blanket next to the wagon.

"But will they do what we want?" Fargo persisted. A lot depended on it. Their lives, for one thing.

"I cannot predict," Li said. "Some of them have been held captive for so long they are like sheep. Others want to fight but can do little against bullets with bare fists."

"Once we have whittled the odds more, there won't be as many bullets to worry about."

Li Dazhong rolled on his side so he faced Fargo. "Would you mind if I asked you a question?"

"Depends on the question."

"Why are you doing this? Why help us? You are not Chinese. You never knew any of us until you came here."

"That seems to be a popular question these days. I was hired—"

"To find May Ling," Li interrupted. "Yes. So you have told me. But you did not leave with her when you could have. Instead you stayed to help us. I ask you again, why are you doing this?"

"It has to be done," Fargo said.

"That is no answer," Li responded. "You might as well say we eat and sleep because it has to be done."

Fargo chuckled. "It does."

"You are not going to tell me, are you?" Li asked, making no effort to mask his disappointment.

"Ever been made a fool of?" Fargo rejoined.

"*That* is your reason for opposing a man like Cain? With all his money and all his killers?"

"He has known who I am almost from the start," Fargo related. "He let me think I had pulled the wool over his eyes and all the while he had pulled the wool over mine. Every step of the way, he was one step ahead of me." Fargo paused. "The short and the true is that Tobias Cain made a jackass of me and I want to pay him back."

"I see. Well, whatever your reasons, in case things do not go well tomorrow, I thank you in advance for helping us."

"Don't make more of it than there is." Fargo was uncomfortable talking about it.

Li coughed lightly. "I have a request to make of you."

Mildly surprised by the appeal that came into the other's tone, Fargo responded, "What kind of request?"

"From what you have told me, I gather you very much want to deal with Tobias Cain yourself."

"There is nothing I want more," Fargo admitted.

"I ask you to reconsider. I ask you to look at this through the eyes of my people. We have been wronged, terribly wronged. Our plight cries out for justice by our own hands, not yours."

"So long as Cain is taken care of, what difference does it make?"

"A lot, if you have been made to work as a slave. A lot, if you have been torn from your loved ones. A lot, if someone has used you to become wealthy. A lot, if you have been treated like an animal. A lot, if you had been forced to bow and scrape and lick the boots of others." Li ended his litany.

"I've seen what the Chinese have gone through," Fargo said, "but I won't make a promise I'm not sure I can keep. There is no telling what will happen once the leads starts to fly."

"All I ask, on behalf of the Chinese captives, is that you consider my request and act accordingly if you can when the time comes."

With that, they turned in. Fargo lay with his head on his arm, pondering. A lot more people were likely to die before the whole business was done, and their deaths would be in part on his shoulders. He was the match lighting the fire. His was the spark that would consume more than the buildings already razed. But it was either that, or ride off and let Tobias Cain go on lording it over Death Valley.

Fargo could not allow that. It was as much a clash between Cain and himself as a fight to free the Chinese. It was a duel. A duel to the death between a man who placed no value on human life, Tobias Cain, and Fargo, who had always been of the opinion that life was kind of precious. Some might think that silly, but the alternative wasn't much to crow about.

Fargo was not one of those who went around doing good for the sake of doing good. He preferred to mind his own business and preferred that others do the same. But life did not always respect someone's wishes. Life could be hard. Life could be cruel. Life could be deadly. And when Fargo found himself in situations like this, where it was kill or be made coyote bait, he would as soon the bait was the other fellow.

Fargo felt sorry for the Chinese, but no more so than he would for anyone in their situation. No one had the right to lord it over someone else. Tobias Cain thought he did and Lord knew, there were a lot of others roaming the vast wilds west of the Mississippi who thought the same. The West was chock-full of bandits, badmen, and hostiles, and it had been Fargo's luck in his wide-flung travels to run into more of them than most.

Fargo had a rule he lived by. He had never thought of it as a rule before, but now that he did, it qualified. The rule was this: He did not go around stepping on the toes of others, and he would be damned if anyone was allowed to step on his. Those who did, those like Tobias Cain, had to be taught that stepping on toes could cost them.

Sleep began to cloud Fargo's mind. He was on the verge of dreamland when a slight sound penetrated his mental fog. Instantly, he was awake. He did not move except to slide his hand to his Colt. He listened but the sound was not repeated. Convinced it had been nothing of importance, he tried to drift off again.

But the harder he tried, the more elusive sleep proved to be.

Disgusted, Fargo sat up. He needed rest, and lots of it. His wits and his reflexes must be razor sharp for the conflict to come. Idly, he stretched and glanced at Li Dazhong.

Something was not quite right. The blankets did not have the shape they should. Perplexed, Fargo quietly rose and cat-footed over. He did not want to wake Li if he was asleep. But he need not have bothered.

Li Dazhong was gone.

Whirling, Fargo grabbed his Henry and ran to the rim. He plunged to the south, running flat out. The ground was flat and open. Soon he should spot Li. But he covered a quarter of a mile and the only sign of life was a scorpion that scuttled out of his path.

Fargo came to a stop, sucking the night air into his lungs. In the distance gleamed the lights of the Oasis. Cain always kept lanterns glowing in the coolie buildings, and the gun sharks standing guard always kept a few campfires going.

To venture farther was pointless. Li did not want to be found. Fargo was baffled as to why. He suspected it had something to do with their talk. But exactly what Li hoped to accomplish eluded him.

Fargo bent his steps back to the wash. He lay on his back and gazed at the stars and tried, again, to get some badly needed sleep. But Li's running off played havoc with his frame of mind. Without Li, he could not let the Chinese know when the time was right to rise up against Cain. Without Li, he was left entirely on his own, and unaided, he stood a snowball's chance in hell of bringing down Cain's kingdom of blood.

Finally, a couple of hours shy of dawn, fatigue refused to be denied. Fargo slept soundly. More soundly than usual. He was stunned when he opened his eyes and discovered the sun was well up into the sky. By his reckoning it was between eight and nine o'clock.

"Damn."

Fargo saddled the Ovaro. He left the other horses in the wash and rode west a ways, then reined south. He went slowly, with frequent halts to use the spyglass.

Cain once again had Chinese sifting through the mansion's ruins. Others were hard at work clearing the burnt timbers that had been part of the stable and the cookhouse. Those remaining were in the fields, and they were few. The field workers were to the east of the mansion, not the west.

The point where Fargo approached the Oasis had another advantage. A few acres of corn, the tallest crop the Oasis boasted, were well along, the stalks shoulder high.

Still wearing the slicker over his buckskins, Fargo rode into the center of the corn and drew rein. Dismounting, he looped the reins around a stalk. He was, in effect, hiding the Ovaro in plain sight. Anyone passing the corn might notice the pinto, and then again, they might not. He judged the risk worth it. He wanted the Ovaro handy in case he needed to make himself scarce in a hurry.

The rows ran east and west. Fargo jogged east. The smell of the manure used to fertilize the corn was strong. His boots sank in the soft irrigated soil.

Crouching when he came to the end of the row, Fargo unfolded the spyglass. He quickly scanned the vicinity. No one had any idea he was there. He focused the telescope on the stable, saw Krast whipping a Chinese worker.

"Soon, you bastard."

Fargo surveyed the fields beyond, noting where Cain's men were. He was not interested in the coolie buildings since they were supposed to be empty at that time of day. But that changed when he happened to pass the spyglass over a window in the coolie building nearest the mansion.

Stiffening, Fargo focused on that window. He had glimpsed a face peering out, low down, near the sill. The face was still there. There could be no mistake. "So that's where you got to."

It was Li Dazhong.

= 31 =

Through the spyglass Fargo saw what happened next as clearly as if he were mere feet away instead of hundreds of yards.

Li Dazhong signaled to someone working at the stable. His fingers moved almost too fast for the eye to follow.

A young Chinese, more muscular than most, made an answering sign. Then he whispered to the man next to him, who, in turn, whispered to the next worker he encountered.

Fargo had no idea what the hand signs meant or what was being whispered, other than the captives were up to something, and the something they were up to had apparently been orchestrated by Li Dazhong.

Cain's overseers were oblivious of the secret message being passed. They cracked whips now and again, usually to spur workers who were not working hard enough or fast enough to suit them, or who talked without permission.

Soon all the Chinese at the stable had received the message. One of their number carried a saw to the mansion and whispered to one of the workers there. The message was spread so slickly, so carefully, that Cain and the hired guns were unaware of what was taking place under their very noses.

Fargo had to hand it to the Chinese. As rapidly as

Li's instructions were being relayed, before long every captive the length and breadth of the Oasis would know them.

But what came next? was the question Fargo couldn't answer. He decided to stay where he was and await developments.

An hour trickled past. Two hours. Noon was near, and campfires were started to cook the midday meal of vegetables and rice.

Li Dazhong had vanished from the barred window. Fargo thought Li might slip out either of the doors at each end of the building, but if Li did, Fargo failed to spot him.

The aroma from the cooking pots was enough to cause Fargo's stomach to growl. He had neglected breakfast.

Tobias Cain had a chair brought. He was so huge, he dwarfed it. Flanked by hard cases, he sat down with a flourish, like an emperor of old deigning to visit his pathetic subjects. About half his men were permitted to eat. The rest had to stand guard until it was their turn.

Some of the Chinese wore crude hats with wide brims woven from straw. Hats they had apparently fashioned themselves to ward off the sun. A little man in black wearing one of the hats was walking toward the cook fires from the direction of the coolie buildings. The hat was pulled low, hiding his face. But Fargo did not need to see the man's features to know who it was.

Amazingly, none of the guards challenged him. Maybe because other Chinese were moving about. Maybe because they did not consider one man much of a threat. Only Fargo noticed the rippling wave of tensed backs, the epidemic of sharp glances in Li Dazhong's direction.

Only Fargo, and one other.

Tobias Cain was talking to Krast when a nearby coolie half turned and adopted the posture of a hunting dog about to be unleashed. Cain sat up in his chair and glanced in the same direction the coolie was staring, at Li Dazhong. Through the spyglass, Fargo saw Cain's eyes narrow, saw the bloom of suspicion, the fleeting shock of recognition.

Fargo opened his mouth to shout a warning even though it was doubtful Li would hear him. But Tobias Cain roared first, coming out of his chair like a cannonball and slamming a sledgehammer fist into the coolie's jaw.

"Look out! It's Dazhong! The Chinese are up to something!"

Li threw off his hat and shouted in Chinese, one word over and over. Then he switched to English. "Now! Now! Now!"

The plan was simple. At Li's yell, every worker, every Chinese, whether male or female, was to rise up against their overloads, relying on their far greater numbers to prevail. Had they not lost the element of surprise, the plan might have worked with little spilled blood.

But Cain's roar proved critical. It galvanized his men into unlimbering their artillery, with the result that the initial rush of Chinese was met with a hail of lead.

A mad melee ensued.

Revolvers and rifles crashed like thunder. Screams, wails, and oaths in two languages swelled the bedlam.

A score of Chinese, probably previously chosen, swarmed toward Tobias Cain. With Cain dead, resistance would crumble. But slaying him proved a daunting challenge.

The giant did not wait for his slayers to reach him. *He* rushed *them*, wading into the foremost like a breaker crashing onto shore-locked rocks. His enormous fists flashed right and left, cracking skulls, pulping faces, shattering ribs and throats and shoulders. Cain was a one-man wrecking crew, an unstoppable juggernaut who reveled in the broken bodies that littered his wake.

But even Tobias Cain could not long stand against rising numbers. For every two he vanquished, four hurtled to take their place. The Chinese threw themselves at his corded arms, at his tree-trunk legs. Eight or nine were clinging to him and he was tottering like a stricken redwood in a thunderstorm when the cavalry came to his rescue.

Krast and those with him were not particular about who they shot. Revolvers and rifles blasting, they dispensed death equally to men and women. Those swarming Cain fell to the leaden scythe.

Elsewhere, pockets of Chinese fared better. From one end of the Oasis to the other, they rose in long-delayed revolt, desperation lending strength to their worn limbs and hope to their hammering hearts.

Fargo snapped the Henry to his shoulder. An overseer had wrapped his whip around the throat of a Chinese girl and was strangling her, his knee against her back. Fargo shot once, and the man folded.

Another Chinese was on the ground, a guard straddling his chest and about to beat the life out of the Chinese with a jagged rock. Fargo planted a slug in the guard's head.

Tobias Cain was running toward the bunkhouse. Krast and others protected the giant's broad back.

Fargo emerged from the corn. He needed clear shots. But thanks to the swirl of fierce combat, they were distressingly few. He fired, shifted, fired again, and came as near as he had ever come to having his brains blown out when a slug nicked his right ear.

The shooter was a salt-and-pepper killer in Cain's employ. Fargo remembered the man saying he was fond of killing women because they were fragile flowers, ridiculously easy to dispose of. The same could be said of the killer. A single shot from Fargo's Henry and the slayer's days of destroying flowers were over.

Bodies sprinkled the Oasis. A lot of bodies. Some were motionless but others convulsed in agony. Plenty were Cain's men. Plenty more were not.

Fargo decided he would be of more help to the Chinese if he were closer. Accordingly, he spun and sprinted between the rows of corn toward the Ovaro. He thought he heard boots pound the soil as swiftly as his own and glanced to the right. But the tall stalks had tricked him. The sound had bounced among the rows, and what he thought came from the right actually came from the left. He found that out when a battering ram caught him in the ribs and lifted him clear off his feet.

Why the hard case did not shoot him was a mystery. But Fargo was grateful for any stupidities that lengthened his life. He grunted with pain as he was slammed to the earth and a knee brutalized his groin. A swarthy, sweating face with breath that reeked of onions oinked like a tusker boar. The oink became a startled gasp when Fargo's fingers clawed piggish eyes.

Fargo shoved the man from him, stabbed for his Colt. The hired gun did the same, but his arm became entangled with a cornstalk and he could not clear leather. Fargo jammed the Colt against the other's sternum and thumbed the hammer twice.

Pain slowed Fargo as he rose to his knees. The Henry was within easy reach, but he could not find the spyglass. He groped among the stalks until a piercing scream reminded him the Chinese needed his help.

Mounting the Ovaro proved difficult. Fargo's groin hurt so much he could barely raise a leg. Gritting his teeth, he managed it, and reined toward the battleground. The number of fallen had doubled. Gun smoke hung in wreaths above the dead and dying. Splashes of scarlet decorated the green. Here and there pockets of savage conflict raged, but the main clash was centered on the bunkhouse.

Tobias Cain, Krast, and others were inside, resisting a tidal wave of enraged Chinese craving for revenge on those who had for so long tormented and abused them.

Lead buzzed past Fargo. Drawing rein, he hurriedly shed the slicker. Now was not the time to be mistaken for one of Cain's killers. Even in his buckskins, in the madness of the moment any one of the Chinese might seek to end his life. So when he spurred out of the corn he did not make straight for the vortex of violence surrounding the bunkhouse, but circled to the north.

Although outnumbered, Cain and company were holding their own. The Chinese had guns taken from those already slain, but they did not have a lot of ammunition. Some had knives. Others wielded farming implements: rakes, hoes, shovels. Again and again they rushed the bunkhouse. Again and again withering fire from the windows and doorways drove them back.

Finally calmer heads prevailed. Commands were shouted, and the Chinese withdrew into an encircling ring. They were still in rifle range, but the firing from the bunkhouse ceased. Cain was wisely not wasting bullets.

The wounded were made comfortable and tended to. Women were sent to the coolie buildings for blankets. Water skins were brought.

Now that their initial bloodlust had faded, many of the Chinese were exhausted and glum. Their revolt was stalled. So long as Tobias Cain lived, they were not safe.

Only a few unfriendly glances were thrown Fargo's way as he roved among them keeping a watchful eye on the bunkhouse. The man he was searching for was issuing orders like a military commander. The straw hat was gone, his black clothes spattered with red.

"Do I call you general?" Fargo asked as he swung down.

Li Dazhong grimly smiled. "It did not go as well as I hoped. The cost has been too high. We have lost far too many, and the monster is still alive." A man ran up and spoke in Chinese. Li listened, then gave orders.

"Your best bet is to burn them out," Fargo suggested.

"That is exactly what we will soon attempt to do," Li said. "That man is in charge of gathering every lamp and lantern left."

"You don't aim to rush them again in broad daylight, do you?" Fargo asked, his tone implying it would cost them too dearly.

"No. Many want to. Many do not care how many lives have been lost. But I care. We will wait until night falls and move in under the cover of darkness."

"Let's hope Cain sits still that long," Fargo said. If he were in the giant's huge boots, he would attempt to break out.

"Have you any idea what Cain will try?"

There, Fargo was stumped. Cain did not have enough men left to break through by force of arms. He must try something else.

Quiet fell, except for scattered groans and moans. The heat, as always, was stifling. Li gave orders that every third Chinese could lie down and rest. Li did not include himself. He stood with his arms folded, regarding the bunkhouse with the intent stare of a hawk longing for its prey to show itself.

Fargo voiced a question that had been nagging at him. "Why did you sneak away in the middle of the night?"

"To be frank, I did not trust you."

"Me?" Fargo said in surprise.

"You refused to promise to let us deal with Cain. You do not understand how important this is to us. He must die by our hands and our hands alone."

Fargo gazed at the many dead and wounded. "Important to them or important to you?"

"Think what you will," Li said.

"Have you seen May Ling?" Fargo changed the subject. He was thinking of the thousand dollars he would collect if he could get her back to San Francisco in one piece.

"Not since the shooting started, no. She is not the woman she was. The spirit has drained out of her."

"I wouldn't count on that," Fargo said. Her greed made her unpredictable. She might yet cause trouble.

Li Dazhong studied him. "If I asked you to leave, would you? Ride off right this minute and never come back?"

Fargo hesitated, and not just because of May Ling. For Li was right. He did want a crack at Tobias Cain.

"I thought as much," Li said, and sighed. He addressed several men behind him. Suddenly rifles and revolvers were brandished, pointed at Fargo.

"What the hell is this?"

"Hand over your weapons," Li directed. "I will have you escorted from the Oasis. Then, and only then, will we give your weapons back. But make no mistake. You are not to return or you will be considered our enemy."

"Damn it," Fargo growled. "I'm on your side. You need me."

"You overestimate your importance. And while we are both on the same side, we are at cross-purposes. Tobias Cain is ours. Since you will not honor that, I must reluctantly send you away."

"Be reasonable," Fargo said, to stall. "You can't

blame me, after what Cain has done. What if I give you my word that—"

A flurry of excited shouts drowned him out. A score of fingers were pointing. Li gave a start and took several steps, bewilderment setting in. "What is this? What is that fiend up to now?"

Smoke was rising from the bunkhouse. From every window and door gray wisps grew into gray columns.

The Chinese were dumfounded. Setting fire to the bunkhouse bordered on madness. But Fargo noticed that the heaviest smoke was pouring from the far end. A thick cloud had formed and was rapidly spreading toward the Chinese, and toward a dozen or so stray horses the Chinese had rounded up.

Seconds later rifles boomed and revolvers crashed from out of the cloud. Chinese dropped in droves. Their line was crippled. Gaps appeared, littered with the blasted.

The cloud disgorged a flying wedge made up of Tobias Cain and Krast and others, fast as they could, mowing down what resistance remained between them and the horses.

Li Dazhong, shouting commands, rushed to stop them. Every Chinese within earshot flocked to his side.

They forgot about Fargo. Two steps, and he was on the Ovaro and reining to the west, not toward Cain. Since he could no longer depend on Li, he would take matters into his own hands.

32

May Ling had materialized in front of the Ovaro, her hand thrust out. "Wait! Take me with you!"

Fargo would just as soon leave her. But he did not have time to argue, and there was that thousand dollars. Bending, he hooked his arm around her waist and swung her up behind him. "Hang on!" He glanced back.

Furious Chinese, rushing to intercept Tobias Cain, were being cut down. Twenty more yards and Cain would reach the horses.

May Ling, strangely, did not ask why Fargo wasn't trying to stop them. As docile as a lamb, she clung to him, her cheek on his back.

Fargo brought the Ovaro to a gallop, continuing toward the black hills that fringed the Oasis. He had an idea how he could outwit Cain—and Li Dazhong.

If Tobias Cain survived the battle being waged, and Fargo was willing to bet the giant would, then Cain would head for the best protected spot in all of Death Valley, the spot where more of his men waited, the one spot where there was water: the spring.

Fargo slowed when he came to the hills so as not to raise much dust, and reined north. The spring was not far off. He would get there well ahead of Cain. He could conceal himself, and when Cain showed, one shot from the Henry and it was over.

May Ling stirred and put her hands on his hips.

"Tobias does not love me anymore," she said forlornly.

"He never did." Fargo rose in the stirrups. He could see the gigantic rock slab but not the spring under it or the men guarding the spring.

"You are wrong. He loved me very much once. I could tell. I was special. He said so many times."

"He was lying." Fargo was in no mood to spare her feelings, not after all she had done.

"You do not know that for certain. You were not there. He is your enemy, so naturally you speak ill of him. But deep down, Tobias is a sweet, caring man."

Fargo snorted. "That will be the day."

As if she had not heard him, May Ling said, "I need to get back in his good graces. I need to prove to him I am worthy of his love. Only then will he take me back. Only then will things be as they were."

"The mansion has been burned to the ground. The captives are out for Cain's blood. Nothing will ever be the same again."

"Again you are wrong," May Ling said. "The mansion can be rebuilt. The captives can be made captive again. Everything can be exactly as it was." She leaned against him and whispered in his ear. "The first step is to prove how much I love Tobias by giving him a gift."

"What kind?" Fargo asked, not really caring.

"The one who is to blame for all this," May Ling answered. "The one who has nearly spoiled everything."

"Li Dazhong won't let you take him prisoner."

"Silly man," May Ling said. "I was not talking about him. I was talking about you."

Fargo felt his Colt slide from its holster, felt the muzzle gouge his back. He drew rein, careful not to make any abrupt moves. "What do you think you're doing?" he demanded.

"I have explained that," May Ling said with infinite patience. "You are the means by which I will regain my lover's heart."

"You're not thinking straight," Fargo said. "Cain doesn't give a damn about you. He'll kill me and tell you to go jump off a bluff."

The Colt gouged deeper. "Stop talking about him like that. You do not know him as I do. Keep riding and soon I will prove you wrong."

Fargo debated whether to throw himself from the saddle, or to seek to wrest the revolver from her grasp. Either might end with him taking lead, an unappealing prospect. He tapped his spurs against the Ovaro.

"For a few moments there I did not think you would do it and I would have had to shoot you," May Ling said. "I would like that, very much. I would like to watch you die and then spit in your face."

Then and there Fargo gave up any notion he had of ever earning that thousand.

"It is good you did not make me shoot you, though," May Ling rambled on. "I do not want to deprive Tobias of the pleasure of killing you himself. There is nothing he would enjoy more." She giggled.

There was something about that giggle. It had a shrill quality that hinted it was made by a mind not entirely sane. A quality that brought a chill to Fargo. "I take it you don't care about seeing your father ever again?"

Now it was May Ling who snorted. "My father! All those years he kept me a prisoner. All those years he prevented me from discovering the truth."

"What are you talking about?"

"I was raised in strict Chinese fashion. I was not permitted to be with young men my age unless chaperoned. There was no touching allowed. No holding hands. Never so much as a kiss." May Ling giggled some more. "I was a virgin when Tobias had his way with me. I fought him. I was so scared. I thought terrible things would happen, but it was the most exquisite delight."

They were near the slab. Under it the surface of the spring glistened. The shack door was closed, and no guards were in evidence.

May Ling slid the Colt's muzzle up Fargo's back until it was pressed against his neck. The metal had been warmed by the sun and was almost hot. "I have not forgotten that you left me to die."

Denying it would be pointless so Fargo said nothing.

"I will ask Tobias if I may shoot you between the legs or cut off your manhood before he kills you. It is a small favor. I am sure he will grant it."

Without warning figures stepped from behind the shack and rose up from behind the boulders sprinkled around the spring. Seven, eight, nine grim men, their rifles trained on Fargo. He reined up.

"What do we have here?" demanded a squat troll with tobacco stains in his beard and on his shirt.

"It's me, Seever," May Ling said, and giggled her peculiar giggle.

"My eyes work right fine," Seever snapped. "But what are you doing with this one? And where's the boss? Mr. Cain told us to stay put no matter what, but all the shooting and yelling has us worried."

May Ling lithely swung down, never once taking the Colt off Fargo. "Let's see. In the order you asked, Fargo, here, is a gift for Tobias, who was caught by surprise when those damn Chinese tried to kill him."

The man called Seever blinked. "But you're a damn Chinese yourself, lady. Or haven't you looked in a mirror lately?"

"I would watch my tongue, were I you," May Ling retorted. "Tobias will not take kindly to you insulting me."

"What are you jabbering about? Mr. Cain booted you out of his bed. We all heard about it."

"What you know and what you think you know are two different things," May Ling said with sugary sweetness. "Whereas what I know and what I think I know are one and the same."

"You've been eating loco weed," was Seever's considered opinion. "But we'll get to the bottom of this pronto. Here comes the boss."

A trio of riders was racing along the main irrigation ditch. Tobias Cain had survived, as Fargo predicted. With the giant were Krast and another hard case.

"Why are there only those three?" asked a guard. "Where is everyone else?"

So far no one had told Fargo to dismount, so he stayed where he was. He started to slide his hand toward his boot, and the Arkansas toothpick, but stopped. Several of the guards were still watching him.

May Ling clasped her hands, and Fargo's Colt, to her bosom, and spun in a circle. "My Tobias has come! My Tobias has come!" She tittered and clapped her hands in glee.

"Crazy bitch," a man muttered.

Cain's hat was missing, his hair disheveled. His clothes were torn and spattered with crimson. He had been cut on the cheek and a slug had grazed his side. He was in a foul temper, and his mood did not improve when he swung down and May Ling threw herself at him.

"Husband! You are safe! Not that I doubted you would prove to be their better." May Ling rubbed her cheek on his chest. "Now that we are together again, all will be well."

Tobias Cain scowled. "Where the devil did you come from?" He sought to push her from him.

"Don't be like this," May Ling said in sudden panic. "I have brought you a gift to prove I truly love you."

"Let go, you stupid cow." Cain shoved harder but she was like a spider wrapped around a beetle.

"Look!" May Ling cried, gesturing at Fargo. "It is the one you hate the most. The one you want dead more than any other. I give him to you."

"I don't have time for this," Cain snarled. "Your friends will be here soon and I must be ready for them."

"My friends?" May Ling giggled. "No, dearest one. I am not part of their stupid revolt. I am yours, now and forever." She rose on her toes, puckered her lips, and went to kiss him.

Intense loathing twisted the giant's features. His entire frame shook, and seizing her by the shoulders, he flung her to the ground. *"Don't touch me!"* he raged. "Don't you ever touch me again."

Bewildered, tears filling her eyes, May Ling clutched at his legs, mewing, "You do not mean that, husband. I am yours and you are mine. No one loves you as much as I do."

"What will it take to get through that thick skull of yours?" Cain fumed. "Everything I say goes in one ear and bounces out again." He drew back his right boot. "Maybe this will get your attention."

May Ling did not try to protect herself or dodge. The kick caught her on the temple and slammed her flat on her belly. Briefly, her eyelids fluttered, and then she lay still.

Krast had drawn his six-shooter. "Want me to take care of her for you, Mr. Cain? After all those we just killed, one more won't hardly matter."

Tobias Cain glanced to the east. His former captives had given chase, some on horseback, the majority on foot, and were spreading out at they neared the spring. "The killing isn't over with," he declared. "And since there are not enough of us left to hold them off, we will arrange a little surprise."

"Do you mean—" Krast began.

"That is exactly what I mean," Cain confirmed. "I

should have used them sooner. But they are a last resort. It is why I keep them so well hid." He flicked his fingers. "Get to it, and don't drag your spurs."

Krast, Seever, and another man hastened to the shack.

Fargo was wondering if he could rein around and get out of there before someone thought to put lead into him. He wondered a bit too long, for the next instant fingers as thick as railroad spikes had hold of the front of his shirt and he was torn from his saddle and hit the ground so hard, his ribs nearly caved in.

"Not too smart of you to stick around," Tobias Cain said. "You must be a glutton for punishment."

Fargo painfully picked himself up. "I don't want to miss your last stand."

Cain balled his enormous fists. "Do you honestly believe Li Dazhong and his rabble can beat me? I always plan ahead, as you and he are about to find out. For you it will be the last sight you ever see, for him it will be the end of his rebellion." Cain slammed his right fist into his left palm. "Things will go back to being as they were."

"That's what May Ling wanted," Fargo remarked, and was clipped with a backhand that sent him staggering. He grabbed at the Ovaro to keep from falling.

"Worry about yourself," Cain said. "You have brought nothing but trouble down on me since you arrived. Soon it will end."

"If you say so," Fargo taunted, only to have the taunt shoved down his throat when Krast and the others stepped from the shack. Each held a barrel of black powder.

"Didn't expect that, did you?" Tobias Cain gloated. "They were under the floorboards. I keep them handy for emergencies." The kegs were placed at his feet. Each was fitted with a short fuse and contained enough black powder to destroy half a San Francisco block. Combined, the three could have brought down the mansion, were it still standing.

"How do you want us to do this, Mr. Cain?" Krast asked.

"Tie the kegs onto three horses, light the fuses, and send the horses toward the Chinese," Cain instructed. "I don't expect more than a few dozen to escape the blast. Rounding them up will take no time at all."

Most eyes were on the advancing skirmish line. Only Fargo noticed May Ling open her eyes. Only he noticed the deep sorrow they mirrored when she stared up at the man she had professed to love. Only he was aware when she started to crawl toward the three kegs of black powder. And only he saw her touch the Colt's muzzle to one of the fuses.

But they all heard the click of the hammer.

Everyone looked, and froze. Except for Fargo. He vaulted astride the Ovaro, hauled on the reins, and used his spurs as he had never used them before. The Ovaro went from standing still to a gallop in the blink of an eye. No one tried to stop him. No one snapped off a shot. They were riveted to May Ling, to the Colt, to the fuse.

"Don't you dare!" Tobias Cain thundered.

Tobias Cain could have said many things. He could have apologized. He could have told her he loved her. He could have implored her not to squeeze the trigger. But he did none of those. What he said next was, "Did you hear me, you stupid bitch?"

May Ling giggled. Her finger twitched.

The explosion was everything Fargo expected it to be, times ten. He was safely out from under the gigantic slab but too close to escape the concussive force of the blast. A wall of wind bowled the Ovaro over as if the stallion were a feather. Fargo left the saddle and cartwheeled through the air. He hit with a marrow-jarring impact and for a while was too dazed to move, let alone sit up. Then questing fingers gently closed on his shoulders, and he was rolled over.

Tu Shuzhen was there, and Ni Ting, and others Fargo did not recognize. They parted for Li Dazhong. The question Li asked seemed to come from the end of a long tunnel. "How badly are you hurt?"

Fargo flexed his arms and legs, patted himself, and grinned, incredulous. "I'm not." The Ovaro was already up and shaking its head but otherwise unharmed.

Li stared at the massive sections of the shattered slab, and the dust rising from under it. "You had to be the one to do it."

Fargo set him straight. "Not me. May Ling."

"Ah. It is ended, then."

That it was. Tons of solid rock had plugged the spring for all time and crushed the tyrant who had used its precious life-giving water for the most vile of ends.

"I call that fitting," Fargo said.

Li mustered a smile. "Perhaps I can interest you in leading us out of here. You know this country. You know how to live off the land. We can make it worth your while. A thousand dollars from my own pocket, and more from the others. What do you say?"

Fargo draped one arm around Tu Shuzhen and the other around Ni Ting. "If these charming ladies are willing to keep me company, we have a deal."

They were.

And they did.

No other series has this much historical action!

THE TRAILSMAN

#284:	DAKOTA PRAIRIE PIRATES	0-451-21561-3
#285:	SALT LAKE SLAUGHTER	0-451-21590-7
#286:	TEXAS TERROR TRAIL	0-451-21620-2
#287:	CALIFORNIA CAMEL CORPS	0-451-21638-5
#288:	GILA RIVER DRY-GULCHERS	0-451-21684-9
#289:	RENEGADE RIDERS	0-451-21704-7
#290:	MOUNTAIN MAVERICKS	0-451-21720-9
#291:	THE CUTTING KIND	0-451-21733-0
#292:	SAN FRANCISCO SHOWDOWN	0-451-21783-7
#293:	OZARK BLOOD FEUD	0-451-21803-5
#294:	OREGON OUTLAWS	0-451-21821-3
#295:	OASIS OF BLOOD	0-451-21833-7
#296:	SIX-GUN PERSUASION	0-451-21891-4
#297:	SOUTH TEXAS SLAUGHTER	0-451-21906-6
#298:	DEAD MAN'S BOUNTY	0-451-21919-8
#299:	DAKOTA DANGER	0-451-21935-X
#300:	BACKWOODS BLOODBATH	0-451-21975-9
#301:	HIGH PLAINS GRIFTERS	0-451-21991-0
#302:	BLACK ROCK PASS	0-451-22001-3
#303:	TERROR TRACKDOWN	0-451-22018-9

TRAILSMAN GIANT: IDAHO BLOOD SPOOR

0-451-21782-9

GRITTY HISTORICAL ACTION FROM
USA Today BESTSELLING AUTHOR

RALPH
COTTON

JACKPOT RIDGE	0-451-21002-6
JUSTICE	0-451-19496-9
BORDER DOGS	0-451-19815-8
GUNMAN'S SONG	0-451-21092-1
BETWEEN HELL AND TEXAS	0-451-21150-2
DEAD MAN'S CANYON	0-451-21325-4
GUNS OF WOLF VALLEY	0-451-21349-1
KILLING PLAIN	0-451-21451-X
THE LAW IN SOMOS SANTOS	0-451-21625-3
BLACK MESA	0-451-21382-3
BLOOD LANDS	0-451-21876-0
TROUBLE CREEK	0-451-21792-6
GUNFIGHT AT COLD DEVIL	0-451-21917-L
BAD DAY AT WILLOW CREEK	0-451-21998-8

Available wherever books are sold or at
penguin.com